SHARRON L. ENSIGN
Mara
ENTERING THE BOOK
WORKBOOK PRESS
RECOMMENDED
LITERARY BOOK COMPETITION 2020

This publication contains the opinions and ideas of its author. It is intended to provide helpful and informative material on the subjects addressed in the publication. The author and publisher specifically disclaim all responsibility for any liability, loss or risk, personal or otherwise, which is incurred as a consequence, directly or indirectly, of the use and application of any of the contents of this book.

WORKBOOK PRESS LLC
187 E Warm Springs Rd,
Suite B285, Las Vegas, NV 89119, USA

Website: https://workbookpress.com/
Hotline: 1-888-818-4856
Email: admin@workbookpress.com

Ordering Information:
Quantity sales. Special discounts are available on quantity purchases by corporations, associations, and others.
For details, contact the publisher at the address above.

ISBN-13:   978-1-953839-67-1 (Paperback Version)
              978-1-953839-68-8 (Digital Version)

REV. DATE: 30/12/2020

CONTENTS

Chapter 1

Finding allies

"Mara, where are you?" called a frustrated woman.

Receiving no response, she returned to the pattern she was trying to get put together as she sewed a new dress for a customer. Somehow things were not coming together. The woman who was sewing pledged never to ask her daughter to help with sewing while she was in school. She had graduated in May at sixteen, and Grace felt that she still owed her the time until age eighteen. Her birthday was in June, making her seventeen next month. Mara was always ready and willing to help so that Mother had the time needed to sew to keep all bills paid. Due to some unexpected aid, Mara could play every musical instrument the music department had on hand. Now it was summer, and in the fall, she would start college. For now, it was her time. Her dad's death insurance paid for her college, while an unknown had paid for the music lessons. Her mother refused to touch the money left for her education.

"Yes, I know she called; however, if we go now, we will be there the rest of the day, and I already helped get everything else done so she could sew," said the seventeen-year-old in a whisper as if receiving a reprimand.

Receiving no response, she continued the story she was reading. She had first heard of Thunder Press when a friend mentioned a new series that was out.

Upon opening the book, the words seemed to come alive as she met the young woman who was an expert with the sword and sent all over the planet to serve as the law where they had none. She was currently on one such assignment, where she had to ride for two weeks to get to the location in question.

Her team of two hurried as quickly as they dared. There were road bandits to avoid, towns she had to take them around, campgrounds that had warnings on them, and many other dangers. They stopped when they could to get some rest then continued to ride to their destination. That is when Mara met Thunder and asked if she would object to a replacement for the story.

Thunder had been working hard and needed a little time off. She had a hidden home with funds to support her, and she seemed to be thinking before she replied.

"If you don't get me killed, sure go ahead. I can use the rest," replied the woman.

Mara then took over the story.

In her mind, she became a young warrior trained in the sword and other skills. She was riding a horse that was solid black and even shined when cleaned up. Now, the animal was covered with mud and plodding along like a farm horse.

"We have to be careful here. This town is known to give women trouble, which is why I changed how I looked and did the same for you. Do not let them catch you, for it will be the last time we are together if they do. Shira is watching from nearby. First on the things to do is find a place to stay that is clean, dry, and honest with stable for you and Shira."

When they reached the entry gate, she dismounted and walked by her horse, for she saw a sign that said no riding of horses in the town itself. The Guards at the gate just waved them through. They were to watch wagons and large groups. However, a single young boy was no threat, was their thought.

Mara thanked the one God for the provision and moved on at a steady, though not hurried, pace. When out of sight of the gate, it was time to find a source of information. She saw a child of about ten leaned against the wall of a building.

"How well do you know the residents of this town?" she asked in a more resonant dust-filled voice.

"Well enough to know who to avoid and when to find a hole and hide," was the response.

"Would you be willing to use that information on my behalf, and in return, I will do my best to keep us both safe?"

"You would look out for me?" he asked in surprise.

"Yes, though you will need to give an oath not to tell anything you learn about me," she responded.

"What do you pay, and how long do you want me to do that?" he replied, now all business.

"Let's discuss that out of the public view, okay? First on my list is to find a place to stay that is clean, dry, and honest dealing plus has space for my friends. What would you suggest?" she asked the ten-year-old. "There may be times when my duties call me away for a short period. However, I promise you we will be together again as soon as possible."

"The owner at the Wren's Nest is very kind to me. Would you like to try it there? They have a stable. I do not know for sure where you prefer. If you want a place where the Sword Dancers go, that is the Pointed Sword. On the other hand, there is the Darkened Den where most with hidden business go," he advised, for he had seen the sword calluses on her hands.

"Do you read or write?" she asked.

"No," he replied, looking at the floor.

"Well, that is one thing we will change as soon as possible."

She walked along looking at various shops they passed, for she initially decided on the Wren's Nest. In time, she might need to stay at them all. However, they would have to start someplace. When they were near a bookstore, she asked the boy to remain with her horse while picking up a couple of books.

He held the reins in his hand once she told the horse it was okay.

The boy leaned into one leg of the horse, still holding the reins, and watched the area around them. He saw a group coming that was a danger.

"Mister Horse, we have to hide you. Those men steal horses and women," he told the riderless animal.

The horse pushed him with its head into a nearby alley. Then she turned toward the entry after moving as close to the dark sidewall as she could. The boy ran although it was behind her. He found the back door to the bookstore and slipped inside.

"Missy, your horse is hidden, and you need to be," the boy whispered.

She quickly paid the bill and followed him to where the horse was in time to see the group riding by. Yes, indeed, she wished to avoid that bunch, for she was not ready to deal with them. Once they were gone, she moved out of the alley with her friends and chuckled when she saw Shira across the street coming from another alleyway.

Suddenly the wolf turned and ran down an alley, then jumped a fence and was gone. At the warning, Mara quickly put the boy on her horse then hurried toward an opening she had noted that led to a different street. She ran to the other end of the alley block, then ducked into a separate area and hid the three of them from sight by telling Pi to lie down behind some tall bushes. They saw the riders as they ran their horses in the street, which was illegal, yet no one tried to stop them.

"How far away is that place you recommended we stay at?" asked Mara

"Follow," was his reply as he scrambled out of the hiding place and then ran in an entirely different direction.

The horse and rider followed slightly slower to not bring attention to themselves, yet they kept close tabs on the boy. Suddenly he was gone. She could not see him anyplace.

When Mara looked up, she realized she was standing under a sign that said Wren's Nest Inn. She saw a sign saying

'Horses' and followed the direction given by the arrow on it. The first thing was to get the horse secure. The new guide was waiting and had a young girl with him.

"This is Gwen, and she will care for your horse. She knows horses and takes good care of all she watches over," said the boy.

"There will be two in the stall, a dog and a horse. Pianto, call her in," directed Mara though she usually called her horse Pie. Soon a dirty canine appeared.

The owner had spotted a water chute at one side of the well-kept area, for she had been looking for just such a device. It was a place for washing horses when they came in muddy. She pulled the channel to her, and the dog moved her direction immediately for washing. They were at the edge of the stable area where the water had a ditch to drain into a distant field. The horse was standing as if next in line, and she received the same service. Mara had already moved the gear inside the stable, where it was dry.

The girl and boy took the rider's gear to the stall where the animals would be. Shutting off the channel once more, which allowed it time to refill, the young woman removed her boots, hat, jacket, and vest before again opening the sluice box, only this time, the water flowed over her body. Her weapons were in the saddlebags except for two knives, which remained nearby. The youngsters watched her, then realized her intent and took the horse, dog, and additional gear to a stall that would be theirs if they remained. Mara drenched herself thoroughly and washed as much dirt off as she could, for they had been on the road for weeks. She even allowed the water to flow into her mouth and hair. The woman was so dry her voice was almost gone. When she turned off the water, Shira was there with two towels. She toweled herself off then followed the guard into the stable where she was directed to a stall to change her wet clothing for dry, for she washed the clothes at the same time by continuing to wear them. With the boy's help, the stablehand had wiped down the two animals while the woman took her unorthodox bath, and they had even wiped the dust from her gear with an old piece of cloth. Once changed, she asked for directions inside and the cost of the stabling.

"You are with Kennet; you will pay what you can afford not to exceed what everyone else pays," replied the girl in a firm tone.

"My partners are dry and even fed. You did not ask for payment first and seemed willing to aid. Here is a tip, and we will pay the going rate. At the same time, I may have some questions for you later if you don't mind. Please do not let anyone near the animals. Warn them if trouble comes, and if necessary, move in with them, for my friends will not harm you. Anyone else is fair game to include those we just saw," directed Mara.

Gwen looked at Kennet with a question in her look.

"The RIOT is in town. You need to be on the watch. If you can hide the horses, this might be the best time," suggested Kennet to Gwen.

"Oh no, not them again, I will get the horses out of sight! Thank you for the warning. Please tell mom."

The girl ran to a post and hit it. A panel opened, and the lever she pulled lowered the entire stable below ground. A platform that looked like ground dirt took the place of the stable. The girl dropped with the horses by jumping inside the stable door as it moved downward.

Mara and her guide walked toward the inn back, where there was an entry for those who rode in. That doorway was open to the stable only. Behind the establishment was closed off by two mountain legs, which met the building at a corner and was as tall as the inn.

Once inside, the boy quickly disappeared to return as speedily, leading a smiling woman in her late forties.

"I'm told you need to keep a low profile and a secure place to rest. You can stay in one of the rooms. Kennet suggests you might like the hidden hotel," the woman told her in a soft voice.

"Would you allow my guard dog to come and go? She is watching over your daughter and horses," asked Mara.

"Yes, I will allow. Kennet put her in location two since Gwen is in number one. Are you going to your regular hideout?" asked the woman.

He looked at Mara for the answer.

"I have hired him as a guide. He will remain with me if you have no objection," replied Mara with a smile.

"If you take care of his well-being, I have no objection. He said he was waiting for his mom that he has yet to meet. It sounded a bit cluttered to me. Those who are regulars here are notified and have moved to the hidden hotel. I'm dropping too since they seem to want to take me along when they leave. Not going to happen if I have anything to say about it," she added. "Oh, by the way, I am Mrs. Boyer or Star if you prefer. I sang under the name of Wren once upon a time. Now own the inn and have three children to raise. Friends will take over the building for us once they get here. It will be before that bunch does."

"If you run into problems with them, let me know. I might be of some help," said Mara with a smile.

"What name do you want me to register you under?" asked the Inn Keeper.

"Depends on who will see it, if you are the only one Mara Jacobson would work. On the other hand, if you plan on it being visible, maybe Thunder Press would work."

The first name brought no response. However, the second one got some startled looks. Even the boy was shocked. That was a name well known.

"It is not my intent to bring you problems. There is a reason I am here, which cannot be shared now though it might be later. The boy, horse, and dog are my entire company. I need to find a few friends who are willing to aid me in various ways. Your hidden hotel would be beneficial. The warning of who is in my vicinity, by the boy, is another aid. Should trouble follow me, I will leave, although your the offer of the hidden space is very timely if not withdrawn," the woman told them.

"If no harm comes to me or mine from you, why should I remove the offer? Kennet said that you warned my youngest daughter about the group in town and offered her aid by staying with your animal friends should trouble come her way. No, I do not withdraw my offer. You are welcome, for currently, I have not seen anything that would cause me to change my offer. Rumor always makes a person seem giant-sized even when they might not be, though there is always some truth in a story. You are accepted as you are and welcome."

"Thank you; it is gratefully received. We need some time to rest as we have been on the move for quite a while. I will pay the going rate for the room and stabling for the four of us. If the opportunity comes up to get a horse for my new friend, it will add another. That is all I am anticipating presently."

Mara stopped reading to think for a time. The story would wait where her reading ended. She was trying to recall what would be needed to know to aid those she had recently seen.

Once again, she heard her Mother's call.

"Right here, mom, what do you need?" the young woman asked, for she heard her Mother's call unless too far away. However, the book was in the attic, so not far at all.

"I need some more blue thread. This has to be ready by the time the woman comes for it, or we don't get paid," said the harried woman.

"Mom, you know they will wait for a year for one of your productions. Sit down and have a cup of tea while I go to the store. Would the Max work for the color you want?" asked Mara with a smile. She always helped when she could, and in turn, her Mother allowed her time to do what she wanted to.

"Yes, of course. Thank you, dear; I don't want to stop what

I was doing and worked on other parts until you returned. Now I must get it done."

"On my way," responded the obedient daughter.

Mara ran for the door and jumped on her bike. It was faster than walking, for the store was only about six blocks away. She had grabbed the old spool to be sure she got the right kind and color.

When she entered the store, she noted that the place appeared to be empty. Thinking the clerk was busy someplace in the store, she stopped at a counter of books relating to building underground. She felt as if her control and training were back as Thunder. She checked out the whole place by looking at various mirrors on the walls. When she saw what the problem could be, she moved to a sports area. There she found a few baseball bats and picking up one; she moved to where a man in a mask was pounding on a store clerk.

She walked up behind him and hit him on the head. He collapsed over the woman on the floor. Her new learning told her where, when, and how hard to strike the man.

"Can you call the authorities while I keep an eye on him?" she asked the clerk after moving the masked robber to one side.

"I thry, he mashed some toofs," was the response of the severely beaten woman. Now she was no longer scared, just mad as the full pain had not hit yet!

"Okay, let me pick up a couple of things, then I will call the police while you hold the bat. If the man wakes up, strike with the bat, only not to kill because they need to find out who, what, when, and why of what he did to you."

Mara ran to the book row,and got the book she had seen. Then the thread row where she blue thread selected. To be on the safe side, Mara picked up two large spools, for she knew if not used for today's sewing, her Mother would need it in time for it was an attractive color. Next, she used the store phone to call the police. She selected the blue thread.

"This the Max store. The woman who works here was beaten severely by a man in a mask. He is now lying on the floor with a lump on his head. Please come as soon as you can, for she needs medical aid, and the man won't be out forever," she told them before returning to the clerk. For some reason, she wiped off the phone and the money before returning to the woman.

"They are on the way. Will you be okay? I have to get home right away, so here is the cost of what I have," she handed over the money and ran for the door. She hoped her fingerprints would disappear by the woman trying to hold onto the bat. The payment was a little more than owed, although she would not wait for change as she had a story waiting. Almost immediately, the sirens began, which greatly relieved her mind, for she hated leaving the woman alone in such bad shape.

Her bike was by the side of the building sitting in a bike rack. Mara lived six blocks south of the store. Therefore, the police did not know she had even been there when they arrived from the northwest.

Law enforcement arrested the man and put him in jail; the officer in charge called the store owner and an ambulance. The woman was severely injured, though she could hold the bat in her least injured hand, which was rapidly swelling. The other arm had more than one break. In the hustle, no one asked about the one who rescued the clerk, for they felt she had overcome her assailant by herself, and he was still out when help arrived.

"Here's your thread, Mom. Need anything else? I still have some things I want to do if that's okay," said the daughter.

"Thank you, dear. I must get this done so that work can begin on Margarette's blouse for the dance. I will try not to bother you again. I appreciate your helping me get everything done. Love you," said the mom, who returned to her sewing and the daughter to her hideout where she read. The short rest was enough for the woman to be able to find her error and move on.

Mara picked up the new book she purchased. She read

quickly about the structure and building of an underground home. Once she had a general idea, she switched to her story once again.

"Sorry, I was thinking. You said your Inn is hidden, or one of them anyhow, how do you keep others from finding out about it?" she asked her host.

"Anyone who goes there is oathsworn not to recall anything about the location, regardless of who asks. Ken said you had him swear an oath and that if he swore an oath to you, he was protected. Does that mean those here are as well?" asked the woman.

"Yes, only let's make it official. I promise to guard this woman, those she hides, and Kennet if they do not divulge who I am or anything about me. The same will be kept confidential about them," replied Thunder Press.

"My full legal name is Mrs. Star Jacoba Boyer or Star. Here they call me Mrs. Boyer, for there is a warrant out on Star Jacoba. I was once called Wren and a lot of other names along the way. When my kids came, I settled down to raise them. Then a man killed my husband, Dart. I tracked down the killer and ended his life, resulting in the warrant out for me. I have worked alone since then, except for my kids and those I hired. When my kids can take care of themselves, I intend to leave. We have now been here since Dan was born, and he is the eldest at fifteen, with Eva being fourteen, and Gwen, whom you met, is twelve. Dart has been gone for ten years now.

"What is it you seek?"

"I would like to find a place of peace, where we don't constantly have to watch for trouble."

"It won't be on this planet. You need to appreciate what you have, including your children and friends, then settle in to make the best of your opportunities where you are. You had your fun time when you were younger, and it won't be coming back. You are an intelligent woman and need to continue at something you are secure doing. The setup here is fantastic. You worked hard to make it this way and have an adequate income. What would happen if this sanctuary should fall into the hands of people like those coming? How about your friends? Don't they need you as much as your kids do to see they are safe? Didn't many of those friends help build what is here? Friends are the most valuable commodity that a person can have, and if they are entirely trustworthy, they are worth more than gold. People on the road never know where the next meal will come from, and the thieves are everywhere. Women become targets. Both males and females live in the open due to lack of housing and pull a blanket over them if they are that rich, and sleep where they fall."

"You must be kidding!"

"I assure you I am not. What greater privilege is there for each of us than to be needed? I use a sword and am required to keep the peace where there is no peace. They pay me well. However, when they bury me, they will train another to take my place. Life is cheap, after all," added the Warrior.

"I'm sorry to hear that. You are welcome here whenever you are in the area. Thank you for the offer. It will be an honor to have you. If that bunch just hit the town, they will be here in about two hours. It is time to be out of sight," Star told her.

"That sounds good to me. May I get something to eat and maybe a snack for later? Can pay my bill daily or weekly, whatever works best for you."

"Kennet said you are a friend of his. Therefore you stay as long as needed and can pay when you are ready to leave. There is also a kitchen in the hidden area so you can get what you want there," replied the woman in a firm voice.

"Again, thank you, now we need to get out of here, for your adversary has changed their schedule and just entered this street," warned Mara, whose senses were on high alert as were those of her keen-eared wolf guard.

The three of them ran to the backdoor of the inn; Star pulled a section of shelves from the wall and directed them to hurry inside. As soon as the panel closed, they could hear shouting and knew they had only seconds to spare. They quietly ran down the stairs though they could listen to the shouts above them.

"Where's that woman? I want that woman. Bring her out here," cried a voice.

"Oh dear, he is dead drunk this time. We now have a male chef, and all the table attendants are men as well. They pack weapons in case this bunch gets rowdy," said Star with tears falling, for she knew the damage they would do when they didn't find her. She had moved all things of value below as soon as the UC was secure enough to do so. Now those items were safe. Nonetheless, it would be costly to repair whatever that bunch damaged.

"I must get some sleep; would you please show me where you want me. I will call for Shira, and once she knows where I am, we will settle in. If you need me, send Ken or Shira, and no one else, for they won't get close," warned Mara.

When all agreed, Kennet went for Shira, and Star took Mara to the food location, where she ordered what she wanted to bring to her room. Then Star showed her where she would be staying. It was one room with a bed and a dresser. The bed's foot had a box with a padded top like one might sit on and look out a window though only candles and a lantern light were there to illuminate as there were no windows underground. It seemed like a possible place for Shira. The room was spotless, and a box with ice in it served to keep her meal fresh. However, she ate it immediately. A second meal was for Kennet and scraps for Shira.

Chapter 2

A day to dream

When Kennet went to get Shira, he recalled that Thunder took a bath as soon as she could, so he did the same, for he would be sharing a room with her. He was quick and arrived at Mara's sleeping room with Shira soon after Thunder and Star reached it.

When Shira joined Mara, she identified the inn owner who allowed her to remain loose in the underground area. Once Star departed and Shira returned to the stable, Ken and Thunder were ready for some rest. Ken moved to the bed and, at a nod from Mara, shed his jeans and shirt, for he left his shoes at the door. He climbed onto the bed and was asleep as soon as Mara was, though Shira was left to run in the hotel and would warn of trouble. Gwen also showed her how to reach the outside.

Soon Thunder was asleep though her mind was on watch for any strange sounds or another trying to enter her area that was unknown. The wolf, Shira, returned to the horse in the stable to ensure it remained secure now that she knew where to find Thunder.

Mara found herself back home.

She sat for a time, thinking about her new knowledge and the beginning of her adventure. The boy was a lot of help, and she planned on keeping her promise to teach him to read and write. The trips back and forth had made her weary, and she was soon asleep though alert for any calls from her Mother.

Mara was soon dreaming and back at the inn location where she heard a strange sound. Therefore, she moved to identify. A man was placing something on the wall opposite her room. When he finished, she put him out of commission. A quick hit on the head with the hilt of a sword did the job.

Next was a closer look at what he put into a hole in the wall. It was a device that would activate at any sound and discharge a fatal dart at her door. She deactivated it and put it in a secure location within her clothing. Now it was time to go home and do some research on this one. The man she struck disappeared from the area.

"Thank you for your help. I knew something was wrong yet couldn't find it. You are right that one was too modern to fit in this setting," said a quiet voice.

She looked around and saw no one.

"You are welcome. May I ask who you are?" asked Mara.

"The author, of course, who else could make those kinds of silly errors?" replied a female voice, and one felt she was smiling.

"I hope you don't mind my joining the story. It is rather fun to be someone else for a time. My name is Mara Jacobson," she told the woman.

"Welcome, and you may join any of my stories if you will fix what is wrong in them along the way and preferably before they reach publication," was the response.

"Let me finish this one; then I will help gladly. I love the way you write. Just as a few suggestions: that stable that dropped needs explained better in keeping with the times. The inn needs running water. I'm not sure how to accomplish that at the current time, although I understand that they used wooden channels. I will suggest that they use metal sheets to direct the water to where the horses need it. Once that is tried, we can have them do the same in the living area. The seams need to be at the top of the metal's length and then use more metal to seal the joints. I think that wax would work to seal the seams to keep from losing all the water as well," replied Mara with a smile of her own. The book she was reading at home would make it easy to find who the author was and locate her on the net.

"Thank you; I will look it up. I appreciate the help. I will let you know when my research is complete," replied the author.

Mara returned home and the interrupted sleep. When she awakened the following morning, the first place to go was the kitchen, where she found her Mother at the table reading the local news.

"Mara, you went to Max yesterday for my thread, and you never said anything about the clerk getting beaten up and a man arrested," her mother said.

"When I got there, the store seemed to be empty," she started.

"Oh, it must have been over by then, I guess. The news says here; the woman had many injuries though she managed to hit the man over the head with a baseball bat and knock him out. He is in jail. She is such a lovely woman. Why would anyone beat her that badly? She has a broken arm, teeth knocked out, glasses broken, and bruised all over her body. They think that someone must have paid her for an item as she had money in the hand of her broken arm. She held the bat in the left hand though that arm too was beaten and swollen so badly the medics had trouble removing the device used to knock him out, it says. Probably a broken collarbone; I hope they put him away for good," said the woman without pause for breath.

Mara didn't say anything, for she was trying to decide how much trouble she would be in if she told the truth. She knew that to lie was never worth the cost, and refusing to tell her Mother what happened was not a good idea.

"Mother, let me tell you what happened," Mara began.

"Let me finish reading the paper, dear. I may not get another chance to sit down. Have a lot of orders to get done today. You did such a good job helping me get all other stuff out of the way; let's just let it go for today. Do whatever you like today because we have the laundry on Monday and will need your help with that," her mother responded.

One does not interrupt a mother when she uses 'that' voice; therefore, she did as her Mother said and got out of the way.

When settled in her reading hole in the attic, by the only light which she purchased with some money earned, Mara opened the book, and the story continued. The teenager had been surprised to find an electrical outlet available in the attic.

Awakening in the inn, she stretched her joints, checked to see where her sword was, put a knife nearby, and then used the pitcher of water on the stand to do a quick scrub before dressing. Once properly attired, she noted her gear lying on the dresser. After thinking a moment, she removed one of the knives and used it to dig a hole in the wall behind the clothes chest; she was careful to cut out the wood in front of the hole in such a way that it would not be apparent. She placed her pack inside the hole to include her sword still encased in leather for travel. Neither the woman nor her sword should be identified this early in the game, and that sword would declare who she was.

She awakened Ken, who also washed up and redressed in the clothes he had been wearing. That would be next. Her to-do list was growing. However, he had to have some suitable clothing. They departed for a meal.

In the dining room, they saw Star.

"Good morning, you two; how was your night?" she asked.

"Hello Star, we slept well and now thought we would fill up the void. Did your inn have a lot of damage last night?" Mara asked.

"You know it was the strangest thing. The men started making trouble and then disappeared. Their horses are still in the back area though the people are gone. We put the horses below with the others where they were unsaddled and rubbed down. Bet that they were an ill-used lot," replied the woman who had received the report from her daughter, Gwen, though Star had not seen the horses.

"It's a good thing you enlarged the stable. If this is my starting place, then most likely, the villains will come to me. That means you may acquire a few extra horses. Interesting," commented Thunder.

"True, we had to, to accommodate those who are also underground. We can now shelter five hundred people and a thousand horses. Yours are all in one area with this last bunch added."

"You are putting them under me? Why?" asked Thunder in surprise.

"Because you told me I am best off where I am; therefore, I do not need horses. On the other hand, you have a mission, you said, and therefore might need them. As to breakfast, we have ham and eggs, fresh fruit with blackberry pie and oatmeal, if any of that interests you," chuckled the woman.

"Please, may I have oatmeal and some pie?" asked Ken.

"Of course, however, keep in mind that you will need energy for the day, and dessert won't aid much with that," commented Thunder.

"Okay, then I'll have ham and eggs, although that will cost more," the boy replied, half in apology and a half in longing.

"That will be okay; I will have the same," Mara told the boy though he also received the piece of the pie.

"Mrs. Boyer is there anything else I need to be aware of?" asked Thunder.

"Yes, one of my longtime renters disappeared. Someone said they saw him in the hall by your room, and now he is gone," she paused a moment in thought. "Not that he is any loss, you understand. Never was comfortable with his presence."

"He was an inside man. You won't be bothered further by him. Wonder who he was inside for?" said Thunder.

"*That would be nice to know,*" whispered a now-familiar voice, though Star and Ken didn't seem to hear a thing.

"Guess he was hoping to gain control over you and the

inn. Saw the worth of it and wanted it to be his. He must have felt I was his competition. Little did he know," Thunder replied to both. Her instincts said the men were keeping track of the inn owner through the man.

"That works," said the distant voice though Thunder wasn't sure which scenario the author would use.

"Good thing I can still trust my instincts. I get good vibes from you and terrible ones from that gang leader and him," replied Mrs. Boyer, who Mara invited to join them for breakfast.

Star had a cup of tea before her as she sat and visited. The place was empty, for it was at the end of meal hours.

"I have a favor to ask. Now that I have some rest, those horses need checking, then the two of us need to wander around town. My horse will remain here if you don't mind. Shira might decide to travel with us. Would you please stay here, below ground, while we do some checking before you return to the public level? By staying below with your family, maybe you could keep an eye on my room for me. It is necessary to find out the state of the city," Thunder told them.

"Yes, I will do that. I'm sure you know more about what is going on here than anyone. Watch your back, and if you can get some hidden weapons, that would be better than packing a sword in the open. Haven't seen any here in years," replied the Inn Keeper.

"Do you think ones like these might work better?" asked Thunder quite seriously as she lay two knives, a shortsword, and an assortment of devices that looked very deadly, to Star, on the table.

"My goodness, yes, only I would suggest you not let anyone else know you have them, at least until they are needed, for that group will take them away. The ones in charge will not let anyone carry arms except themselves. I am much relieved to find you are armed. That sword was not visible until just now. Put it back where it was," warned Star, who even looked to one side as Thunder put them away.

Ken took note and turned with her.

"Thank you for your concern. Few will ever know what I carry for weapons. Best to keep them guessing. If you lead me to the horses, that duty will be covered, and thank you. I may need them."

Thunder had only shown a few of the lighter weapons, not the many she carried. Most of her defense tools had been in her saddlebags when entering the town, for she did not want them damaged or stolen, and Shira would hide them if trouble came on the road.

Everyone put their dirty dishes away and followed Star as she moved to a different part of the hotel. They passed via a tunnel from the inn underground to the stable underground.

"They must be taught to remain silent. Pi, please advise them, for they will give away this location if they continue to greet anyone who comes in," Thunder informed her mount.

Immediately all were silent.

As Thunder looked around, she noted that Pi and Shira were now in a stall underground near the new horses she had inherited. The trunk where she put her gear for Shira and Pi to watch over when the first arriving was now in place in the lower chamber. Nothing had been bothered as near as she could tell.

Thunder saw that the stable girl had removed all saddlebags and put them in a stall next to where Thunder's friends were. She even put sawhorses outside the horse stall of each animal, and the saddles were placed on the wooden frame to dry. The horse's bridle was looped over the saddle horn so that Mara soon knew what gear went with what horse. Each horse wore a halter, and Gwen explained that she found them tied to the saddle's back on leather ties. Each animal had been brushed down and fed.

"These are racers! My goodness, what did they plan to do with them?" asked Thunder.

"One time when they were here, they said they could outrun anyone trying to catch them. It looks like RIOT takes excellent care of mounts," replied the girl who had checked them over.

Gwen and Star departed, leaving Thunder to look at the gear that the horses had carried. She found several things she was not expecting. When it was all sorted, she found they lost value in what she had inherited. A couple of the horses carried so much gold; it is a wonder that it could support a rider, but then maybe it hadn't.

She went back to check on the horses once again and realized four pack animals were in with the racers. She returned to the stall and looked for the packsaddles from those. She estimated that there were around two hundred pounds of gold in some of the silk-lined saddlebags. There were masks and other clothing to serve as disguises. There were at least forty new pistols in individual containers plus bandoliers with shells. Now it looked like there were forty-four horses, and each had a valuable load. There were more knives than she had ever seen in one place except for a smith shop. She also found wanted posters. There were fifty when she counted, hefty awards on them too. After Thunder had sorted everything, she locked the bounty in the locker that Star put in the stall with her horse. Saddles, blankets, headgear, and pack boards were airing in the tack room where Pi and Shira could keep an eye on them. The horse and gear each had a number to keep track of what went where. Shira could quickly jump the wall if anyone entered the tack area, for the wall stopped at the rafters. Star also put a saddle blanket on the top of the trunk, allowing a soft place to rest for Shira. The packs were each inspected as the saddlebags had been. With the tasks completed, Thunder returned to her room, where she found Ken waiting.

"Why did you leave?"

"Mrs. Boyer said it was not my business unless you said it was. She never tells me lies, nor do I tell her any. That's why I came back to our room while you sorted the stuff she said is now yours. Are we going out now?" Ken asked.

"Yes, we are going now. First, what do you want for pay, and how do you want it? Should I credit you whatever you ask for and hold it for you, or do you want to carry it yourself?"

"Oh, don't give it to me. If I had that much money, it could get me killed. Even a dollar is worth killing someone here. Please keep it hidden. Whatever you chose to pay me will be okay. If I want something, would you buy it and take it out of my wages?" Ken asked.

"What do you think you would like to purchase?"

"You said maybe one day I could have a horse. Could I have one like yours that understands human talk?" he wanted to know.

"We just inherited about forty head of horses. Why would we buy any?" she chuckled at his notion, for she planned on keeping this youngster.

"I can ride okay, though still too small to fit an adult saddle, so guess it will be walking for me yet for a few years," he replied.

"Will see about that. First, those horses must be tested and see how gentle they are, plus how firm their mouths are. Don't want them to run away with you," Mara explained.

"No, Ma'am wouldn't like that idea at all," he replied with large eyes.

"I'll consider it the first chance I get," she told him.

"Before we go outside, please tell me: what do you want to find, where do you need to go, and who are you trying to avoid?" the boy asked.

"I need to locate a shop that sells musical instruments. Then we will look for a saddle maker that knows his or her craft. We need to find new clothing for both of us. I wish to speak with a goldsmith. Does this town have a bank? It is important that we not be identified by the local non-law enforcers," she explained.

He chuckled at her words.

"Yes, there is a money changer if that is what you mean. You can probably speak with a goldsmith at the mines. I will need a little time to find out how honest that person is first."

"Let me know when we can speak with that person," Thunder responded.

"Then follow me. Do you want Shira to go with us or to stay with Pi?" he asked.

"That is her choice. I told her we were going shopping, and when I left her, she was settling down for a nap," Thunder said to him.

"She wouldn't do that. Shira would make sure someone would guard you. Pi can handle himself if it is needed," Ken replied, for he did not know that Pi was a mare.

"And how do you know that? Do you think I cannot take care of myself?"

"Well, Pi hid when the riders came as I told him. You trusted Shira to stay hidden, so you always have someone lose if someone captured you. Then you told me to keep you from trouble with those who live here. We will guard you as best we can," the ten-year-old promptly replied without commenting on the question of did he think she was capable of; His motto was never to tell all you know. It had kept him alive.

A fair response was her thought, for he had not seen her do much to present time.

"I know you will; however, all I want you to do is get me where I need to go, warn if danger comes, then find a place out of the line of fire," she told him.

"Would you be willing to trust me with a knife? I had one once, and the rider took it from me, said it was too dangerous."

"Certainly, I will trust you, think we better have some lessons first, and that won't be until later as these errands need to be taken care of, and along the way, we might find out what is going on."

Kennet had the answers he needed, and after checking outside through a peephole, he exited by a back way. She followed him through a couple of dry water beds to her first location. The main river had changed where it flowed, and the empty water beds remained. The hidden Inn and stable were now under those same beds while a swift-running river ran between the inn and the meadow. Water ran from inside the mountain and met the river at the opposite end.

Thunder stopped a time or two to look at something in the stream bed then followed her trusty guide.

"Why did we use that route?"

"Because no one must know about the hidden lodging, we use a few different ways out to not let anyone see us and to keep those inside safe. We don't want anyone to see the hidden valley. Mrs. B hopes she can one day buy that acreage behind her place. That way, there will be more room for those she will hide," he replied.

She nodded agreement, and they entered the music store.

"Hello, Kennet, what brings you our way?" asked the man behind the counter.

"My friend needs something from your store, Mr. Spritzer. Please treat them fair," replied Kennet.

"Of course. Now, what may I do for you friend of Kennet?" said the smiling man.

"I would like a six-string guitar, full size, and one the size of Kennet. Sheet music won't be needed at present though probably later. At the same time, I would like to know what you know of the area," she told him.

Mr. Spritzer shared what he knew about the area and its people. Then he added a few observations he had as he selected the instruments Thunder requested. He first asked her to play an instrument he handed her. It was a twelve-string guitar, and she played it like a professional. She had asked for a six-string guitar, and that is what he sold her.

When the bill was before her, and she paid for the amount due.

"May we leave them here until our return? We have a few things to take care of along the way and should return in two to four hours."

"That will be okay. I will put your purchases in the box by the door, and you can get them if a customer is here," he replied, then matching words and action, he wrapped each instrument in a custom bag and put them in the box.

"Thank you," she replied, and they departed.

Next, Kennet took her to a saddle maker.

"Myster has trouble with his legs. However, his hands work just fine. He makes the best and sturdiest saddles in the area though many won't deal with him because of his legs. It's a shame because he is a nice man and works hard at what he does," Ken told her.

Upon entering the store, Kennet again received a greeting.

"Hello Kennet, what can I do for you today?"

"I have a friend who wants to purchase something from you. Please give them a good deal and honesty," replied the boy.

"Gladly. Thank you for bringing this lady to my shop. Friend of Kennet, what can I do for you?"

"Need a saddle to fit this young fellow. Must go on a full-sized horse and have all the long-distance straps as well as a few hidden places for things of value or weapons," Thunder told him.

"Let me show you something. I have a boy's saddle that will fit Kennet, and it was for a boy his age. It has all you are asking for and more. The youngster doesn't need it anymore. Would that work for you?"

He opened a cabinet in one wall and pulled out a beautiful

saddle.

"Was that Jackie's saddle?"

"Yes, though he never got to use it," replied the man with tears in his eyes.

"Thank you, we would like to purchase the saddle," Mara said without any questions. Those could be answered by Kennet when they were in their room once again. No need to embarrass the man further.

"If you like, you can put it in the box by the door and pick it up on your way home. That way, you don't have to pack the saddle all over," the man told her.

Later Kennet told her how those riders had run down the boy, and their horses killed him. To them, it was fun; to the grieving father, it was murder. Myster lost his leg trying to save his only son, the man would spend the rest of his life on crutches.

Next, Mara saw a shop selling knives and swords. The knives she now had were for adults and were good quality; Ken would need a shorter version. She hoped to have a secure storage area for all she found in the saddlebags. The box Star loaned would work for now, with Shira to guard. The problem was it was stuffed full, and some items were behind the container.

"Kennet, could we go to this shop?" Thunder asked.

"Yes, though there is another that I would recommend. This man is not always honest, and he does not like kids," replied her guide.

"In that case, lead on," she told him.

They moved farther down the road and to the back of a building.

"Be right with you," said a rough sounding woman's voice.

"It's me, Mrs. Daz. Have a friend who wishes something."

"Ah, Kennet, bless you. Hello, a friend of Kennet. What

may I do for you?" Thunder heard as a broad-shouldered woman entered the room. She wore a blacksmith's apron and looked to be unyielding.

"We need some weapons to fit his hands. He will be given proper training before using them. I assure you," responded Thunder.

The boy's eyes sparkled, yet he said not a word.

"I will pay the going price for your wares swordsmith," Thunder advised.

"In truth, your purchase should about pay my rent for another week," replied the woman.

"May I speak privately with you for a moment?" asked Thunder.

"Of course. Kennet, mind the shop, will you? We will be in the inner chamber," said the woman.

"I cannot give you my name now; however, may I know yours?"

"They call me many things hereabouts. My name is Marjory though friends often call me Maggie. What can I do for you?" she asked.

"Maggie, I have a mission here and might need your services. Would you be willing to aid in regaining this town for its legal citizens?"

"I'm too slow to be of much use as a fighter. If you are talking weapons, you bet! Can make all you need at a reasonable price, though I will need a place that isn't as open as here," replied Maggie.

"Here is a retainer," said Thunder reaching into an empty pocket. Then she moved her hand upward inside her pocket lining, which accessed more funds. Never do to have too much money visible regardless of the form. The rest was in the trunk that Shira was using as a bed.

"No, Ma'am, you are a friend of Kennet. When he vouches for someone, we know there is no need for concern. If you need me, either send him to get to me, or he can bring you to my lair. All I need is enough for my rent. Maybe one day I can purchase this place or one like it," said the woman who was thinking how wonderful it would be to have a secure location where people couldn't come on her unaware or that what she was doing was scrutinized by everyone.

"Thank you; we will be in touch. When do you want us to pick up the knives for Kennet?"

"I have them now. Would you please wait and return in two days for them? May have some information for you by then," was the response.

"We will be here," Thunder replied, for she had asked this woman about any knowledge of the area and its peoples.

Chapter 3

Meeting the collaborators

They exited the shop, and Thunder saw a feed store on another street visible through the alley. Again, she asked if she should go to that place.

"Depends on what you need. Your horses and dog get fed by the people at the inn. Mrs. Boyer buys her hay and grains from Jennie Parsons, for she lost her husband and has three kids like Mrs. Boyer. What do you need? Oh, Gwen said to tell you that Star ordered in extra hay for your horses. Also, some grains," he told her.

"Let me look around the store, and I will decide. Not sure what they have available. Needs to be a treat for those horses so I can teach them to work for us," Mara responded though she was looking at the cost of the new mounts. Then she recalled that the author told her the funds would be available as needed.

"Oh, Mrs. Nutter makes molasses sticks and the horses like those. She makes a different kind of thing for dogs, and it is in little pieces to make it easy to feed."

"Lead on then," said Thunder, and they moved onto a side street for the stores were on the main road, and the residents were mostly on back streets like the inn.

He led her to a well-kept home on a different street. There she met Mrs. Nutter and her wonderful animal treats. Thunder met the woman's three dogs and a small horse she kept as a pet and tested her training aids for the larger animals. Mara was pleased with what the woman had for sale. They purchased a large order as there were forty horses to be retrained.

The next place was an open market where new and used clothing was for sale. Ken and Mara both made selections.

Mara saw some canvas bags and bought four of them. She had some ideas. Mara showed Kennet how to use the ties as carrying straps over his arms to put his clothing inside. Then she did the same with her own. Next, she added another of the canvas packs to take the animal treats to the inn. They still had many items to pick up on their way back.

"I will check on the Goldsmith once you are again in the underground, also the money changer. I will be back as soon as I can," Kennet told her.

Then it was to retrace their steps and pick up their purchases before returning to the underground living space. They went in the same way they left.

"Let's get something to eat, and then we will spend some time in our room. You can run your errand right after we eat. Have an idea," Thunder told Kennet.

"He smiled a broad smile and led her to their room, where he put the guitars and saddle away before continuing to the serving room.

When the inn owner came by, Thunder asked to speak with her a moment.

"What can I do for you?" asked Mrs. Boyer.

"Would you be willing to stop by my room after lunch? I have an idea that I would like to discuss with you."

"Certainly. I need to make sure the kitchen staff knows what is for the evening meal and pick up Dan's shopping list. Today is farmer's day, and he needs to get things while they are fresh. The vendors set aside what I require for the inn, and he picks them up first thing in the morning," she explained, for Dan was her eldest child.

"That will work for us. See you then," responded Thunder.

The boy would have to wait for his Mother to write up the order of any additions or changes she wanted. Otherwise, he carried the same order time after time. It seemed there was always an addition of some kind because someone had a preference or different things were in season for harvest.

When a large crop came in, Maggie would order large boxes of stuff to preserve them for off-season use. Things like strawberries and corn were always on her list when in the season, as were potatoes, peas, corn, beans, and the like.

Kennet excused himself when done with his meal and walked away though he was running once he was outside. A path led from the edge of town and moved upward.

"Hello Kennet, what brings you out our way?" asked a rider who was a guard for the mines.

"Need to talk to your goldsmith. Who is the best money changer in town?" Needs to be reliable and honest in their dealings, especially with women," replied the boy.

"Then climb here, and let's see what we can do."

He did as the rider told him and was soon at the mine headquarters. The man said he would return to give Kennet a ride back in a few minutes.

"Well, hello, Kennet, didn't expect to see you here. What can I do for you?" asked a different man who came to the guard's call.

"I'm on an errand for a friend. She wants to know about you. She said she needed a goldsmith. Are you one of those?" he asked politely.

"Yes, I am. No doubt, you could tell me what I need to know; however, I would prefer to meet the person who wants my services. She must be honest and deal fairly with me. Otherwise, I will refuse the request though no one will know we met."

"Can you meet us at the east end of Wren's Inn just before supper? I will have her there. Thank you for seeing me," said Kennet, who then departed and found the guard waiting to take him to the town's edge.

When Mrs. Boyer reached Thunder's room, which was in a hall by itself away from the inn's rest, she stopped a moment and listened. She was hearing a guitar and wondered where the sound originated. Then she tapped on the door, and it stopped.

"Ah, so you are the artist," commented the woman.

"Yes, I play several instruments. However, this one is most welcome for use in my day to day life. What would you like to hear?" asked Thunder.

Kennet had been gone such a short time, due to the guard's ride, that he was in place when Star arrived, and he sat in rapture listening to the music played. At times Mrs. Boyer became Wren and sang the tune played. Even Thunder joined in on occasion. He loved it. His life didn't have much music, for he could not afford such luxuries.

After an hour of playing, Thunder lay the guitar aside and turned to Star.

"Do you have an underground practice range here? It must be soundproofed and set up with targets for many different types of weapons. Knives, swords, and handguns must be first, followed by training in rifles and axes."

"My husband always wanted such a place, and we hoped to purchase the lot across the river to put it in. The inn's idea has proven a good choice; I would like to buy that property to put a range and another stable there. That way, you could have room for all your horses, keep everything hidden, and everyone safe," replied Star.

"Let me show you my idea and see what you think," replied Thunder.

She drew out the meadow that Star was referring to in shape. Thunder had asked the author to describe the valley in shape, size, and such things as water. The land beyond the center of the hourglass-shaped piece appeared to be part of the mountain. The back section had an offset entry that everyone thought was part of the hill while allowing it to be a hidden entry to the back section. Then she began to cut the front part of the valley into quarters as she explained what she had in mind.

"If you cut it this way, you could put all your horses on that side of the river with a tunnel passing under the river that is tall enough for the animals to walk through. Remodel this side of the river and make it all rooms for those you keep secure. Put any businesses on the outer edge of the new location to allow everyone access. On the outer edge, away from the horses, would be a good place for a target area. A range that size would allow a dozen to practice at once without a sound heard outside the range. Also, I need a workout room for another type of defense that everyone should learn. If possible, I would like a full home built on the horse side of the river with easy access to you, my animals, and the dining room," Thunder told them.

"I have wanted to purchase that property for years; however, funds have not been available. Since we are just dreaming here, why not put a tunnel on the east side by the mountain, giving you a straight shot from the back area to where the new range will be. You and I will have the only entry keys. That way, you could have a single stall by your hidden room where Pi could stay and be on hand when needed," Star said.

"Currently, I have some extra funds. Let's talk to the owner and see their asking price to purchase the area we are discussing. It will more than double your capacity for both people and horses underground, while your lodging will still accommodate only so many inside the Inn, which would be those who are only looking for a place for one or two nights. You will have room for the entire town in this lower level, though you will need to be selective," advised Thunder.

"We will be selective, I assure you. That is your money, not mine, how I would like to do it, though," Star replied.

"Then let's do it this way. I will pay for it, and your half is running it if we go, partners. I want a place for me and mine to stay without crowding out anyone who needs to be here. It could be all the women and children of the area as well as your regulars. Now, if you put children below, you need to make sure there are teachers for them. I bet that some of the women have the training to do that. Also, if it is necessary to have a group of volunteers to get things back on track, then there is a hidden place where they can practice and have meetings," responded Thunder.

"The first ones we need to secure are those who are friends of Kennet. He has a way of making his presence felt."

"I agree with you. Could even put a copy of the town underground," replied Thunder with a smile. She could see that Star was already trying to figure out how to make it happen.

"Will you be available right after the evening meal? Need to take you to meet someone, and for that, I must change who I am," said Star with a glow on her face and a sparkle in her eyes.

"We have an appointment later today, that is important. After dinner, would be all right," responded Thunder.

They agreed to meet later.

At the agreed-upon time, Kennet took Thunder to meet the Goldsmith. The man was waiting in the area as he didn't have access to the back of the Inn. Kennet let him in, then left the conversation to Thunder.

She showed the man the samples she had picked up from the riverbed. Then she asked him to wait while she ran for something else she wanted to show him. She dropped to the underground and the stable, where she picked up fifty pounds of the gold she had hidden. This way, she could see how good his work was and how he dealt with the required security.

Once they agreed, he departed with the gold, for which he gave her a receipt. He explained that the pure gold, once refined, would be worth about half again what the raw gold was worth. What she had was genuine, for no one had melted it down and bricked it. He would do that. It increased the value and kept it from flaking and losing some of the gold.

Thunder knew what her next course of study would have to be. If she guessed right, she might also own a gold mine.

The next item to take care of was a meal. It seemed

like the pair were always busy, and if not working, it was eating. Mara and Kennet were discussing when they were interrupted by a knock at the door. When Thunder opened the door, she nearly closed it again though Kennet reached for the door handle very quickly when he saw who it was.

"Hello, Mr. Danson. Are we going with you today?" he asked.

A nod of the head and Thunder put the guitars in safekeeping, for she had discovered the box by one wall was empty and used it to store them. Mara secured the room, and they followed the man in a different direction.

When they exited, they were in the tree line, yet Thunder did not feel they had passed under the river.

"Sandor lives in a house set apart. Let's see if he is home, shall we?" spoke Mr. Dawson in a gravelly voice.

Ken and Thunder continued to follow.

They finally reached a shack on the hill. Dawson knocked on the door, waited for a count of three, and again knocked. The door immediately opened.

"Hello Sandor, I'm here with a friend of Kennet to speak business. Will you hear our request?" Dawson asked.

"About time, almost gave up on you. When do we start work?" the man asked.

"Tonight, we plan and pay the fee. Tomorrow we go to work. What do you want for the meadow behind my inn?"

"You know the terms," he responded.

"Yes, however, Kennet's friend does not. Would you please explain to her?"

"I get a room for the rest of my life; you pay the bills, which will be just my daily needs like food, clean room, friends, and a way to be useful. The latter part is digging, and I'm ready. Show me what you have in mind. Kennet said that help was on the way and to get my crew ready to move. A few things have changed about that property, though. Why don't you three come with me?" said Sander.

They rose from their seats and moved to the back of his house. He pushed on a wall panel, and it swung inward. The group entered, and the man locked the board. They found themselves in a cave. He followed a well-worn path for quite some distance.

Mara's direction sense said they entered his house facing north and began following the mountain trail to the east, then moved south.

Thunder chuckled to herself. Her feelings told her that they were within the mountain behind the property that Star had in mind. The hills proved to have caverns built by nature. She could even smell hot springs, which she planned on finding the first chance she got. The meadow was open at the town end, where the fast-running river protected it from much use, and Wren's Inn blocked it from view. The sides had high rocks that were so flat sided one could not climb them. She liked the security the meadow offered and was glad it would be in friendly hands. Many would not live there, for they felt hemmed in, although the valley became wider widened once anyone entered the narrow end. She was already dreaming of a private ranch in the back part of the valley, one where she could also have an above-ground home.

"The dampness in here would not be right for living or business area. However, it makes a good route to reach your area above the ground without going under the river. Also, no one can hear a conversation held in this area. The crew has been working about sixty feet below the surface. We need a blacksmith to move to the area and give us some steel beams to ensure the roof doesn't fall on anybody. I need her to work on-site due to the weights of the ground and timbers. A fellow told me the formula to make the rails. The mines have the equipment for that at their refinery, for they make the rolled railroad tracks, and it follows the same principle. If you can give me enough to pay for the steel we need, that work will start. Also, need money for nails, spikes, shovels, and timber," he muttered to himself as he stopped by a large flat stone where he pulled a piece of paper out of his pocket and figured a little, then gave her the cost.

"How can you do it that cheaply?" asked Thunder in surprise, yet her friendly voice replied.

"The economy was different. For that time and place, that was a lot of money. You have the funds, and more will be available if needed," the author told her.

"Steel beams? It seems to me that those kinds of things had yet to come into being at the time of your book," Mara said to the author.

"There were steel rails for the railroad to run on, so my guess would be they also had the process of making steel beams. At the same time, mines used wood beams to protect the miners. If your blacksmith could make steel-encased beams for the ceiling, would that work?" asked the author.

"We will see," replied Mara, who then saw the group activated and continued the conversation in progress.

"The lumber will come from Jame's Mill, the nails from Palmer Hardware, and get Marjory to do the steel which comes from Prizer Mines. Already have the tools we need until something breaks. Been buying up what we could from traveling folks not to use all that was available in town or set off any sparks. Pete took his pack train and wagons to the riverboat and picked up a full boatload of stuff we need. A train also carried a lot of what we might need. We hid everything until needed. Those involved chipped in to pay the cost. Show me that idea you have," said Sandor.

Thunder reached inside her jacket and pulled out the paper she had shown to Star.

"It would make it easier if you could dig up the whole area. The problem with that idea is then everyone would know what is going on. My thought was to remove an area the size of the town. Simultaneously, only Kennet's friends will be allowed to stay in the new city, which means there needs to be room for a street of shops for those who must move their items of value to the new location. Those who live there will still need access to the talents and products from those shops. There must be a soundproofed practice range for weapons of all kinds, and the dirt between the top of the city and ground level will serve as a buffer, so no one will know anyone is even here. Before you panic, the stores will be in the area that is now the underground stable. The horses move to this side of the river if we can make a crossover to allow the owners access to their mounts," commented Thunder.

"We already have that. You see, the trail we are on ends about a mile into the mountain. That allows the workers to come and go through my place. The same happens on the other side of the valley mountain. The stable for the Inn is part of the tip of that mountain. If we cut a ramp from the mountain to the underground, any horses needed could be brought up when required without anyone except the stable keepers knowing the way. Her inn blocks access to that meadow. The back part seems to have only a solid mountain. Star's husband was very security-minded and built accordingly. The area was blocked on purpose, to work on the underground inn, without anyone being the wiser. He blocked the whole area though he also put in gates to allow the residents to do business in town if they needed to. With the stable once again above ground, Star will have lodging for those staying at the inn, plus a way to get mounts outside without undue notice. People on either side of her have agreed to sell her their places in return for a safe refuge. The cost is the same charge as mine. Dart made a deal with me to never sell this property unless it was to someone entirely trustworthy. I know he wanted it to be him and his wife; however, they were low on funds due to helping everyone else before doing their tasks. We, in turn, helped him. This valley is in my name; in truth, I am only safeguarding it for Star. To be safe, we will give all we have. When the town is again ours, maybe we will purchase our original homes, or we may all agree to stay in the underground area. I like underground idea, especially at times like winter or an invasion. There is nothing like peace and quiet. Time will tell," said Sandor.

"Now that this Lady owns the valley, would you object to her suggestions?" asked Mr. Dawson.

"I am all for it and like the new ideas. The ceilings in this new area are eight feet high. If you are moving horses here, it should go to at least ten feet high or more. I don't want an animal rearing and getting hurt in the underground, for it could cause damage to the area and occupants. I will tell the crew. Since the basic plan is going well, it shouldn't be a problem to raise the ceilings once we have beams. I see here that you want the range farther into the valley with a meeting room and three sets of private quarters. Did you want them places like the inn has? That should be an easy adjustment. A note signed by all involved says we sold you this property in return for security and a home. Don't leave it anyplace, though, or someone else will soon own your property," he advised.

"Since I am the one purchasing, no one else will know of the note other than those who signed it and us here. I would like to see a five-room house containing a kitchen, front room or meeting room, three bedrooms, and a direct path to the stable where my mount is. The side that my horses will be in needs to be accessible by me only. I like the idea that you have to move the animals through the caves and the stable to get them into service if needed. Once the action begins, we will be sleeping when we can, and that might mean that day and night get reversed. Since I sleep lightly, a home where no one can reach me without warning is a must. Is there a fresh water source that could feed into the stables? I have many horses housed there. We may work my horses in the meadow if we can do it without anyone getting too excited. Since no one can see the area except those in Wren's Inn, I might get away with it," Thunder commented.

"That isn't a problem. There are no windows on the back of the Inn; it's the way he built it. You can do whatever you like, and no one will even know unless you tell them. Yes, there are a couple of springs in the valley used for drinking water plus a stream. A water trough placed on the ground and sealed with spring water running through it would allow the stock easy access to water. If you bring the horses up for water, that will help too, for it would give them a chance to make waste where no one must clean it up," commented Mr. Dawson, who was Mrs. Boyle.

"That sounds good to me."

They continued to discuss what would be needed, the cost, and how many would live underground. The work crew was working around the clock to get the work done before the expected trouble came. The task had been going on for ten years without Star, even knowing what was happening. Everyone was thankful that this new woman had ideas they had not thought of themselves. It was almost like she could see into the future and knew what would work and what wouldn't.

Thunder already had an idea of placing a barricade where the valley narrowed to a quarter-mile. That way, she could allow her horses to run in the area for exercise and only bring them in for training or to be out of inclement weather. The hourglass shape was somewhat different when seen. The first section, known as The Meadow, would protect the resident's horses underground. It would work great with animals on one side of the river and the town on the other. She requested a stable for one hundred horses underground by the separating gate on her property side. That piece was to have a spacious home, while the back of that portion would allow Thunder to check out her idea that a mine might exist within the mountain. Her horses could move underground until they reached a private entrance to the ramp-up and into the mountain leg.

It was late when they returned to the underground, for they saw what the workers were doing, how much area they had done, and what would be needed next. Now was the time to call in Kennet's friends and move them, if they were willing. The following morning would be a moving day. Any prepared to move that night could since Star had that schedule ready.

Thunder was resting because her duties were during the day.

Thunder did her best to cover all the duties she had set for herself, for once things began to happen, she might be the one in charge of keeping everyone safe. If that became the case, time to help plus get her ranch done would be hard to find. In time her turn would come to bring out Lightning, her sword. In the meantime, there was work that needed doing.

Star got everyone settled in while Kennet made the rounds to let folks know that they were moving as soon as possible. All those Thunder had met were transferred in the dark of night. Thunder was cleaning her gear and getting ready to go to work.

Two men moved the leathercrafter, for his legs would not maneuver with the stairs and all. They helped him get into a buggy that a single horse pulled to get him to the new location. After securing the carriage and the horse, the men took him to his new home.

The Music man had his products moved ahead of time and rode out of town in the evening only to double back and enter the stable. The stablehand put his horse below, and he moved into the underground.

Mrs. Nutter asked to be taken to the inn in the night, for her belongings were packed in wagons, ready to go. The lady and her animals took the ramp built for the horses and carriages to get belongings below.

Maggie was one of those who moved in the night, and she asked for Kennet. When he wasn't available, Star met with her.

"I need to find the newest friend of Kennet. Have some information for her," Maggie told the inn owner.

"Tell you what, she is resting and will be at breakfast, then I will locate her. Until then, you can set up your new home and get comfortable," then Star departed.

Early the next morning, Star knocked on Thunder's door. She knew that was when Kennet received his training.

"Thunder, Maggie is here and says she has some information for you. There is an empty room near yours; why don't you use it for such meetings? That way, you won't be giving out information before you want to. Even after you move to your new home across the river, you can continue to use these rooms for meeting with people, not to end up giving away where you live," offered Star.

Thunder finished Kennet's training with a smile of thanks before they both departed to the eating room. She knew that Maggie would find her soon enough.

Kennet guided those who had not been underground before, like those who had entered by the back way. Two men who already had rooms there would be remaining inside.

Thunder had bought the leatherman's gear and placed it in his new store underground.

"Hello, Maggie. Would you mind coming with me? It is a little noisy here, and if they see us, we will get put to work," laughed Thunder as she approached the waiting woman.

"There is truth to that," replied Maggie, who then followed the young woman.

Chapter 4

A new form of training

Once inside the room and the door closed, they sat down to talk.

"Kennet told me that you knew about the underground. That is right, for you may well be the one to rescue us, whoever you are. I told you there would be some information to share in a couple of days. He said that you were busy and could be here. I have a few informants that roam around to keep me advised of what is going on in town to allow time to hide if necessary. They tell me that the gang will be here in three days. It seems someone found them wandering around in the mountains without their mounts. None of them has any idea where they had been or where the horses and gear were. As for me, I'm not a bit sorry they lost them," Maggie began.

"The horses didn't get lost, just transferred to a new owner," responded Thunder with a chuckle, for this woman was under oath and knew the consequences of telling what she knew.

"I hope that is a good thing," said Maggie.

"You and me both, you see the new owner is me, though that isn't for publication."

"I was certainly hoping so. The refinery is working at night to get some iron ready for me. Sander said he would have it moved by wagon to the new Smith site. It is so much better than the old one. It has better air circulation, and they built the fire chambers as I asked. Star knows that I wanted to purchase the new location. She said it was not for sale, however, to ask you for a lease. Since I now have a place to work will get the materials for the miners done. Those knives you want are in my room. Pick them up anytime you like. Saw the music man and he is in his shop here. The animal treat woman is here as well as a lot of Kennet's friends. Amazingly, Star had the shops and homes ready for everyone," replied Maggie, who had a soft spot for horses and purchased some of those treats when she could to make her 'horse customers' more comfortable to handle when she had to put horseshoes on them. Maggie's new shop was right behind the stable yet not disturbing the horses and still making her available to shoe a horse if needed. Behind the horseshoeing area, she had her hidden home, for she liked a place of her own away from people. She did not have to watch her back that way.

Thunder did not mention her involvement unless to one of the leaders, and currently, that was her and Star. Maggie did not need to know.

"Thank you for the information; we need to help get folks settled and take care of what happens next. We have to all work together if this is to be done correctly and protect you all for years to come," Thunder advised.

"Glad you are here. I understand you have been working with everyone to get things done that they didn't know how to do. It is greatly appreciated for no telling how long we will be living here," replied the blacksmith.

"There is truth to that. Now I must get busy, and that means going where people can find me. You take care, and I will chat with you another time when there isn't so much going on," Thunder told her.

They moved out of the room and were soon helping settle in the various Kennet's friends. When Thunder saw Kennet, he was to get something to eat and return to their place for some sleep. It appeared he had been up all night.

Knowing that the gang was due in three days had people working hard to accomplish all they needed. They soon had everything in place. No one got much sleep; however, the underground residents were now in place. All of Kennet's friends now lived under the ground. Their former shops and homes above ground were empty, and the contents now were below. New signs appeared in the windows of the businesses and homes. All they said was: SOLD.

The schedule Thunder set up in her mind was: work on reading, writing, and music with Kennet before breakfast, for once seen, someone would require her services. As soon as possible, she moved to the second underground to check work progress.

Then five of the horses were transferred to the meadow and tested. By the end of three days, they would come at a call, with help from Pi, who joined the training session. Then it was back for lunch. After that, she checked on the first underground and gave many suggestions for issues that came up; then, it was time for supper. After that, she called for Kennet. He needed to ride daily to get used to the new saddle, which was with the horses.

Thunder also managed to spend time in the new underground building for Star. to supervise the tasks to include time in her new underground home. She also had a surface home nearby with a chute to drop below immediately if trouble came. She wanted secure hideouts in her houses that allowed her to keep items she did not want anyone else to know existed.

One of the underground workers said he would take the oath, and if she wanted him to, he could make her hiding places, although he chose not to know how she planned on using them. She agreed as she was running out of time. He would get paid when he completed the project as it was not part of the town and stable that Star had ordered. Since he had helped build the new hideout, she knew he could be relied on for Kennet approved him.

Another blessing was Gwen. When she asked her to help with the horses, she readily agreed.

"You would let me ride the racers? Sure, I would love it. I have the morning shift, and my sister takes the afternoon one. Would that work? If not, I will see if she will trade me shifts so that you can still do what you had planned," Gwen told her.

"We will try it out with your current schedule. If it is too hot for the horses in the afternoon, we might have to adjust it. In the evening, I ride with Kennet maybe that would work best for you." Thunder suggested.

"Oh, yes, and I want to help. Thank you for allowing me to ride. When do you want me to meet you and where?" asked Gwen.

"Try supper, and if that doesn't work, find Shira and ask her to find me," replied the woman with a smile.

Mara had gone home a couple of times to check on her mom and found her asleep in the living room on the couch. She tiptoed to the attic and returned to her adventure.

"Ken, Gwen will be helping us work the new horses. She is coming this evening if nothing else interferes," advised Thunder.

"She loves horses, although her mom won't let her ride due to fear she will take a horse and run away," offered Ken.

"Oh, guess I better see what I can do about that," replied Thunder, who departed to find the owner.

Mara found Star sitting in a corner, staring into space.

"I understand I'm in trouble, so thought I best come direct," began Thunder.

"That makes two of us," replied the woman.

"In that case, shall we adjourn to my room and discuss in private?" asked Thunder.

"Good Idea," replied Star, and the two rose to depart in that direction.

Once inside the room and the door shut and secured, they sat down.

"It is my understanding, although after the fact, that I did something you wouldn't approve. I hired your daughter Gwen to aid me in riding out the forty. I do not have enough riders when there is only Ken and myself. Now I understand that you are against that idea. I never intended to upset you or do something you disapproved of."

"I'm glad you didn't know. That is one comment that I regret. It was hobbling the child, and so I put her to work in the stables, thinking it would give her time to be with the horses, which was like rubbing salt in an old wound. That was never my intent, and I could not figure out a way to reverse the comment. She should have the same freedoms of choice as everyone else. She's a sweet child and does all that I ask of her without a word of complaint. Please teach them all you can," asked Star with tears in her eyes.

"She will be paid and will train in the evening with Kennet and me if you have no objection. The forty will be taken above ground and worked there due to the number. I will train them both in weapons and riding, not just any horses, racers. At the same time, they must ride normal horses. They need to be able to train any horse that is available for use at a given time. They both need to know what the animals and weapons can do and when to use them and when not. It is not my intent to injure either of them. They need the training while they are young and flexible. I may not be here a long time and want to do as much as I can while my services bring me here," Thunder told Star.

"This is personal to you, is it not?" asked Star, who had some questions in her mind.

"Yes, and here your oath comes into play. My dad lost his life when I was six. My mom raised me and saved the insurance for my education. She works long, hard hours to keep me fed, clothed, and in a secure home. I have been trained since an early age to protect myself. A time came when I saw a man beating a woman almost to death. He was popped on the head and is currently in legal custody. No one else knows I was even there. The woman hid those thoughts in her mind, and her rescuer was long gone when the police got there. These two need to know how to defend themselves and when to run. If you have no objections, we could pick up another guitar and include her in the guitar lessons if Ken doesn't object to sharing his space. Let me ask him first, though he is so thrilled at the lessons."

"Tell you what, I will pull my daughter aside and suggest she begin singing lessons from me. I can also teach her how to play guitar though not near as well as you do. As far as music goes, we will practice when you and Ken do, though in a different area. The horse and weapons training is all yours since I do not have the knowledge or talent for that," responded Star.

"I will get it done. Now, what can I do for you?" asked Thunder with relief.

"I went out today, though in disguise, due to a message I received to meet a woman and small son. Someone had beaten her severely yet managed to hide the baby from anyone knowing of the child's existence except me. If he remains here, it is a death sentence for them both. They are in a secure room inside the top floor of the inn. The child is six months old and silent. A doctor needs to check him over. I know you must leave from time to time. You seem to pause in your speaking; then, it is often on an entirely different subject when you continue. If you have that ability, can you get them out of here?" asked Star.

"I am oath-bound not to share my story. Your assumption is correct. However, that is all I can tell you. Take me to where the child and mother are; then we shall see if I can help."

The two women moved up the stairs from underground to the surface business. After checking with all senses, they entered Wren's Inn. Everything was quiet, for it wasn't yet time for a meal. Star signaled to the man who popped his head out of the kitchen, and he left as he came, silently.

Star tapped lightly on the door of one of the rooms, and it opened just a crack.

"I have someone who wishes to speak with both of you," Star told the woman.

The door opened wider until the two were inside, then it was shut and secured once again.

On the bed lay a small infant. He was moving his feet around and playing with them. Not a sound did he make in the process. However, the little boy would smile and seem to laugh, yet it was all silent.

"He has never made a sound. Please, I do not want him killed, and if found, he will be. This woman says you might be able to help. Would you be willing?" asked the woman of about sixteen.

"If he is gone, then what happens to you?" asked Mara.

"I will run and keep running so they can't find me. There is no other way."

"Mrs. Boyer, have I your permission?" asked Thunder.

"Yes, for it will be too easy to find her here. Get oath first, though," replied the innkeeper.

"Follow me in an oath," began Thunder, who then led in the oath of silence.

"We need to follow the silent trail to the meadow," said Thunder.

Star looked a little puzzled, then realized what Thunder was thinking. She nodded, and they departed by a door at the back of the inn. The stable was again above ground, where it would remain since the lower level was living quarters for those rescued. The housing was under one side of the river, and the stable was underground on the other. They moved into a building and to the end while the girl watched their back trail while Thunder opened the secret panel. A scarf covered the girl's eyes when led by Thunder to the new location. Star carried the child as they moved into the mountain and followed the trail that would lead them to the underground entry.

The young woman and her child went to one of the housing units that Thunder ordered. The building was not close to her home, which kept it from anyone finding her except Star.

"Now that we are secure, may we have a name for you?" asked Thunder as she removed the scarf, and Star handed Joey to his mom.

"What is she doing there? I didn't put her in my story?" the author commented.

"It appears that I now am about to become grandmother and mother to a mother and her child."

"How old are you in truth?" asked the author.

"Seventeen a month ago," replied Mara with a chuckle.

"Where do you live?" the voice asked with a matching laugh.

"In Jacoran on the Tiera Sea within the town of Promise," responded Mara.

"No, I'm not asking about Thunder; where do you live?"

"Oh, sorry, when not here, I live in Prescot City, Montana, the state in the USA," replied Mara.

"At least you aren't the whole continent from me. Rather than explaining this to your mother, I thought you might be open to a different suggestion."

"I haven't gotten around to telling her about you either," laughed Thunder.

"You work for me now, and I will raise the mother and child until you leave home, and then we will discuss it. I raised four children who are now a lawyer, a doctor, a dentist, and a techno-geek. All of them have moved away and hardly ever write to me. The next question is, how do we get you and me together without anyone else getting involved?" asked the author.

"That's easy. I wait until my sleep time at home, come here and get the two, take them back if I can. Next, notify you they are coming and catch a cab to your house since you live about four miles from me," replied Thunder.

"I'll pay for the cab. We can catch up on who owes what later. When you get here, we need to discuss your goals for your new family. Adopting is an option and one I highly recommend. I am betting the child needs medical attention, and the mother will as well."

"Before any of them wake up here, I better get them squared away. Will get this done this evening, for we have a gang due in tomorrow," Thunder told the woman.

"Give me a call. I will be listening," replied the woman.

When there was a moment of silence, the women and child began again to show movement.

"Star, would you be willing to get this woman set up with some food and maybe some clean clothes for tonight? By daylight, we will have departed," Thunder told them.

Star immediately departed to get what would be needed.

"My name is Joy though they called me Pricilla. I ran away from a man who beat my mom and me. Now have no place to go and can't let Joey get into their hands. My step-dad will kill him because he is different; he said that I too would be killed cause I'm a cripple," the girl told her rescuer.

"You are to eat what Star brings for you. Then take these straps and put them where they will be handy to strap the child to your chest. I will be here as soon as people settle into their homes in the area. You will be departing with me if you have no objections. I will become your child's grandmother by adopting you. An exceptional woman is going to help until I am free of these duties to aid you. Do not be surprised at anything that happens either here or where we are going. You and the child will have a medical checkup to take care of any medical needs. I was hired to do a job here and must return for now," *actually two of them*, she thought with a chuckle.

"I have a couple of training classes to give so, please excuse me. I'm a bit late," Thunder told Joy.

When Star returned, she had a nightshirt, jeans, a shirt for the young mother, a blanket for Joey, and a meal with the load.

"This will tide you over until tomorrow, at least. I'm sure there will be food where you are going. Trust your guide, and you will be in good hands. Have faith that all will happen as it should," directed Star.

"She feels very trustworthy to me. I wish my mom had been like her," replied the teenager.

"Would you like some company?" asked Star of the shaking young woman.

"If you don't mind, I can't seem to stop shaking," Joy told her.

"You probably missed a few meals though I note that the child has not, such a happy little boy. You have done well by him," Star told her.

"I have tried my best. I did not let anyone know about Joey until you found us. My stepdad saw him once though he thought I was watching the child for someone. Know that people are looking for us, and we must not let them catch us. I will leave him with you and go if it makes them stop searching."

"No, I won't be the caregiver the other woman will be. Trust her, Joy, for she knows a lot that we don't. I've seen her care of her son, and you could not have asked for a better person," said Star, for that was how she saw Kennet in relationship to Thunder.

When Thunder returned two hours later, she was tired and dirty. She brought a pail of water with her for bathing and sent Ken to jump in the creek. Once again, clean, she felt much better. On one of her outings with Ken, she picked up some clothing that would fit her so she could change often. She preferred to be clean.

By the time Ken returned, with a very wet head, he was about ready for bed. She toweled his head dry and told him it was time for supper.

She stopped by the second home and knocked. When Joy came to the door, Thunder introduced Kennet, then explained that they were going to dinner and asked if she wanted anything.

"Would it be alright to have a sandwich? I can't leave Joey alone, and someone might tell that he is here," Joy told them.

"We will bring you a full meal. I'll take those dishes from lunch back to the kitchen at the same time," Thunder advised the girl.

"Meat would be best and a glass of milk since I am nursing," replied the young woman.

"Be back soon," Thunder told Joy before she and Ken departed. Her new area would keep the transient area separate from her home and private stables. No one could enter if she were on site, and all was secure.

"What do you want for the evening meal, Kennet?" asked Thunder when they were passing through the caves.

"I always want something I shouldn't have, or that is too much food for me. Please order, and I will eat it," Kennet replied with a smile.

"That makes no sense. Let me see; I plan on having a steak with potatoes and gravy, then some vegetables and maybe a dessert. That means I'll have to work harder to keep my weight down. However, I'm hungry tonight."

"Me too, if I cannot eat all my meat, maybe I can give some of it to Shira?" he asked with his eyes sparkling.

"She doesn't like her meat cooked. We will see what we can work out," said Thunder. When they got to the lunchroom, she spotted Star.

"Mrs. Boyer, could you have your chef fix two steaks? One is to be medium-well while the other steak is to have one-quarter cut from it. The one-quarter is for Kennet's requirements. We will take the uncooked portion with us for Shira," directed Thunder in a soft voice, for she did not want others to hear her speaking with Star.

"That will be okay. Will get it ready," laughed Mrs. Boyer.

"Don't forget the meal for Joy," Ken told Mara.

Thank you, for I probably would have. Have a few things on my mind," Thunder said to him.

He ran to the kitchen and told Mrs. Boyer about forgetting

to order for Joy, then strolled back to the table and sat down.

"Thank you for the reminder. How did you like having Gwen join us for your evening lessons?" asked Thunder.

"She has wanted to ride forever, and now she has permission. She is thrilled, and I don't mind sharing, maybe not all the time, though sometimes. When I was looking for a place to stay, she didn't seem to care if it was here," Kennet explained.

"That is the way we all should be. Being selfish keeps us from having friends; however, we have to be careful who we trust with our friendship, too," replied Thunder.

"Yes, I know that. Have only honest people in Kennet's friends. If they aren't honest, they are not encouraged to ask for me. I'm so glad you found me right away. Tried to be where you were most apt to see me," Ken told her.

"How did you know I was coming?" asked Thunder, for she had not told anyone of her posting.

"The voice said you were to be trusted and were on your way. It never leads me wrong," Ken replied.

"May I ask what voice?" asked Thunder.

"He is talking about me. We have never met; however, he too needs a good home. Would you object to him coming with the girl and baby? That way, I can get a picture of him, and we will get them adopted by you if that works for what you want to do," replied the author.

"I was not looking forward to leaving him behind when I return home. Yes, that works, though he must remain here with me until I finish the story, and we finish our assignment," responded Thunder.

"Is a story every finished?" asked the author cryptically.

"Mara?" called another voice.

"Yes, mom, on my way," said the girl as she grabbed Kennet by the hand, and they departed.

"Ken, not a word, please. My Mom does not know of you. However, I needed to be sure you could come and go when I do. Please stay up here until I come back, for a lot needs to happen before we go get Joy."

The boy nodded his head in acceptance and found a blanket in a corner where he lay down to sleep, for this was his nighttime.

Mara ran lightly down the attic stairs and then to the main floor, entering as if from the kitchen.

"What you need, mom?" asked the girl.

"We need to get ready for church. It starts in one hour."

"I met a young boy yesterday, age about ten, and he was asking me if he could go to church with us. Would you mind?" Mara asked.

"Not at all, bring him along," replied her mother.

"Author, you wrote the story. Would you please write in some decent clothes for Kennet and a full night of rest?" Mara asked the author.

"Done," was the response.

When ready, she moved to the attic and awakened Kennet.

"We are going to church, and you are coming as well. I know you must be tired. However, we may get a chance to sleep later," Mara told him.

"I'm ready. I went back and slept the night, then picked up the new clothes you got me and am ready," replied Kennet.

"You will act as if knocking at the back door, which I will answer. The story is you asked me to let you go to church with me, and you will meet my mom. I didn't want to leave you in a strange house alone. This way, we get a snack at church, meet a few people, then return here," Mara explained.

"Never been to church before, will there be a lot of folks there?" he asked.

"We only have a hundred or so on Sunday," replied the young woman. "Please do not mention where you call home. That must remain our secret for now. Let's say you are from here and let it go at that."

He followed the directions given and soon knocked on the kitchen door to be let in by Mara.

When they reached the church, people were milling around and visiting though they first selected a seat and left something to show reserved.

He did as she said, spoke when talked to, and observed all around him.

"Aren't you, Mara Jacobson," said a new yet familiar voice.

"Why, yes, I am. How did you know?" asked Mara.

"By asking, and this must be your son Kennet," said the woman, yet all around them remained frozen for the conversation.

"Hello, Mrs. N-Sign; how are you today?" Kennet asked the tall, gray-haired lady.

"Happy to meet you, Ken. I imagine we will see more of one another in the not too distant future," replied the woman.

He smiled and nodded.

"Now I can relax and know my charges will be in good hands. Thank you for helping me make this happen. I leave for college on August twentieth, so I must have everything done before then," Mara explained.

"Would that be Prescot University?"

"Yes, I am much looking forward to it," Mara replied.

Chapter 5

Learning the keys

"You will be right out my back door. Drop-in and see your family whenever you wish. You have the address and will be most welcome. Who knows, I might even be able to help you in your studies. I will contact the Dean of Students and see if it would be alright for you to live at my house," replied Mrs. N-Sign.

"That would be great. I would like to have Kennet and Joy in school since neither has any education. We will need to see that they have medical exams and any issues resolved. I wish there were a grant we could apply for to cover their living expenses until I make an income to support us all," commented Mara.

"There is, and I know just the person to apply for it. At the same time, I am thinking about having an application done to put a second home on my property for Joy and her son. I am so looking forward to having them spend time with me. They have to let me write, however, for that pays my bills," chuckled the woman.

"I will tell them," said Mara though she could feel Thunder looking on in the background.

When she felt the switch, she began to look around the area. She saw a man moving along the wall toward the back of the church.

"Kennet, stay with Mrs. N-Sign it appears I have some work to do," she told them before moving toward the man. When she caught up with him, he was at the door to the Pastor's office.

"Hello Graeson, what brings you this way?" asked Mara of the man.

"Oh, I just wanted to meet with the pastor before service." The man was startled and trying not to let it show.

"Then let's speak with him together, for he sent for me", replied Mara.

Having no option, the man went into the pastor's office with Mara following. She saw him reach into his coat, and she noted the handle of a gun. She picked up a large paperweight on the desk. She intended to hit him with it when she noticed that it was now a sword in her hand. She knocked the man out. The Pastor sat with a look of shock on his face.

"Sorry, Pastor, I saw the gun and thought you might need a little backup. Please call the police," Mara directed though she wondered why the man wanted to hold up the pastor before service. The money wouldn't be in his office until afterward.

He heard her yet now thought he was the one to knock out the man with the gun. He reached for his phone and dialed the police station. He asked for the chief.

"Chief, this is Pastor Riser. A man just entered my office with a weapon. Would you be so kind as to collect him as it is nearly time for service," the pastor told him.

He set down the phone and looked around.

"How am I going to explain this?" he asked himself.

"Try by saying he pulled a gun, and you hit him with a paperweight," whispered Mara, who then slipped out of the room just before the Police Chief entered, for he had been visiting with some in the waiting room since it was also his church. He had received the call on his cell.

Mara returned to Kennet and Mrs. N-Sign.

"Good job. Now it is time to find our seats. Would you mind if I joined you and your mom? She is an amazing seamstress. After service, I would like to talk to her about a dress I need for graduation. Might also see if she is willing to make a suit for this young man," commented Mrs. N-Sign.

"Hello, Shelly. I haven't seen you in a while. How are you doing?" asked Mara's mom, for she turned to see her standing nearby.

"I was telling your daughter that I need to order a garment for spring. I will also need a suit for this young man," explained Shelly.

"I would be honored to do that. Didn't someone tell me that you are now a writer?" asked Mrs. Jacobson.

"Yes, and it is such a wonderful way to meet new people. Your daughter will be working for me starting Tuesday, for I understand you need her on Monday for laundry. She has to proofread my books before they go to the publisher. Tuesday through Saturday will be times when she will do my books in the evenings, and the rest of the time, she will be in college working toward her degree. Mara, didn't you say you have a free ride scholarship? You will be staying with me then. I have a large home and take in young women who don't have money to pay for their lodging. I like the young company," Shelly explained.

"I will miss her company; however, know that once Mara starts college, she won't have time to help me anyhow. I'll hire someone to be of help in her place," responded Mrs. Jacobson.

"Time to start for here comes the Pastor," Mara commented.

She was not surprised to have Shelley join her and her mom for a meal after church. Her mother always cooked things on Saturday to serve those she invited home on Sunday. Today they had a rib roast put on a timer ato be ready when they reached their home.

Kennet immediately asked Mrs. Jacobson if he could help in any way. Mara set the table before they left for church. Now, all it needed was the roast, which would be done at half past the hour, and with it came the potatoes and veggies. The cold drinks were in the refrigerator and hot drinks set on a timer, which would have them done soon, for they went off as the group entered the home.

"Tell you what, come with me, and we will get two pies from the freezer. I will put them in the oven to thaw and be ready by the time we want dessert," Mrs. Jacobson said.

"I love pie of any kind," Kennet replied.

"Shelly, how do you come to have such a following?" asked Grace as she and Kennet returned with the pies.

"I wrote a book, and that opened several doors to new friends," replied Shelly.

"What kind of book do you write?" asked Mrs. Jacobson.

"Adventure, I guess it would be. It might be fantasy or could be Sci-Fi, I imagine. However, my aim was just for good reading. It is fun to watch a story unfold and become a part of it for a time."

Mara managed to keep a straight face by distracting Kennet.

"Rather than have anything spilled, why don't you tell me what you want, and I will dish it up for you?" said Mara with a smile.

"Please, may I have some of everything? It all looks splendid," he replied.

Since he seldom walked anyplace, always running, he didn't have to worry about weight gain. Mara was so proud of him. He was honest, obedient, didn't get upset at different things happening, and was willing to help in any way he could. Kennet had called her mom during one of the riding lessons and didn't even seem to notice. When she didn't object, he now used that title all the time. She liked the sound. He was learning the morning training quickly. Only three days yet, he recognized all the letters and numbers. Now was trying to put them into words.

"Grace, would you object if Mara came to my home this evening? I have some young folks coming by to see if we can get along, for I have room for about fifteen young folks to stay with me, and some of the students cannot afford to stay in college dorms, so my home gives them another option. Like the laughter and company of those youngsters," Shelly told Mara's mother.

"That would mean she gets home late, and we have a busy day planned for tomorrow," replied Grace with concern.

"Then, I will keep her overnight and have her to your house immediately after breakfast if that will work for you," Shelly replied.

"What are your thoughts about it?" asked Grace of her daughter.

"I think it would be fun. I would like to see where I will be staying to get ready for college," replied the girl though she left it to her mother to decide.

Kennet stayed busy with his food.

"Okay, when you finish eating, go get your overnight pack, and you can go when Mrs. N-Sign does. It will save her from making another trip and you from riding your bicycle that far.

They spent the afternoon with Mara playing the piano and a floor harp. Everyone sang hymns and enjoyed a time of relaxation. When Mrs. N-Sign suggested that it was time to go, Mara ran upstairs and put her book, nightclothes, and everyday clothing in her bag before returning to the main floor ready to go.

"Mom, I'm taking care of Kennet until his folks get back. He will go with me. Mrs. N-Sign says it will be okay. They left him in my care," said Mara.

The three were soon on their way to the author's home though the driver stopped at a clothing store for women and children. They purchased clothes in a variety of sizes to take with them. The baby would need some items, as would Kennet. Things that were theirs and not just whatever came to hand.

"I live forty miles from town. I have an address in Prescot for those who wish to locate me. However, my main home is farther out. When I told you that the college is outside, my back door that is true if you don't have a concern about distance," laughed Shelly.

When they reached their destination, it was a large home with a well-manicured lawn encircling it. Stables were in a row in the back area beyond the mowed grass. In the distance, one could see the spires of the college.

"You two make yourselves at home. Then you need to get our other two guests. They should have nothing to fear here," the woman explained.

"May I call you Granda?" asked Mara. "My grandmothers are both gone, so never got to know them. I think you would make a wonderful grandmother."

"Thank you, child. You honor me. It would appear you have some other questions you would like settled before you continue your mission," Shelly told her latest guests.

"I know there is a way to accelerate learning, for I used one form to get through high school by age sixteen. Since I now have a family to support, I need to earn some degrees to understand better how to take care of them."

"What degrees do you have in mind?" asked Shelly with interest.

"Business, veterinarian, medical, and precious metals degree, which I know is called something else though can't recall it this minute. I need to learn to ride properly, run a ranch, get Kennet, Joy, and Joey educated, then take what I have and make it the best possible. I need to learn about those grants too. Want to pay as much in subsidies as can be so that the money you gave me will last," Mara explained.

"The money I gave you?" questioned Shelly.

"I filed on the property behind Star's Inn as soon as the paperwork was in my possession. I made sure I got water and mineral rights, as well. It seems that part of what I purchased is a Motherlode of gold. I brought some with me to see if it would make the transfer when Kennet and I did. It does," she said and handed the woman a one-pound lump of melted gold and did not mention the pounds she still carried.

"Have you any idea what that is worth here?" asked Shelly in surprise.

"I heard that gold was five hundred an ounce a while back. That would make it eight thousand a pound. Therefore, fifty pounds would result in four hundred thousand. That should be enough to get started here. You offered to help tutor me. I can pay for that. The book time I offered, and there is no charge at all. Most important is to take care of Ken, Joy, and Joey. If Joey and Joy can get a doctor's appointment soon, there is money to pay for it. I will be in school the first week in September; therefore, if everyone can have a medical checkup before then, maybe you would go with us to see that I do everything right. Now comes the part I'm not sure how to handle. How long will it take for the adoption to go through for them? Otherwise, there could be problems due to my age and their needs," said Mara.

"I filed the paperwork as soon as you asked to replace Thunder. The approval came through yesterday. A special courier brought it. Here it is," said Shelly, who handed the young woman a sealed envelope.

Mara opened it with eyes glistening and read the documents. The envelope contained other materials; it turned out. In her hand were official certificates showing that Mara Jacobson had adopted Joy and Kennet. The other showed a request for a name change to Thunder Press.

"Wow, I don't think Thunder will much like that idea. I only asked to be Thunder for one book."

"She was offered a chance to retire while still alive and took it once she saw how you were operating as Thunder. I gave her a home some time ago that is secure, and she has many friends she has helped along the way. Lightning, Pi, and Shira have agreed to become your partners. I am betting that the forty-four will transfer over as well. Let's not test it just yet, though. We need to get Joy and Joey out first," Shelly responded.

"Then let's get it done. We can discuss this when we

return when we return or as time goes on once we move here. I wish mom had help now cause then I could sign up for some summer courses and begin College now. The sooner I get started, the sooner I will be finished. Where we were, I must take care of problems. Promised to train Star's daughter in riding and arms plus that gang is still a problem," Mara told Granda.

"It is a bit late tonight to deal with that, plus it is Sunday. Let's go a step at a time. I cannot enter my books. It causes me to lose control of the story. That means I won't be able to go with you and help. The best I can offer is to back you up from here," Granda advised.

"That will work fine. Now Kennet and I need to get back and see how things are going there, and as soon as we can, we will return with Joy and Joey. I think it is time to bring Pi back this time. It will tell us whether there is any chance of bringing the forty-four here. Shira can watch over the bank while I am gone. You will have fifty pounds of refined, bricked gold when we return. I need the funds to get things working here. Kennet, change into your story clothes, and I will do the same. We need to leave," directed Thunder, and Kennet felt the urgency too.

Mara grabbed the book, placed it on a stand, and opened it to the page they had been reading.

"Wait, if you are bringing Pi, hadn't you better put the book in the stable? She might not appreciate being in a house that might not support her weight."

"Thank you hadn't thought of that," replied Thunder, and they ran for the stable. The book was opened and set on the floor in the center of the barn. As Granda watched from one of the stalls, Thunder and Kennet disappeared.

They landed in their rented room in the underground and could hear sounds in the hall. After opening the door cautiously, they moved into the corridor. People were breaking up things in their sight. Thunder returned to the room and opened the secret hiding place to pull out Lightning.

"Kennet, hide!" she ordered as she walked toward the mayhem.

"What is going on here?" she shouted at those causing the destruction.

"We are here to get what belongs to us," said one of the men.

"And what might that be?" asked Thunder.

"Our horses and gear, we know you have them, for we left them here," said one of the men.

"What do you mean? How would we keep horses underground? You can't be serious!"

"We backtracked where we had been, and the trail led us to The Wren's Nest Inn. Some folks saw the horses here, and now they aren't."

"They aren't here; you took them with you when you left. Why blame us for your loss of memory? Now get out of here and quit destroying private property. Move, all of you!" Thunder directed as she pulled her lesser sword.

They started scrambling.

"Make sure they forget about the underground and never to return unless to drop off more horses," commented Mara.

"Done, they just left you a few more," replied Granda.

The two laughed at how easy it seemed, yet both knew they were lucky.

"Star, are you here?" asked Thunder.

"Oh, thank you! The RIOT will kill us without you. They found Gwen in the stable and have her tied up to take with them. Please, she needs to leave. Will you take her as well?" asked Star.

"Yes, if she is willing. We must hurry for a lot has to be done this night. Kennet, where are you?" called Thunder.

"I'm here, mom," he promptly replied, for he had followed

her yet tried to stay out of the way of anyone injuring him.

"Go to Pi and Shira. Tell them the plan and stay with them until I get there. Find Gwen on your way and keep her with you. Star, you need to stay underground and do not go upstairs for anything. I mean that, not for anything! Send someone else though I suggest you tell them to move through the outside gates, not the one that connects the upper and lower areas," she could see that her guess was right, for Dan stood by Star. He was the one who gave away the entry.

"I am sorry he was warned and would not listen. Now he sees the damage he has done. Now maybe he will listen and learn. He will not be leaving the underground. His poor judgment nearly cost the lives of many people. Had you not returned, mine would have been first followed by his sister's. Now hurry, you must finish what you started," said Star with tears in her eyes.

Kennet was long gone, and Thunder moved out of the underground by the back way. She then entered the caves and ran for where the horses would be. From there, she dropped to the home to reach Joy.

Tapping lightly on the door caused it to open quickly.

"Thank goodness it is you. Something felt so dangerous and wrong we were packing up to run," said Joy.

"Yes, we are going to do that. Here let me help you with the straps. Gather up anything that shows you were ever here. Put it all in that piece of cloth, and tie it with the smaller strap, then put it on your back. Now come with me, for we must get a few things done, and now is the time," Thunder told her in a gentle voice, for she did not want to frighten the child.

They moved to where Pi, Gwen, and Kennet were waiting.

"Shira, will you please watch over everyone? I will return as soon as I can," said Thunder.

She had moved the gear for the forty-four to the back ranch. Mara would have to remove everything along with the gold, weapons, and other items found with the horses. As she watched, the horses walked by her, and as they did, saddlebags, saddles, bridles, and pack gear moved to the back of each of the animals.

"Pi, you need to tell them to move nose to tail and touching. You are all going back with us. Shira, we will return as soon as we can."

Joy and Joey rode on Pi, Kennet rode his saddle on one of the racers and led. Thunder mounted another at the end of the line. In a short time, they were moving through an opening in the side of the mountain, and when they exited, it was in a stable on Shelly's ranch. She was still in the stall watching them arrive.

"Trouble, I take it," Granda commented.

"You could say that. The gang came early due to a report by one of the citizens and caught Star's son as he used the hidden stairwell to go from the underground to the inn. They tried to smash up a few things. Thank you for loading all the gear on the horses so I could move them all at once. RIOT will be back, I'm sure, although they will not find a thing that says we have their horses," said Thunder, for she was still very much in place.

Large boulders in the ground formed a barrier on the meadow side of the property between her valley and the horse stables underground. The author felt the same way and put it in place, then locked the gate above ground that was twenty feet high between Thunder's valley ranch and the Inn Meadow, although it looked like there was nothing except mountains beyond that location.

"Gwen, would you help me get the horses settled? There are stalls for all of them. I will put the saddles up if you will remove them and place them in front of their stall," that was when she realized she still had Lightning with her.

She looked around for someplace to hide it and spotted the box in Pi's stall. With a chuckle, she put the sword inside.

Once the horses settled, Thunder felt that she had put

in a full day shoveling. The tack room had logs built into the walls to hold the saddles and accommodate up to a thousand horses from the days when this was an operating ranch that raised thoroughbred horses. Each post and stall had a number on it. The gear matched the horse in that stall, for each animal took their usual horse stall from their place in the book.

"Granda, I know I'm tired, though I shouldn't be. How many saddles and pack frames do you see?" asked Mara.

"I see about a hundred plus the stud; why?" she asked.

"No wonder I'm tired. We left with forty-five horses and arrived with a hundred and one? Okay, where does the stallion go?" Thunder asked no one in particular.

"He is in the stallion holding area. Kennet asked Pi to tell him what was going on and where he was to go," Gwen replied.

"Thank you. Granda, please order enough hay and grain for that many horses. For tonight they will remain where they are. I will see what tomorrow brings for Kennet, and I must return to the book. Gwen, will you care for the stock here while we go back and take care of the rest of this mess? Your mother asked that I remove you, and she knows you are in my care. Granda can answer some of your questions, I'm sure. We will return once things are okay there. Didn't want that gang to find the horses, or there would be a lot more trouble," Thunder explained, for that was who Gwen knew.

"I will make the appointments when you return for otherwise, no idea of your availability," said Granda.

"We have to finish what we started. Give me a week, and we will be back. Shira will come next time, as will our operating capital. Or I should say, more of it," said Thunder. "Do you have a vault I can use?"

"Actually, yes, there is a vault here. Your group is oathsworn, are they not?" asked Granda.

"Ladies, speak up, are any of you oathsworn?" Thunder

asked.

"Oh yes," replied Gwen with no hesitation.

"Yes, I am though Joey is too little," Joy replied.

"I am oathsworn too," Kennet said to be sure the woman knew to include him.

"Gwen and Kennet, help me move the saddlebags to a new location. Joy, have a seat over there with Joey so you can feed him. Here is where you put the saddlebags while I take care of other things," said Thunder, concealed entry while the rest of the group gathered up the bags and pack boards, all of which were full of something substantial, so they dragged them.

Thunder stood by a blank wall. The children began pulling the bags to Thunder, and soon the horses pushed the children gently to the side and gripped the bags with their teeth to pull them where Thunder waited. Thunder dropped the containers down a chute near where she stood. Once all were gone, she traded places with Granda to do the sorting.

Mara asked Granda to take everyone else to her home. Mara would join them as soon as Thunder finished her inventory.

The sacks found inside each saddlebag made it necessary to view the contents. Thunder took some of the bags and tied them up once again before putting them in a walk-in vault left open by Granda. Next, she looked for any more pistols like the forty she already had; she put those together in a location near other weapons. She went through sorting what was there. Something was tugging at her mind, though.

Again, Thunder moved to the sacks of gold, and seeing a scale nearby; she used the pan by it to pour each bag into a sorting tray. In each of the bags was an electronic device to monitor the location. Mara went into the hall, and there found a bucket with a waterspout nearby. The bucket was filled halfway and moved to the devices. Each device found was dropped into the bucket as quickly as possible. Thunder removed each of the unique weapons from their containers. The same happened with the electronics found within. By the time she had gone through everything, the bucket was full of sensing devices.

"Granda, if you can hear me when I'm in the book, can you hear me now?" asked Thunder.

"Yes," she heard.

"Ask Gwen to watch over the group there, and please return to the stable. I am still there."

"On my way," was the reply.

When Granda entered the stable, she spoke.

"I am here," she told the girl, for she knew her talents and didn't want to startle her.

"Come down, please," Thunder said.

"What do you have?" asked Granda as she reached the bottom of the stairs.

"Speak in your usual way with me."

The woman thought a moment, trying to understand the information given, then smiled and spoke as usual, which froze all around them.

"A real problem, it seems," said Granda.

"Everything is rigged with technology from our own time. It has been waterlogged, which should short circuit it. That is how that bunch knew the horses were in Star's underground. That also means that those horses could have been originally from this time. Pi is the only exception. While waiting, I asked Pi to check with each of the horses and let me know if that bunch stole them. I gave her options of stolen, bought, or raised by the group. She chose the second option meaning the men bought them. When I went through the pack boards, I found the title sheets, and none show an owner's name. That makes no sense to me. Anyhow all packs are now sorted, and all containers checked," Thunder reported.

"How about we also check them electronically? Then here is a scrambler that will keep any devices from recording any of us. Now use this thing and see what it tells you about the packs, all of them, for pockets can be sewed inside that would hold those devices. After you do that, we will check each horse."

"I'm glad you come equipped. It looks like I need to get a degree in electronics as well," commented Mara with a chuckle.

"At least, find a tech geek that is knowledgeable and can make them for you," laughed Granda, for that is what she had done.

Chapter 6

When it begins

Having checked all areas, they felt better, for the animals carried no sensors within their bodies though there were others in the saddlebags and pack boards.

"Pi, tell them not to let anyone put any electronics in or on them without my explicit consent. We will deal with what is in saddlebags and such," Thunder ordered, and the horse nodded.

Once all was secure, the women returned to the main house. There they found everyone in the front room and fast asleep.

"Joy, time to wake up long enough to put you and Joey to bed. We have a room ready for you both," Thunder told her.

The girl got up and picked up the baby to follow her new mom. Soon the baby was being fed, and then Joy could return to sleep.

Next, Gwen was awakened and moved in like manner. Kennet was left to sleep until time to go. Pi would be ready at a call.

"Granda, we need to look at what we have and where we are. I have a bank account mom opened for me when I started school. It doesn't have a lot in it. However, that might be a place to put what I have acquired," Mara suggested.

"Why not open a new account and call it your business account. It needs to be in a secure location. That way, you can put me on as your second signer to pay for things like hay and grain when it is needed, and you are gone. As your capital increases, you need to find an honest, reliable accountant," advised Granda.

"That's a good idea, also need an account for just the four

additions and their needs. It seems to me if we have these few, we may be getting more. Your book has become a gateway, so we need to use it to rescue all we can, even if we then lose that story from your inventory," replied Mara.

"No, we won't forget the story or lose it. I hold copyright on each of my books. People will not be allowed entry, though. When you return this time, be sure you have plenty of rest, for you may not get sleep at your mom's."

"Since Kennet is sleeping now, my guess is we won't be able to sleep in the book either."

"Didn't you say that the book story stays as you leave it until your return? Why not let all of you sleep here tonight? I will then return you and Kennet to your mom's place. You can help with the laundry. I will contact the Dean and see about getting you in school sooner. Tell your mother, and you can move here full time. It means you will be juggling school classes while you are checking out the book for me. Can you handle that and your new family as well?"

"Yes, I look forward to the challenge. Okay, I agree. I will let Pi know we are not leaving and get some sleep. We will go back the day after tomorrow. Only one thing concerns me. When I returned the last time, the men were inside, and the battle was ongoing. If they can do that, those in the inn are in danger, and we need to be there."

"You have a point. Come with me," said Granda, who led Mara to another part of the vast mansion.

It turned out to be her private area, which had an exclusive lock that only her handprint could activate. She had a master suite to include her writing area. They walked over to the table, and Granda picked up a book. She opened it to where they now were.

"Record: full security at Wren's Inn, regular customers to not include the RIOT, a time of rest only. No action until Thunder can return to deal with it."

"Granda, you have my oath as well. I will not say anything about you or those you work with ever. Thank you for trusting me and allowing me to use your stable, house my new family, given me access to your vault, and now are aiding me in getting started with college soon to get the degrees I will need," said Mara.

"To be honest, I am thrilled to have someone who knows my book so well and that is also willing to allow me to aid in your adventure. It makes me feel younger and full of life. You have my oath, or you would not be in my book," laughed Granda.

"I suggest we get some sleep for tomorrow will indeed be a busy day at my mom's. We did the bedding last week, so it should not be a massive undertaking. However, if it is a light laundry, mom also does the fabric she is making into something to be sure it does not shrink after being made into an order. Usually, it is a twelve-hour day. On Tuesday, she will get her fabric orders. She can't order a whole bunch at a time, for we don't have the storage room she needs. I wish she had a store near our home she could operate out of and use her house home for herself and any company. We each have a bedroom on the second floor. There is an attic, which is where I go to read and not be disturbed. Then there is the main floor with front room, sitting room, kitchen, bathroom, walk-in pantry, and all of that is needed for her sewing, except for the pantry and part of the kitchen."

"We must find her someplace more suited to her needs. She would need one with an apartment for her live-in help. It needs to be in the city limits where she is accessible to everyone," suggested Shelly.

"Do you know of a goldsmith? Have a lot of gold that will become bricks, and it is in your vault. Once it is in that form, no one can identify where it came from, a Goldsmith told me. We will leave it in your safe until needed. Would you be willing to go house hunting with mom? We need to come up with an idea first to have her join us once we find something. Must find someone willing to work with and for her. Mom isn't hard to get along with; only a bit distracted when working on something. I run errands for her, except for help with the laundry and the weekly chore list. If that person could also keep house, it would free up more time for mom to sew, which she loves and is good at."

"We will see what I can find. Now next question: The Dean wants to know what subjects you wish to study. I told him lapidary, vet, physician, surgeon, equestrian, business, accounting, ranch running, flying a plane, overseeing a full staff, real estate, and whatever you add later. He said you could do it if you are willing to do some of it online due to time constraints in doing too many classes at the same time," advised Granda.

"That is under a dozen, so should be alright. Do you have degrees in any of those that would help?" asked Mara.

"Yes, I have the first six and can oversee a staff plus buy and sell real estate. I do not know how to fly a plane, although I can run a ranch."

"Then add them by all means. It sounds like fun. That will make you my tutor, and we need one for each of the additions. I have no idea how much education Gwen and Joy have. Kennet has what I have given him. I need to look at a way to bring the heavy stuff back with me. Also, we might need rides if more folks need to come here. You said you did not write Joy and Joey into the story; therefore, we could get others. At the same time, you did write in Gwen, yet she is here, which could mean her family will be following," commented Mara.

Mara returned to the story the night laundry day ended. She was scheduled to meet with the goldsmith and found him waiting. It was just four PM in the book world.

"Glad you could make it. It seems things have been a bit rough around here of late. Someone tried to rob the mine night before last. We know that people broke into places of business as well. I wish I had a place to hide and preferably far away from here. They don't pay me enough to put my life on the line for some gold that isn't even mine," he told her.

"Pack up your gear and meet me here at six in the morning. Load a pack animal with what you want to bring with you.

For now, we need to take care of some other business. I will see you then," Thunder advised.

"On my way and thank you," he replied, then handed over the fifty pounds of gold bricks, which meant five of them.

"Be sure to bring whatever you need to make more. Have some to process where you are going," Thunder said to the goldsmith, for the man had taken the oaths.

Thunder took the gold bricks and hid them with Shira, then went looking for Star. She also advised Shira they would leave together this time. She stopped in the leather shop and asked the owner to make her a vest. It would have to hold ten to fifty pounds each with the full load, not over two hundred pounds. He got her measurements, and she departed to look for Star.

She went into the underground kitchen and asked if anyone had seen Star.

"Not today," replied the cook.

"What time is it now?" she asked.

"I would guess about midnight. We are the night crew here to fix breakfast," he responded.

"Then she is probably sleeping. Thank you," she told the man and departed.

"Something is amiss," she said aloud once in the caves of the mountain.

"Have you any idea what?" asked Granda.

"Star is missing; there is no guard on duty, and the men in the kitchen are not the ones that should be there. I hired a Goldsmith who is leaving with me. He said that last night, someone robbed several businesses. Kennet is sleeping with Shira now. I entered from the front of the inn, and no one questioned me at all."

"Did you take Lightning with you?" asked Granda.

"No, it is in the stall with Pi," replied Thunder.

"That is what is wrong. I will awaken Pi and send the sword back," Granda told her editor.

"Tell her to come to the back stable. That is where Kennet and Shira are. I am on my way there," she responded and departed on the run.

When she reached the ranch home, she took the secret passage underground. Much to her relief, there sat Star and her last two children.

"Forgive me; I should not be here. However, there is chaos in town. Someone burned some businesses, and I'm scared. Tell me what to do, please. Some men I don't know showed up at the underground Inn and said they were the new cooks. All I could think of was hiding here until you returned. Then I noticed that all the horses are gone, and it frightened me. What is going on?" Star asked.

"It is time for me to go to work. Do you want to leave and join Gwen? You will be meeting my mentor, and she will see to your care until I return. It is now time for me to settle things here and take care of the gang for the last time. We need to find out who they are, where they are from, and know their intent in terrorizing a town. Whether I win or lose, you will be safe with Granda."

She heard something and moved to the underground stable. Pi was entering the end of the main hall.

"Thank you, Pi; I should have remembered Lightning. My apologies; you and Shira must take Star, her two kids, and the goldsmith back with you. It is up to me to finish the job that put me here. We have learned that the horses were from my home time. Kennet will need to go with you, as well. As soon as the Goldsmith gets here, you have to go," directed Thunder.

"I got that; he is in the first room though his horse is in the upper stable there. Do you want them where you are?" asked Granda.

"Yes, please. Those who are going must leave immediately," replied Thunder.

She looked up and saw the man leading two packhorses laden with as much as it could hold.

"Take the halter for your pack animal and hold onto Pi's tail. Star mount up. Your daughter can walk with the goldsmith. Your son is to grasp the halter of the pack animal and the tail of Pi, though don't pull. She is aiding you to safety," Thunder told them.

Everyone did as she ordered, and the animals waited. Nothing happened.

"They can't leave, for something is holding them here," said Thunder.

"You are the key; they can only leave if you do as well," replied Granda.

Thunder was now wearing the sword and new vest, which was full of gold. It weighed her down. However, she moved out to grab Pi's halter and lead them to safety.

"Granda, they are here. Please take care of them. Here is a vest that needs put in the vault. You will need it if I don't get back," said Thunder.

"You will return; I will make sure of it." Granda told her with great determination.

Granda asked Gwen to put the animals away while she took the new guests to her home. She managed to drop the vest down the chute without being seen.

Thunder moved toward the place where the animals had landed, and as she stepped through the doorway, she felt she had company. Once in the book, she found Kennet, Shira, and Pi with her.

"It is their battle, too, you know," said Granda in a whisper.

"I tried to make you safe. Now you could well die here," Thunder told them with sadness.

"Make sure we don't!" said a different voice only in her head.

Thunder checked her weapons, took the stirrups off her saddle, and removed Pi's bridle before realizing she had two horses with her. One wore the leather device the leatherman made, with Kennet on it. Those stirrups she left in place for he would have to remain on his mount, to have any chance at all. As for herself, she might fight mounted or on the ground. She began in the saddle, and at her word, the team moved from the upper stable, where they had landed.

As the Thunder team was preparing to fight, Granda was securing as much as possible. She closed all access to the other side of the river. Next, the underground stables were closed and hidden. She had already placed a steel barrier above ground where Thunder's private property began and blocked all underground areas from anyone except the T-team. The room that Kennet and Thunder used initially had to be locked as well as the interview room. Next, she secured the underground city in the same manner. Making sure there weren't any unknowns in those areas first. She also locked all the exits from the inn, whether underground or above level. No one would be able to enter the underground that was not already there. With some persuasion, she got rid of the phony cook crew. She sent a few bees to visit them. Then she sat listening for the next clue as to what was required.

"Kennet, remember what I told you to do. Tell me about the problems, then find a place to hide. I do not want to lose you. You are my son and much loved," Thunder told him.

Ken nodded in agreement and tried to move as she had shown him to make it easy on the horse he was on because he would not always be ten years old. At the same time, he was watching for Shira. She had disappeared again.

"They come," Kennet said and looked down one street they had crossed.

"Find a hole," she directed and turned to face the incoming.

He looked to the side and saw Shira. He moved in her direction then waited as he felt the tension. She bared her teeth at the incoming riders and then looked at him.

"Yes, I am willing to fight if that is what you are asking. If you tell me what to do, I will do it. Can you talk to Granda?" he asked.

Shira nodded.

"Tell her, and she will tell me then," he responded.

"She says you are to call on Kennet's friends. Since most are locked underground, who does she mean?" Granda asked.

"I know. Duster, get me to the mine," Kennet directed, and the horse moved slowly at first to be sure the rider was secure before racing away.

Shira remained.

When Kennet reached the mine area, the guard stopped him.

"The Goldsmith is not here anymore, my friend. What can I do for you this time?" he asked.

"I know, although your help is needed. Thunder Press is here and has no backup. We need to help because they outnumber her. She said that the gang needs stopping. There are some questions that she must ask before deciding what needs to happen with them. Will you leave a guard here, and the rest of you come help?" asked Kennet.

"You know, I will. I owe my life to you. Wait a moment while I call out the troops," he replied, reaching for a horn that hung from his saddle, which he sounded.

Men on horseback came from many directions.

He quickly explained, and everyone hurried to do his bidding. They, too, had reasons to appreciate Kennet.

They moved toward the town where the riders dismounted and entered buildings along a line from the street they were now on, near where Wren's Nest was located and moved toward the main gate forcing those who should not be there ahead of them. Each horse followed the rider once outside the buildings. The group of felons continued to grow.

Meantime Thunder was watching the incoming for the first one to draw a weapon. Her sword would remain in its case until that time. She sat calmly watching around her, though her focus was on those who would soon be in her court. She felt, rather than saw, the force behind her.

"Don't turn, mom; they are friends. Keep your focus; we will help. The unwelcome ones are going to the gate. If you can meet them there, maybe there won't be as much damage to the town," said Kennet.

"You know I can do this, don't you?"

"Yes, for no one else would be able to," he replied with a smile.

She continued watching; then, she saw the first weapon — the man aimed at her, yet she still had to wait for an actual sign of aggression.

"Pi, left," Kennet shouted, and the horse jumped immediately with the horse Kennet was riding moving in the same direction. Only the animals heard his voice.

The shell passed through where Thunder had been.

Her sword was immediately in her hand, and she moved forward. She saw that the men ahead of her weren't watching her; it was the men behind her. That is when she dismounted and lifted the sword Lightning. She used the weapon as a shield, and by directing the force, she could cause whatever they aimed toward any of her group to return to the sender. It was not a time to kill; it was a time to disable, and she did that sword drew all firing as if a magnet then released it back to the sender.

When the noise quieted, the men with Kennet moved in to capture those who were down. He had warned them not to pass Thunder when she had the sword in her hand unless she first gave consent. They pushed the prisoners toward the main entrance. The men with Kennet grew in number as they walked behind Thunder yet kept the group moving where Kennet suggested.

The gate guards lost their weapons as the moving force

disarmed and ordered them to join the group pushed outside. Kennet's friends encircled those they moved to be sure none were mounted and would not leave until Thunder said they could.

"Who oversees this group?" asked Thunder.

None could deny her questions when the sword remained in her hand.

"I am," replied a man who tried to hide.

"Come before me," she ordered.

He moved as directed.

"Where is your home?"

"Sawtooth Mountains," he replied.

"No, your real home, and while you are answering that one, tell me about what is going on that has you targeting a peaceful community. I know it is for your gain. However, it will not be yours. Now tell everyone here your name and what you planned on doing," Thunder directed.

"My name is Guider Cinderman. There are three gold mines here, and we need the product from them. The town is to be ours," the man told her.

"Since I am the owner of those three mines, how much chance do you think you have?" she asked.

"That isn't what he told me," he responded with a frown.

"Then, he did not tell the truth. I can furnish a deed for each of those mines. These men with me are the guards of those sites. In the last month, most of the businesses in town have been purchased by me. Those who burnt them down will be required to rebuild them or pay to have it done. Men, would you please strip search them and remove all weapons, electronics, which means items you don't know what they are for?"

She sat and waited.

"Granda?"

"Yes."

"Can you open another book while this one is open?"

"Yes."

"Give me one that covers one hundred acres only, flat land with a shallow stream running through it. Put these men in it and close it. I don't dare interrogate them here, for it would give out information that others must not have. We need to find out about the racers, where did you get them, what mines do they own either here or elsewhere? Did the horses come from a ranch on this world or ones in your time?"

"They have each been given a prison cell with food and water for however long it will take to find out what you need to. That way, they cannot gang up on you again. I am removing the items found on each of them. I will check them later. The location where he said he has his home will require investigation. I will get the information and forward it upon receipt. You will have your answers," said Granda with a frown.

The author had seen and heard the battle at her request. Though she feared for her granddaughter, she knew how capable she was. Once Mara pulled the sword, no one could get near her, and Kennet directed the men behind her not to pass her regardless of what happened until she told them it was okay.

When Thunder went to judge the group in the Book without End, her team went with her. She searched her memory and found that she had the book of law for Kennet's world and one for her world. That gave her a master in two places. She was both a lawyer and a judge.

"Okay, listen up; this is the court which will try you. All answers will be given in a voice easily heard, and they must be sincere. Number one, you start it," directed Thunder as she sat on a bench with Lightning lying before her.

"What do you wish to know?" asked the man.

"Please bring silence to all except this man and my team," directed Thunder.

She noted that everyone else ceased to move.

"Where are you truly a resident?" asked the Judge.

"I own a ranch in Jordan, which gives me residency there. Have one in Montana, which does the same. My birthplace is Manassa. However, I hold citizenship in every place I have been to."

"How many of those places were stolen?"

"Not stolen, just taken over when the owners were no longer alive or around to control them," he replied with a smirk.

"Stolen," was her response.

"Please record at least three spreads on three continents as being stolen. Also, research all such enterprises in that name. 0We need to know what his assets are at this moment and who is controlling in his absence. Make your granddaughter the new owner," directed Thunder.

There was a pause to allow time to record or catch up on a list to do later.

"Where did you get the items that were on the horses you left at the inn?" the Judge asked.

"Inherited them," he laughed.

"Stolen," was her response.

"All properties are to be checked out for collectibles, weapons, gems, precious metals, and contraband. All funds freeze until the new owner can sort and determine what should go where. The animals on the properties are to have a health checkup and ownership removed from this man. You are to turn over any illegal substances legitimate law enforcement group. The horses that you were riding are now awaiting my arrival. They no longer belong to you. Who is over you?" asked the Judge.

"No one tells me what to do," the man replied in anger.

"It seems to me I just did. Now answer the question!"

"Laser Pradsor is my boss."

Thunder had him spell it for the record.

"He is to be placed with the rest of this group, in prison. Remove his assets as well. Everyone gave testimony and verification, including this man and who is so called boss, who will remain confined through the rest of their lives. No visitors, except those here now. Lock his cage," directed the Judge.

When he tried to speak, he found he could not.

Each person was allowed to speak and answer the questions; they replied as directed, for there was no way to avoid the Judge or the sword she held.

Everything the felons owned transferred to Mara and thereby to Thunder, who shared all she had with her family if they aided her in owning and managing what was under her control. Since the men would not be there to take care of the animals and property, someone had to, and Thunder would be in control. Upon checking her memories, Thunder found she knew how to manage a ranch, care for livestock, and even medically meet man and beast's needs. She was shocked.

When the court was over, she informed the prisoners that they would not be allowed to converse, for none had voices. The only place they would see on that parcel of land was their cells' four walls, which would be cleaned daily by being hosed down with water.

"Lock this story," directed Thunder, and as she departed the area with her team, she heard the lock being activated and felt a device placed in her pocket.

She put the sword Lightning in the leather case and returned it to its normal position. They returned to the town of Star. There she asked Pi to advise the horses that were waiting that they were going home with her. They lined up behind Pi and nose to rump they followed as they departed through the back wall of the stable.

When they reached Granda's home, they found Gwen and Granda waiting for them in the stable. Gwen put the horses away and took care of them. Granda took the sword in its leather casing to the vault after making sure of other items that Thunder needed to store as well.

"Just drop them, and I will sort tomorrow," she told Granda.

Chapter 7

Getting the Family ready

Kennet and Thunder sat on bales of hay and watched the proceedings, too tired to do much else. Shira watched over them. When the duties finished, the walk to the main house was underway. Upon reaching Granda's home, they smelled good things cooking and knew that Star was filling in. Thunder and Kennet went to their rooms for showers and clean clothes. There was an adjoining door between the two of them, for Kennet liked his mom near.

When Thunder had dressed, she opened the door between their rooms. Kennet immediately entered.

"Thank you, son," said Thunder.

"I only did what you have done before me. Thank you for trusting me. We may not always win. However, we will train to do our best," Kennet replied.

"How do you know I have done this before?"

"The songs, they sing songs of all you have accomplished. It says if Lightning is on your side, never pass the bearer of it. Is that what you mean?"

"Yes, watching my back, doing as I told you, getting help when you knew something I didn't, coming despite my orders and caring enough to tempt your mother's wrath," said Thunder with a smile.

"You are still my mom and would never hurt me. I love you too, mom. Now dinner is getting cold, and I'm hungry," he told her; however, the glow on his face and the twinkle in his eye said it all.

She offered him a hug, and he walked into it, where she knelt on the floor. It took a while before either of them let go. Then they walked downstairs hand in hand for dinner.

"Hello, one and all. Thank you for holding dinner for us," said Mara, with a smile at each of her new family members.

"What do we call you?" asked Gwen.

"When here with Granda, I am Mara Jacobson; if we return to the book, then I become Thunder Press again. Unless you happen to be Kennet or Joy, which makes me mom, or to Joey, he is my grandson. As to how the rest of you fit into my family, if that is your desire, that is your choice," Mara told them, then sat at the table.

"See, I told you, but you didn't believe me. Mara adopted Kennet and Joy, which meant she also is now related to Joey. Let her eat in peace, then you can talk and ask what you want to know," smiled Granda, who was so thankful that Thunder had been able to handle the problem and even sentenced the villains.

"Granda?" asked Mara, and the room stopped motion.

"Yes, granddaughter," she replied.

"I find I am a lawyer, ranch owner, doctor, and vet. Guess I will need testing to see if I qualify for a master's degree. I'm working on the other ones. Thank you for your backup. Kennet was fantastic. Never lost his cool and knew when to change the rules and when to get out of the way."

"I noticed he is one sharp kid. As a little warning, Star and her three would like to remain if you don't mind. In time, I believe that they will want to return and finish what they started. She might decide to turn the underground city over to those who can control it, and they will close that part of their lives. The Goldsmith says if you control, he will work from one location servicing every mine you have in your inventory. Otherwise, he will remain here once you tell him where he is to work," Granda advised.

"You know I forgot he was even here. I now own a few mines. My lapidary skills are improving daily. Discovered we have three in Star's town, for the corporation inherited the ones with the guards. It seems the man who owned the gold mine was one of those sentenced, bringing my total for gold to four. Also, three more are on the list of the confessions of the prisoners. I must do some learning about steel, silver, and copper. That should be enough to keep the goldsmith busy, although he may not work with ones that are not gold, I will have to ask. He needs a home and business location in town though he may be working for only us. The Goldsmith will need a place that is near one of the mines, I would guess. We now own the racers, which are here plus, the other ranches raise different breeds, and this last bunch was an assortment. I think that puts our stock at about three hundred. Not sure until we check them out. Must hire a foreman and wife or forewoman and husband for each of them, for we can't be everyplace at the same time," explained Thunder.

"I researched the places when you got home. Suggest you purchase a bus if you are taking everyone with you to check things out. Another suggestion would be to leave Star in control here while you and I move in a crew cab truck pulling a horse trailer so that Pi and Shira will travel with Kennet, you, and me. If Shira chose to ride in the horse trailer, you could take your goldsmith along if needed. Since Kennet is your son, you might want him to see what you now own. I set up appointments for all the new ones to have physicals tomorrow in the city. Once that is taken care of, we can be on the way. The more you get done before starting your testing, the better," advised Granda.

"I wholeheartedly agree. Please keep me organized until I can get back to just two of me. When I lead a group from one location to another, it makes me more tired though I think that will become easier over time. A night's sleep puts me to rights and gets whoever is required ready to take on whatever happens next," Thunder/Mara told her.

"Would you like to go for a leisurely ride with your family? Like maybe from here partway to the college property to learn the backroads?" asked Granda, who loved to travel horseback.

"Yes, let's do that. We might need another shower. However, think it we can do that," laughed Mara, who objected to no running water yet never complained if that was where the story took her. She felt much better after a full meal and cleanup.

"How would everyone like to take a ride once your meal settles?" Granda asked.

"I would love it. We would get to see some of this new area where we live. Joy, would you like to take Joey and come also?" asked Star.

"Just a second, think I know something that would make that easier," said Granda, who departed to her private area and returned with a baby carrier to wear on the chest.

"Give this a try. Always keep one on hand for my students," she laid it on the couch, and they continued the meal.

"You are an excellent cook, Star," said Kennet, and Mara was quick to agree.

"I always liked cooking, though with so many eating at the inn had to turn it to others to do. There was much to oversee, so I gave it up. Granda, you have a fantastic kitchen and I love the flow it has. Would take that job in a minute if it was open," said Star.

"It is, and you have the job. We have some traveling to do in the future, and we need to go together. If questions come up, you need to wait until we are in a secure environment, like here, to ask them," said Granda.

"Tonight, we rest. Tomorrow morning we will be leaving to take care of some appointments. Our transportation will be here when we get up. Granda has guards that will watch over this area while we do whatever needs my attention. All of you need to be on this trip. It will be just for the day. There is clothing to purchase, a few things for Joey; let us make this a fun time for our family. Only answer questions if I let you know it is okay. In this world, you can ignore a question if you find it unsuitable or intrusive. Shira and Pi will remain here at Granda's during that time," Mara told them, with a warning to herself, that she must be wearing Lightning, though hidden.

After the meal, everyone helped with the cleanup. Once

the food had settled, everyone went to the stable and saddled mounts for their evening ride. They ate earlier than usual to allow plenty of light to ride. It was summer, and a full moon was out, making it possible to travel into the night, or however long the moon shone on them.

Joey was sound asleep as soon as the horses started moving. Joy had a smile on her face as her son slept. Star was watching all around her. Gwen was watching the horses ridden to be sure they were behaving and had no problems. Granda and Thunder were observing all sides without appearing to do so. Pi and Shira were also on watch. Thunder rode the stud while Joy and Joey rode Pi. Granda rode a fiery black mare. Said it reminded her of one she used to have.

Early the next morning found everyone up and doing chores that Granda had assigned. Mara and Gwen went to the stable to take care of the horses. It was time to meet the new stallion.

"Pi, would you translate for the new stud, please?" asked Thunder.

The mare nodded, and her stall opened.

"Hello, Mr. Stallion would like to ask you your name, however not sure I could hear your answer. You are in your new home, and I am your owner. All who live here are family to me. We have some duties to take care of, and when we return, I will work with you. Want all the horses to come to me at a call, in the case of trouble. Will you cooperate with me?" Thunder questioned.

Pi nodded, as did the stallion.

"For now, let's put you on a line and allow you some run time. On second thought, will you remain in the area and return when I call?" asked Thunder.

The horse again nodded.

She put a halter on him and explained that it was so folks would know he had an owner and to leave him alone. Only Thunder or a member of her family would be allowed to ride him. Mara took him to an area that was fenced off and would allow plenty of running room. There she unclipped his halter and closed the gate to watch his movement. He bucked, ran, rolled, and sidestepped. Then she realized he was showing her what he could do. He danced as if to an obscure band; then, it was jumping, running, walking on hind legs, weaving, and many other steps.

The animal was incredible, and she was thrilled that he was now in her care, where she could use his abilities.

"Thank you, would you object if I called you Bolt as in short for ThunderBolt?" Thunder asked.

The animal threw back his head and whinnied in a loud horse laugh.

"Okay, Bolt, it is. I will return in a little while to put you back in your stall. For now, enjoy it."

"Gwen, which of the forty did you take a liking to?" Thunder asked.

"The one with the blaze on her face, I wanted to call her Star. However, that is my mom's name, so I've been thinking about a different one."

"Let's go ask her," replied Thunder, and they returned to the stable.

"I know I'll call her Shooting Star. That is close enough yet won't make mom think I named you after her."

They asked the horse, who nodded her head in acceptance.

"Gwen, how far have you gotten in school?" asked Mara.

"Never been to school, mom taught us to read and write plus numbers. We can read signs, books, and even recipes. We had to learn to make the change for customers in the inn. That is all we have needed," replied the girl.

"Would you be willing to take a test to see how much knowledge you have? Once that is done, a tutor will come and aid you in getting the education you need to live here. For example, if horses are your life's work, you need to know how to do it right. Run a ranch, have a veterinary license, and can instruct others in the process. That is not to say that you must do any one particular thing. Once you have the education, hire others to do what you set up, see what appeals to you the most. You would get paid for it and have whatever kind of business you wanted to work with," Mara told her.

"Is that what you had to do?"

"I am currently getting the education I will need. Some of my horse ranches will need people to run them for me. That makes it necessary for me to know as much as I can about it, for that is the only way I can guide and train those who work for me. Also, have other businesses that were inherited. We need to keep them operating to give people jobs and me an income to help you get an education to do what you want to in life. In a week, I will go to college and take tests to see if my knowledge in those areas is enough or if more is required. It will be an exciting challenge. To serve those in my care, they must have the best I can give. They won't be allowed to be lazy. However, there will be time for fun as well as work," Mara explained.

"Gee, you are smart," replied Gwen.

"Not yet, I am working on it, and you need to as well. We will have tutors and get caught up while living with Granda. Along the way, you may meet my mom. She knows nothing of what is going on, and it must stay that way. If people knew what we have done, they would want to control us to do what they want. We must not let that knowledge be known. Your brother did not follow the rules. He still does not know where we are or how we got here. Until he can follow orders, the knowledge will not be his. If Star wants me to adopt you four, I can. She will become my daughter, making her kids my grandchildren though it will require a name change. It will demand that all of us get an education. That is the key to our lives. The more you learn, the better to control what you become," which was what Mara felt.

"I would like to do that, though I don't know if horses are all I want to know. The thing is, I have no idea what is available to be learned at this new place. Will you help me get started?" asked Gwen.

"Certainly, we will work on it together. You helped me; now I will help you," replied Mara.

"My sister Eva wants to learn sewing. It never interested me much. The way you are saying it, if I want something sewed for me, I need to know what is required so that no one tries to cheat me. Is that what you mean?"

"Yes, that is true. Clothing is ready-made here. However, there is a better example. Say, for instance, you wanted to build a house. If you didn't know how to lay a foundation, drill a well, work with a septic system, wire the house and outbuildings, stuff like that, someone could nail some boards together and tell you it is fine. It would be necessary to read the spec sheets, also called an architect's drawing of what your house should look like when done. It is like seeing the bones of your house. When you build a house, you need many things such as insulation, wiring, plumbing, and the craftsmen and women must do it right to last your lifetime."

"Some folks figure they will sell the house and buy another when it wears out. It costs more each time you do that. If you had maintained the home properly and taken care of it, you would get more if you ever want to sell, besides which it will last longer. Some folks need a big place due to a large family, while others want just a place to sleep when they aren't out enjoying this world. Sit down and think about what you want now. Then put it away and look at what we will see in the next few days as we look over some property. Make a new list at the end of the week and see if your desires have changed any. I think the list will be longer. We will see where it all leads," smiled Mara.

"Now I'm getting excited. Where will we go today?"

"All of you need a physical. That means a doctor needs to make sure you are healthy and have all the medical shots you need to stay that way. When the doctor finishes checking you out, we will eat at a local restaurant unless Star wants to come back and cook. By eating out, you will see some more of the area we live in," advised Mara.

"Then I will go take a bath," said Gwen with a laugh.

"Splendid idea, think I will do the same," replied Mara.

They raced each other to the main house and then went for showers.

Kennet was helping Star.

"She needed some time with Gwen, and I have always helped you. It works now and then. Mom said we were going to the doctor today, and everyone is to take a shower. I did and put on my clean clothes. After we eat, transportation would be here, she said. What is transportation?" Kennet asked.

"I know that is what horses are for, they take us from one place to another, yet that is not the way we will be going. We must listen and learn as we go, then ask her if we still have questions when we return home," responded Star with a smile, for she was enjoying this new adventure.

As Mara was departing her new living quarters, she heard a conversation and hung back.

"Dan, why don't you like us?" asked Kennet's voice.

"I like you, alright, why?" replied Dan.

"Then why are you spoiling our time with your mom and my mom? Your mom cries because of what you are doing, and you don't even care. My mom allowed you to come here with us. She didn't have to do that, and she is the only one who could have invited you. You live with Granda, yet you are so unkind and refuse to do or enjoy what is here. We ride the best horses in the universe, have rooms for ourselves, a roof over our heads, clean clothes, people who love us, and someone to explain when we don't understand. Because of your poor treatment of everyone, your mom will ask my mom to let you return to the Inn. You go back to running errands, being pushed around by everybody, and crying yourself to sleep. Is that what you want? I've been there, and it is not a place I want to go back to," Kennet told the older boy.

"You don't know any such thing. I don't cry. I liked it at the inn. The staff treated me right, and I could come and go when I wanted. It was real life. My friends were my own, and we didn't share with anyone," replied the boy.

"You are wrong. You share with your mom and sisters. You share with those who live in the Inn that your mom runs. There is a roof over your head without leaks and walls that don't let in the cold wind. Did you ever go to bed hungry? Have you ever been beaten so bad you couldn't stand up, and no one cared? Did you wish someone cared and knew that crying about it would only get you another beating? Dan, you have a decent life and are throwing away an even better one. You are hurting your mom and sisters by your actions. We can learn to be what we want and always have our moms and sisters to love. Until you apologize to this family, all you will get is a one-way trip back to the Inn. None of us are going with you, except to get you there, if that is what you want. Today we will be checked out medically. You need to answer the questions asked, and that is all. After that, we will go out to eat. I'm sure that will be a shock to our systems, yet I'm looking forward to it. When we return, tell me what you want. Sleep on it overnight, then tell me. I'll ask mom to take you back if you want; however, you can never return once you leave. Your choice," Kennet told the older boy.

Dan stood staring after Kennet and wondered if maybe he needed to take another look at his life. Kennet sounded like he knew a lot about life. It seemed like Kennet's life was not one anyone would want.

Mara waited until she heard Dan enter his room before continuing to the main floor where everyone was to meet.

"Here comes the van. I will drive," said Granda.

They moved outside and took places in the vehicle. Dan came running from the house and climbed into the far back with Kennet as they were more flexible than the others. Joy was placed in the middle seats so that Joey could sit in a car seat and be following the law. Mara was in front, with Granda, while Star sat with Joy, and the two girls sat behind them.

When they reached the Doctor's office, a nurse met them. She asked who Mara was, and the girl stood up.

"I understand you want your family given checkups. We usually do one a day to allow for the rest of our workload. Our understanding is that all of you must have a physical now, for you are leaving unexpectedly on a trip. Come with me, please," the nurse told them.

"When we get inside, I want all the boys in one line and the girls in the other. That way, they can take you as groups. Granda, if you will stay with the girls, I will see to the boys," Mara said.

"Hey, I ain't getting poked with no needle!" flatly refused Dan.

Kennet walked up to the doc and said, "Me first, please," then got the shot.

Dan frowned then got his.

When each person finished, they moved to the waiting room to find out what was next.

"Boys, you had the easy part. You are done and will need to wait here until Joy and Joey take their turn. Joy was injured and needed to have her whole body checked. Then Joey has some issues too. Please wait here, and I will return as soon as I can," Mara told them.

"Nurse, do you need me for any information on my family?" asked Mara.

"No. Mrs. N-Sign gave it over the phone. I understand you will be paying by check and that you prefer billed to keep track of all records," replied the receptionist.

"Yes, please. We just set up a new account, and the checks have not come in yet. I will pay you on the first of the month. Do you have the information on Kennet and Dan?"

"It is all here. Mrs. N-Sign filled out the females' forms, and she said she would take care of the bill if something delays setting up your accounts. Do you want to sit in on the session with Joy and Joey?" asked the nurse they had met earlier.

"Yes, if I may. As Joy's mother and Joey's grandmother, it is important to understand if they have any issues that need to be taken care of," replied Mara.

"Come this way then," directed the woman and led her to a room located in the hall where patients met with the doc.

"They have not been seen by the doctor yet so that you can be with them. The older woman said she would stay with the boys once you were here. X-ray and labs are taken care of," the nurse advised.

Granda opened a door where she was upon hearing Mara's voice and moved into the hall.

"I'll watch the boys. Star is with the doc, and the girls are in the waiting room. I thought you might prefer to be with Joy when the doc checks her. Once Star can stay with the boys, I can return and join you if you wish," Granda told Mara.

"Thank you. Don't want to miss something important," responded Mara.

She sat down with Joy to wait for the doctor.

"Are you okay?" Mara asked.

"I'm scared and trying not to show it for Joey's sake," replied the teenage mother.

"Whatever it is, we will meet it together. Relax, I'm here, and Granda will return as soon as Star is with the boys. We have to keep an eye on Dan though his medical went well."

"Why is he so unhappy? We have had a wonderful trip, and everyone has been so kind to those of us you brought back with you."

"Sometimes we think what we want is better than what we have. I've always found that what we earn is what has the most value. We learn from our mistakes and do better next time. Life is valuable, and we must put into it to get anything out. You have cared for Joey even through your broken bones and scars. You are paying your dues, and because of what you have been through, you will, with help, be able to raise your son to be a wonderful man who respects those around him and loves his mom, who gave him life," Mara explained.

"That is what I pray he will be. If anything happens to me, will you still raise Joey to be that kind of person?" Joy asked.

"You have my promise, though you aren't going anyplace. All of us will look out for one another," replied Mara.

Just then, the doctor knocked lightly on the door and then entered.

"Hello, ladies. Understand you received a severe beating. The pictures they took on x-ray films, show you have a cracked collarbone, a dislocated hip, and two broken fingers. Also, there are some broken ribs and legs. We will get everything put back where it should be and put you in a body brace while your hurts heal. Do you have someone to take care of you and your son?" he asked.

"Yes, mom will do that. How long will I be in the brace?"

"It can take up to a year. You will come in for x-rays, which will tell us if all is staying put or not. You are young, and the bones will mend once the breaks set, which means the time I cannot promise, though. Someone pounded on your body," the doc responded.

"Yes," the youngster replied, although she said nothing else.

"Will you need to do surgery?" asked Mara.

"Yes, if you want it done right. Some are old damage and some new. It might be advisable to use pins to keep things in place, for some of them were out for quite some time," the doc replied.

"Please explain to us what you will need to do and how

long the surgery will take. We are scheduled to make a trip this week and will be away for at least a week. However, I will put that on hold if necessary for the children to take priority," Mara told him.

"I doubt we can get your daughter in within that time frame. Let me check with my nurse and see if we have an opening."

He stepped out of the room, then returned as quickly. His nurse was with him.

"Sorry, I was taking care of someone else. I show we have a slot a week from tomorrow. Would that work for you? It is for eight AM," the nurse explained.

"Yes, we can meet that. Now how is Joey doing?" asked Mara.

"Your grandson has a couple of problems that may also require surgery. Before we go there, I would like you to take him to a specialist in Bashire. He is the best there is working with kids. I trust his opinion more than my own in this area. I spoke with him by phone, and he asks that you bring him in this week. He will give you a slot on his calendar to see your family if you will advise when you will be there," the doctor said.

"Granda, how far off the proposed schedule would that be?" asked Mara.

"It will be in an entirely different direction and closer to the end of the unscheduled trip. Guess we could reverse the course," Granda replied.

"Okay, we will discuss it when we get home. Thank you, doctor, for the information and for getting us a chance to see the Specialist; I will call him by tomorrow morning. We appreciate your assistance and for giving us contact. A week from tomorrow is Joy's appointment. Therefore, we will be here at that time. Should have a report from the second doc by then," Mara told him.

A nurse escorted them to the exit. Mara looked at Star and put her finger to her lips to signify silence when in the van. No one spoke on the trip to the restaurant.

Chapter 8

A New Ali

Once inside, Mara asked Granda to use her sensor. She felt that there were electronics within the van. Whether inside or out, she was not sure. However, it was there. She returned outside and checked the vehicle. As expected, it had electronic devices on it, which she left where they were.

A change to Thunder and a message to Pi had both animals on their way to guard the vehicle. When Thunder saw them, the wolf and horse were running side by side. Pi moved to a nearby park and hid where she could watch the restaurant, and Shira jumped to the top of the van and lay down.

Inside, Mara asked to use a phone to call the local police station. The waitress led her to an alcove where she could speak privately.

"Prescot Police Station, Officer Preson, how may I help you?"

"This is Mara Jacobson. We purchased a van today to take my family to some medical appointments. When we received it, there were electronic devices installed in the vehicle to monitor our actions. We had to meet our scheduled meetings and ran out of time, so we used the van. Now we are eating and would like an officer to check out the vehicle. When you get here, I will come out as my guard dog will not let you near the vehicle unless I'm in control. Thank you," she hung up and went back to the table. They could see the van and Shira from where they sat.

Each ordered their meal and watched around them. When Mara stood, she became Thunder, and the family remained seated, for they sensed the change. Granda would take care of them while Thunder was busy.

The woman moved outside and toward the patrol sedan

sitting in the lot.

"Hello Officers, are you looking for anyone in particular?" asked Mara/Thunder.

"We have a request to meet a woman here. Are you Mara?"

"At times, yes, just a moment, Ganasee," called Thunder.

The wolfdog departed for the park, where she joined Pi though the officers were unable to determine where she went.

"We are waiting for the electronics expert to check your vehicle. She has devices to do that. Ah, there she is now," said one of the officers.

A blue sedan pulled into the lot and was parked. A woman in jeans, a western shirt, cowboy boots, and a hat departed the vehicle then moved toward the patrol vehicle.

Thunder walked toward her, and they met before the newly arrived person got to the officers.

"Hello, I see you kept up your interest in technology," said Mara with a smile.

"Mara, where did you come from?" asked the woman with a smile of her own, for she recalled the girl with favor.

"I purchased a new vehicle, and it seems someone bugged it before it came to us. Would you check it out, please? When you are done and have given your report to these fine gentlemen, I would like some of your time. Will pay the going rate," said Thunder.

"It will cost you dessert, then we leave here to talk, too public in this place, but do like their pie."

"As does my son," laughed Mara, who now could relax, to some extent.

"Mara, note the black sixteen-passenger van that is now coming into the lot. I am betting those are the ones that rigged the van. They do that when folks have money, then try to get them alone and take over. Names are Jakker and

Ric. Run a scam, and this is the first time anyone is close enough to catch them at it."

The woman who was talking to Mara turned toward the two men moving their way. She slipped a sign to the officers, and they returned to their car though they acted as if using the radio and watching the park.

"Hello Jakker, what brings you out this way? I was going to have dessert with my sister and her family," the technologically trained woman opened the conversation.

"Say I saw a van like that one in the lot earlier. Do you know who owns it? Been looking all over for one of that make and model," replied the man.

"Betting it has contraband," whispered the woman into a collar mike that was instantly heard by the officers.

Thunder called on her senses to see what was in the two sixteen-passenger vans; they were using.

"Granda?"

"Yes."

"Speak and freeze the parking lot," commented Thunder.

Everyone outside ceased to move, except Thunder and the new woman.

"For now, you need to trust me. Mara sent me to you. The two men coming this way have weapons in their van. Cases of them, in fact, also this van has several items hidden in the walls and floor of the vehicle. It seems the car was not supposed to be released, and they have spent all morning looking for it. Would prefer that no one else knows about me, please take an oath," which Thunder directed, and the woman readily agreed to.

"Do you get credit for finding these two and their vehicles?" asked Thunder.

"Yes, if I can prove they own both units and that there are items hidden inside."

"What is your street name here?" asked Thunder.

"Whipcord."

"Thunder."

Thunder whistled once, and Shira came on the run.

"This is an undercover policewoman. We need to help her prove that what these two men possess is illegal. They appear to own the van we are using. Both vans need inspection at the Police garage. Will you please show her where the access is to the contents? All restaurant windows are blank so that no one will see what is going on here."

Shira nodded and moved to the van, which was closer. She crawled under it and growled when she found a sensor. A shake of her head told them that it was all on the outside. Whipcord removed every sensor and secured it in a sealed container. Attached was the information as to when and where found and by whom. Shira then tapped the door handle asking for entry inside.

Thunder opened the door with the set of keys she had. The wolfdog climbed inside.

Shira checked the driver and passenger sides and then moved to the second seat, where she snarled and returned to the passenger seat.

Thunder opened the side door on the passenger's side to allow Shira to show them the combination. She moved cautiously on the floor to the second row of seats. She looked under both front seats and then departed the van. Once outside, a sneeze said it all.

"Okay, thank you, Ma'am. Will you tell me where the trigger is to open the floor? That must be where you found it," directed the policewoman.

Shira sneezed twice and stared at the driver's seat.

The officer moved to the driver's seat and reached back under the driver's seat, where she pushed a button, and all the places lifted from the floor by hydraulic lifts. Inside was much of something. She secured the seats once again, and they moved to the car the men were using. Having found the first activator, with Shira's help, she sat in the driver's seat of that vehicle and repeated what she had done in the van. It brought the same results. She was thankful that she always wore gloves when checking for sensors.

"Thunder, how do we get their confessions legally?" asked the officer, for she felt that that personality had more information to share.

"I will take care of it; however, you can't go with me. Please stay where you are until I return. The men will be leaving with me though they will return when I do."

The officer turned and noted that Thunder was where she had been, as were the two men.

"Did you get what we need?" asked the officer, remembering to trust that it was so for she knew Mara and knew her to be trustworthy.

"Yes, here is your recording. Please make sure none of my fingerprints are on it or in the van. My family rode to the doctors in it. They are not involved and are not aware of my double duties. Now call in your squad, and I will stand watch until they have control. Here is my current address. We will need transportation to get us to the ranch. You can follow us back at that time, for we must talk a little. Remember your oath, though, for not doing so can cost one their life," cautioned Thunder.

"Go ahead and join your family. As soon as I get things wrapped up here, a new van will be available, and I will join you if that dessert option is still open," replied Whipcord.

"It is. Our table is on this side of the dining room, and there are about nine of us," said Mara.

"See you soon. Please, ask your questions far from here," the officer told Thunder.

"I agree with you."

"The van is not operating properly, and a tow truck is

coming for it," Mara explained to Granda, who nodded, for both now knew the reason.

They then finished the meal that was put on hold while the outside mission took place.

"We have a guest joining us for dessert. Remember no questions," advised Mara with a smile.

When the officer joined them, she was still in civilian attire as Mara initially saw her. No one would know she was an officer unless she told them. Everyone ordered dessert, and Mara led the conversation.

"My daughters and their children, as well as my son, are staying with Granda until we get classes scheduled and some medical issues resolved. We must be on the road tomorrow. How is the Zoo doing these days?" asked Mara. She had taken a day and worked with the officer to see how that group operated.

"They got in the bears that were rescued from that bunch trying to make pets out of them. Added a lion and a bobcat, now there is an injured elk, an antelope, some deer, a few geese, and oh yes, a wolf. You need to take the family there when you have time," suggested the officer.

"We will do that. Do you have an idea when the van will be here for us to go home?" asked Mara.

"Yes, it is outside. I didn't come in until it was in place."

Granda was given the keys and took the family outside while Mara took care of the bill and the new lady.

"You need to leave your vehicle here. One of us will bring you back to get it. If someone sees it where we live, it will connect us, and that cannot happen until you have answered some questions for me," warned Mara though there was a six-car garage at the mansion. Once they knew what the officer wanted to do, Mara would make the necessary decisions.

"That works for me; only let me move it more to the front of the building so that someone will notice if anyone tries to mess with it," was the reply.

She jumped into her car and drove it to the front of the building, where the cashier could see it. The Officer retrieved her jacket and suitcase on wheels; she locked up and joined the Thunder group. Gwen and her sister had moved to make room for the new woman at Mara's request.

They stopped at the park, and only Mara got out. She told Pi what they were doing and asked Shira to make sure there weren't any more electronics placed in this van. The wolfdog stuck her head inside the open side door and sniffed. She then checked under the vehicle, and it was clean as well, for she returned to Mara.

"Thank you; we are returning home. I will see you there," Mara told the pair.

Suddenly she stopped and signaled for the officer to join her.

"I have to get home immediately. Will you take my seat up front and guard my family? We will see you at home," said Mara, who moved around to Granda's window.

"Thunder has to be home immediately." The woman mounted Pi bareback and was about to head home when Kennet shouted.

"Mom, wait, you need me, too," he told her.

She gave him a hand up by swinging him behind her; then, she rode across a field.

"Hello Mrs. N-Sign, I am oath sworn. How do you fit into this picture?" asked the officer.

"Can you still hear me?" asked Granda as she changed her tone.

"Yes," replied the woman.

"No one in the van will hear me except you. Ask your questions, for we cannot answer them at home. We have one that is not sure what side of the fence to be on, and therefore we have to be very cautious."

"Thunder is an agent, she told me, or implied it is so."

"She is a lot of things, all of them good. It is my understanding you will be joining us at her request," Granda told her.

"Yes, and she advised that caution is a must. We did not exchange much information in this public place. Since she aided me in a major bust, I wish to know more of her and work with her if possible."

"There is trouble at home. Therefore, we must get there as soon as we can yet don't want to break any laws," said Granda.

"Could call for a patrol to get us there. However, that is a bit public. Where do you need to go?"

"The N-Sign Ranch west on Hwy twenty-two about forty miles. Once we are out of town, it will go faster."

"Take this side street. Now use the road to the right. If you turn here, you miss the light. Turn to the left and then take a sharp right. See that way. Please take it. That is a shortcut to the freeway. Enter the next street sign. You are headed west on Hwy 22."

"Now forgive me, have to concentrate. Please put your seatbelt on," directed Granda as they sped along the highway.

Granda slowed for the turn and needed to drive at a slower pace for the blacktop required repair. It was on her schedule to happen soon.

Thunder was riding through pastures and clearing fences. She was home before they were.

"Star, please take everyone inside. This lady and I will be meeting with your mother," directed Granda.

As they approached the stables, they met Thunder, and she had Lightning in her hand. She moved to the back of the building then to the stud's pasture. There they found a few men face down in the dirt and the stud running around them.

Thunder stepped inside and raised the sword.

"Thank you, Bolt; you did well. Please stand behind me. Which one leads?" asked Thunder.

"I do," replied one of them.

"Come stand before me and explain who you are, where you are from, who is with you, and their duties, as well as your own. Then tell me what you are doing here, and what is your intent toward this family?" asked Thunder.

"This rich old woman does not need this place, and we do. She is going to get booted out of here, and we will take over. We can better use all that wealth she has hidden," said the man.

"You guessed wrong this time. My grandmother will remain here as long as she lives, and others hired to see that people like you do not bother her or what she owns," as she spoke, she noted that someone was trying to pull a weapon. She waited after warning the two women who moved behind her.

At the first shot, she began to move, and when the dust cleared, the men were all down though none were dead. Just shot with whatever they fired at the three women.

"Whipcord, you are now Mara and a lawyer. Question these men, and as a judge, I will see that everything is on record for you to solve this case and maybe a few others as well," Thunder directed.

The UCA nodded and asked where she should stand.

Thunder lowered the sword to her lap as she sat at a justice bench. The new Mara stepped forward and began her questions. By the time she finished, they had solved more than one case, and all the information was on file.

"Your attempt to try to kill my grandmother gives you the death sentence. Your accomplices will get life without parole except for anyone who fired at me, and they get the death penalty with you," Thunder told the man.

The UCA/Lawyer/Mara interviewed them, all with the testimony recorded. When done, the captives signed the various statements, which went to the Judge.

"This way, ladies. Bolt, Pi, and Shira watch," said Thunder, and they returned to the stable.

Thunder sat on a bale of hay.

"Please, will you take care of them? I'm beat," said Thunder to her new friend.

"Most assuredly, the Sheriff's team is on their way, and Highway Patrol is leading them in," replied Whipcord.

Granda helped Thunder to her feet then got her downstairs to the vault while the new woman dealt with the law enforcement.

"Granda, I'm tired. Must have to go back from time to time to reenergize," explained Thunder.

"I have another suggestion. Remember that last shipment of gold? You didn't take it to the goldsmith. Take one of the bags and put that in a pocket. Now let's see if you feel up to being Mara and telling law that yes, the woman is allowed onto this property," said Granda though she was a bit concerned.

"It is best that I put Bolt in the stallion stall before they get here too. They may not appreciate that I left a full male in an open pasture," responded Thunder, who rose from the stool and made her way upstairs then outside where she called for Bolt and put him away, after thanking him for his help.

"Mrs. N-Sign, would you be willing to sign that you asked our agent to come to your property?" asked one of the sheriff's deputies.

"Certainly, only that won't do you much good for my granddaughter owns what you see. It is her signature you will need," responded Granda.

"Which one is she?"

"Since you know me, you appear to know the city official, and that only leaves you one. That is who you ask," replied Granda to the nervous young man.

When he approached Thunder, she turned as soon as she sensed his presence.

"Yes," she spoke, acknowledging his presence.

"We need someone to sign that you requested the officer to be here and not intruding on your property." The police recruit said.

Thunder reached into her pocket and pulled out a badge and an ID for Thunder Press. She showed it to him, then put it back in her pocket.

"By law, I can call on any individual or force that will aid me in performing my duties. This time we got lucky. You have the depositions of those involved and the confessions of those found on this property without said permission. Please remove them. For future reference, this woman is allowed on my property anytime; she feels a need to be here. Thank you for your prompt response," Thunder told them, and they knew they were dealing with a professional that it was best not to cross.

The men were soon in cuffs and removed to a couple of buses as they did not have enough room in the squad cars.

"Okay, time for a chat," said Thunder once the extras were gone, and only the three women were in the stable.

"I am Patricia or Pat Sizerton. Currently serving undercover for the Police Department of Prescot. My field of expertise is electronics. I have a law degree, one in technology, have a few black belts, and am looking for something different," said the woman.

"Pat, you have walked into a situation that you will never be able to explain. You have given the oath to aid me in the fulfillment of my duties. To do that, you need to know who I am. When going to school and learning in this place,

My name is Mara. When we go on the road to take care of some property I inherited, I am called Thunder Press. Ah, it seems you know the name?" commented Thunder.

"Yes, though I thought it was just a story," replied Pat in surprise.

"Not just," replied Granda with a smile.

"You do change persona as you change duties?"

"That is the best way to describe me, I guess. Do you know how to ride?"

"Yes, grew up on a ranch."

"Pack your gear then, turn in your resignation for you just changed jobs, if you have no objection," Thunder told her.

"You best plan on changing residences too because we depart tomorrow morning early, and you need to be aboard," Granda told her with another smile.

"How are we going to accommodate everyone for this trip?" asked Thunder.

"Horse trailer for Pi and Shira, need a communication connection from that truck to any other vehicles in convoy. Why not put Thunder and Pat in that one?" suggested Granda.

"And me," replied Kennet, for he saw the men and told Thunder where they were.

"That will lighten the van load to Star and her three, plus your other two," responded Granda.

"Pat, since you know the technology, how about being the navigator while we travel? There needs to be a headset for each of us so that Granda, you, and I can speak as if we were in the same vehicle. With Granda and me as drivers, we need someone to research where we are going, where to stay, and how to find places. My daughter Joy has an appointment for her and her son Joey with a specialist in Bashire. The appointment is for the day after tomorrow since we will be driving about five hundred miles. His secretary said if we get there sooner to call and he will be ready. Now I need to introduce you to the rest of my team. Shira and Pi, this is Pat, who will now travel with us. She has some talents we may need along the way. Currently, I have suggested she take a week's leave and see if we are a fit or not. If we fit, she will travel with us while getting everyone cared for and the new properties accurately recorded under Mara. Granda is my grandmother and helps keep me out of trouble. This young man is my son Kennet who is part of my team as well," Mara advised.

"While you were busy at the restaurant, Star asked if she and her kids could remain here, said she could clean house or something until we return. I think she is afraid of here unless you are nearby," Granda told Thunder.

"I sensed that, as well. Gwen can take care of the horses then. That is of concern. She can also work her mount. None of them can leave unless we are together," commented Thunder, and Granda understood what was said.

"If you are leaving four, how many does that mean are going?" asked Pat, for it would be up to her to obtain hotel rooms. And see that Pi and Shira received care of as well.

"You, Kennet, Joy, Joey, Granda, and me, which is six if I counted right," Thunder replied.

"Why not use something smaller than a van then? A car might be more comfortable with only three or four in the car. As a citizen of this county, you can request that a Sheriff's car drive by on a staggered schedule, to check on them," suggested Pat.

"Works for me," was Thunder's response.

Granda chuckled. Her house was fully secure and controlled by an AI, so no one could enter any area she put off-limits, like her tower or Mara's room. Also, no one would find the vault in the stable basement, for it took Granda or Thunder/ Mara's handprint to get into it. When her son was learning electronics, he asked if he could wire the entire place for his mom's safety. She paid the bill for the material and got a lesson on how to work it. That is when she began writing seriously.

Granda placed a call to get a smaller vehicle for a week.

Joy had not once complained yet per the doctor she saw; the girl was in terrible shape. She did not walk upright, drug one leg, her head canted to one side, and she could not raise her arms any higher than to hold Joey to feed.

Now that Mara had a guard, Granda could stay with Joy and Joey if necessary while the rest continued.

That evening about seven, a tan vehicle pulled into the yard. When Mara went out to see what that person wanted, she met her mother, Grace.

"Hello, mom, what brings you out this way?" asked Mara in surprise.

"I have no orders for today and thought I would surprise you," replied Grace.

"I'm studying on the internet until they can test me at the college, and that is next week. We are leaving tomorrow with Mrs. N-Sign to take a woman and child to a doctor in another town. I can study along the way, plus this gives a backup driver. Have a favor to ask, though. There is a young girl here who is fourteen. She has a dream to be a seamstress. I think she might like to design as well as sew. With me gone for the year, would you be willing to take her as an employee to help you and teach her your trade?" asked Mara.

"Let me meet her first," replied Grace with a smile of surprise.

They went inside, where Mara introduced each member of the group by name.

Then Mara asked everyone to have a seat. She had something to share. Everyone did as she requested.

"Mom, I refuse to tiptoe around you and have something to share. I met some folks who asked me to rescue them. After some study, I decided the best way to do that was to adopt them. Meet my son Kennet, my daughter Joy and her son Joey, my daughter Star and her three children: Gwen, Dan, and the young woman I mentioned, interested in learning to design and sew clothing, Eva. Now I am learning to balance my studies and their needs. Joey must see a specialist in the east, so we are leaving early tomorrow to handle that. If all goes as planned, we should be back in a week. Oh, sorry, I forgot to introduce Pat. Yes, she is adopted, too," Mara told her mom.

Pat acknowledged the introduction then sat quietly to listen. She was learning a great deal just by doing that. The more her knowledge grew, the more astonishing it all seemed to be. How would she have reacted if in Mara's place? For one thing, she would never have been in that position. When they first met, they were instantly friends. It was at a class the law enforcement group presented to school kids.

Chapter 9

Checked and double-checked

"I always knew you would hit the ground running once you graduated. However, this wasn't exactly what I was thinking. Nevertheless, I accept each of you for who you are. How have you had time to study?" asked Grace with a smile.

"The knowledge is in my head. However, someone needs to test me to see if what I know gives me a Master's Degree in a few areas," replied Mara.

"When may I ask, do you plan on doing that?" asked Grace.

"Let me see Joey sees the doc day after tomorrow. Joy has surgery a week from today. The next day I see the Dean of Students for testing. We all have some learning to do before then," replied Mara.

"I can certainly see that. You seem to have a handle on it, however," Grace observed.

"May I ask a question?" asked Kennet when Grace stopped speaking.

"Certainly, what can I do for you?" Grace responded.

"What would you like me to call you? Are you Mrs. Jacobson, grandmother, or some other name?" he asked ever so politely.

"I thought I was too young to be a grandmother; however, if my daughter can be one at her age, I should be willing to be one at any age as well. Young man, it is an honor to call you grandson, that's if you have no objections," Grace told him.

"I never had one before. Thank you," said the excited boy.

"Would you let me call you that too?" asked Dan.

"Yes, if you are, indeed, my grandson," replied Grace.

"My mother is Star, and she is Mara's daughter, which makes you my grandmother, I think," Dan replied.

"It makes me your great grandmother, for I am Mara's mother," laughed Grace, for she was just forty, and the thought of being a grandmother seemed okay; therefore, why not be a great grandmother if that is what duty required?

"I'm sorry. However, we have a family to get settled in, for we depart very early. Star, do you have any objections if Eva spends some time with mom? She can see where she works and what she is currently making? If you want to wait, mom can get Eva for a day later though her days are usually pretty busy once she starts sewing," explained Mara.

"Please, mom, could I go now? I will behave and would like to see what she does. When she gets tired of me, then she can bring me home," said the girl with growing excitement.

"That is not likely to happen, young lady. It is doubtful that I will tire of you. Now get your night gear and clean clothes for tomorrow, and we will be on our way," the girl ran to do as bid, and Mara saw the tears in her mother's eyes.

There were clothes in Mara's closet that might fit the youngster, and she should make use of them. Over the last two months, nothing would have suited her anyhow due to her work ethic and strength making her body size larger while still very appropriate to her frame.

"Mom, she wants to learn. Please teach her the right way. Thank you for accepting my full family. They will all love you as much as I do, and that includes Mrs. N-sign, who has become my grandmother," laughed Mara.

"I'm glad you still remember I am part of your family. Thank you, daughter mine, for that. Always wanted a large family, now we have one," responded Grace.

"And I have a great-grandmother," Dan said with pride. All knew that he was now on board with what was going on. No one said a word about her, also being that to all who claimed Mara as a grandmother.

Star visibly relaxed. Now her kids would be alright.

Joy requested hugs from Mara and Grace, for they would be on the road early, and it was time to put Joey to bed. Gwen said she would feed the horses, although she hugged Grace before she left. Dan asked for his hugs and then asked Gwen if he could help, and the group split up to do what must be taken care of before bed. Kennet and Pat stood the watch in the main house.

"Thank you for not objecting to Mara adopting everyone, for she wanted to help. Now I have joined your daughter's new family as well, which will give us both a large family. When we get back from taking care of Joy and Joey, hope to have a surprise for you," said Shelly/Granda to Grace.

"Come on, Eve; I did not plan on staying long as I do not much like driving when it gets dark. Mara, since you have moved out, how about a hug for your mom?" asked Grace.

As Mara moved to answer the request and whisper a thank you in her mom's ear, she mentioned the girl's clothes. That was when she noticed activity outside. She looked at Kennet and saw he had seen it too.

"Mom, would you mind waiting a bit? We need to check something out," Mara explained.

Pat, Kennet, and Mara departed at a run while Granda secured all doors and windows. They ran for the stables where Dan and Gwen would be alone. Running through the stable helped them locate the two youngsters. She found them with the stallion, who was in a fighting stance. Gwen had opened his corral, and when he refused to leave, she moved inside to calm him. Dan followed her. The Stallion pulled the gate shut once they were inside.

Shira opened the stall where Pi was, and the two of them waited for the men to appear, now that the youngsters were secure.

"Shelly, does this go on all the time?" Grace asked for she saw a group that reacted as one.

"It happens a bit frequently. A few hundred men are now in prison. The Judge awarded Mara the estates of all the men. Now that there are funds available, I hired a group to start tomorrow. However, that does not cover today. There are three animals on watch in the stables for now." Granda was cautious with Shelly as she was not sure how the woman would accept Mara now handling vast sums of money.

"Why did Mara run to the stables? She can't meet them alone, can she?" Grace asked with concern.

"Mara now has a degree as a law enforcement officer. Pat has the same, and Kennet is learning. They will handle what waits," replied Granda with a voice filled with confidence.

"I am amazed at her every day. She set herself the goal of learning every instrument in the band and succeeded. Then it was to graduate by age sixteen. She could have graduated at fifteen. However, the principal felt she was too young, so she used the time to learn the instruments," Grace shared.

"The thing is you cannot share what she knows, for it would create problems for her. Think of her as your daughter, who graduated at sixteen, and let it go at that. We will know what her expertise is, though outside of this family, no one will know," cautioned Shelly.

"That I can do; I'm so proud of her. It makes me want to shout. With the new challenges, her dynamic must change. She will need the freedom to do what she considers her duty. What is she doing?" asked Grace as she looked out the window and saw some men being moved to a corral with the three from the house following them and something bright in the hand of one woman.

"She is activating Lightning and judging the men in the meadow. Pat and law enforcement will file the report then send them away. Once they are gone, you will be able to return home," Granda advised.

"You know this evening has been a real eye-opener. I'm glad that you allowed Mara and her new family to stay with you. We don't have space at our home, though wish we did." Grace explained.

"I look forward to working with Eva to see what she wants to learn," said Grace.

"Now you have caught the fever too," laughed Shelly, for everyone seemed to want to learn something. She knew how much Mara wanted everyone to be as educated as she was, if in the lead group.

Soon the law enforcement groups came and carted off the prisoners. Pat and Thunder helped get the horses taken care of then ran to the house. When the women left the first horse stable, the computer AI locked all doors to the animal buildings. Now they could get a decent night's sleep, Granda hoped.

"Mara, do you think your mom would drop me off at the restaurant so I can get my car plus move my belongings here? Most of what I have is in storage, and I'll move it later," said Pat. She had Mara's information so she could reach her even if she came in the middle of the night. If that were the case, she would sleep in her car until someone was up to let her in.

"Mom, would you drop Pat by the Pied Piper Restaurant? She needs to pick up her car there," asked Mara.

"Of course, I will, all aboard that is going," laughed Grace, who was having an excellent time and loved the new family.

Soon all except Granda and Mara were in bed, although it was earlier than usual, for they had to be up by five and gone by six for it would be a long drive. The house was quiet, and they were sitting in the kitchen, visiting where they could see the driveway to their home.

Two hours later, they saw the lights coming their way. Mara moved outside and identified Pat when the lights came on. Granda opened the garage to allow Pat to drive inside.

Now they were ready to depart.

Guards would be on the property at six AM, for Pat had taken care of that.

Gwen and Dan would feed and care for the horses while the others were gone.

"Pat, we need to visit a bit."

Pat followed the two women to the sitting room. Granda did not want to keep the children awake.

"There are some things you need to know about me. If you suddenly find me gone, don't be alarmed. I will return as soon as I can. It will mean that duty calls me elsewhere. When it happens, Kennet, Shira, and Pi will be gone as well. Please watch over my family, for it will mean I must be two places at once. It could happen while we are on this trip. The concern is that you and Granda take care of Joy and Joey. We need to know what the little guy's problems are and see that Joy gets the help she needs. She will be having surgery next week, and they will put her in a full-body cast, which could last for up to a year. As you heard tonight, Eva will be with my mom. This way, we are not all in one place to be hit. Star will remain with Gwen and Dan, who can take care of the horses and the house. Bolt will watch over them too," Mara explained.

"I'm intrigued about what is going on. You said the windows of the restaurant would not let anyone see out. I know they didn't, for when I joined you, couldn't see a thing in the lot. Those in the parking lot froze by your order and did not move while you and I checked out the two vehicles. Your horse and guard dog remained where they could aid you if needed, even to getting you home in a faster manner than the vehicles could. Your mother did not seem to notice anything different; however," said Pat.

"My mother trusts me to do what is required. She does not question what that is since I became Thunder. I tried to explain once, and she said she was busy. She will not hear any reference to what I have done as Thunder. I will always be Thunder, for that is my legal name, and I have the paperwork to prove it."

Mara paused a moment to see if Pat had any questions. When Pat said nothing, she continued.

"On the other hand, will the double duty be my responsibility forever, that is not known. Why are men coming here to take away our rights? Something is telling them where we are, and we need to locate the source. If it is on or within one of us, they will follow us on this trip. Part of the medical checkup was to be sure we do not have any electronics in our bodies. If you have any ideas on how to check, please do so. We checked the horses, for they came when we did. At the same time, they need to be verified by you and your knowledge to see if there is a problem we can fix. I know this is not the best timeframe to be going away, yet we have no choice. Joey does not speak or make any sounds. It is important to know why. While he and his mom are out of commission, it will fall to me as next of kin to take care of them. In a week, I will be spending a few days at the university to take exams in some subjects to see if I qualify for any master's degrees. A backup is needed for me. Would you be willing to do this? We must be very cautious about who knows what is going on, and currently, that is Kennet, Granda, and me. Are you willing to give it a try? You cannot ever tell anyone what you know of any of us," Mara told her.

Granda sat listening. She would not say a word unless one of them asked it of her. Mara was in charge and would have to do things her way.

"Granda, do you trust me to do what Mara wishes of me?" Pat inquired. To make this work would require both women to believe in her, or it would not work out.

"Yes, you are very trustworthy. It is not a case of trusting you, but whether you wish to take on this challenge or not. You already know more than anyone outside this family, or some in it, know. Mara must take care of her education, thus the tests. Thunder takes care of all of us and is a law enforcer at two locations. If she is free to cover those duties, someone might have to fill in as her. We are in hopes that Mara can complete the exams before there are any calls. So far, the cases have come to her, and we are trying to keep it that way."

"I will give you my best. I find it interesting, for it seems like I have come home in some way," responded Pat.

When they got up the following morning, Mara asked Pat to check the horses and the wolf. The former police officer carried a device used to scan each of them. Her electronics didn't show any issues.

The group hurried through chores and breakfast, then loaded into the vehicles and departed.

"Keep that gadget with you. Such a device will come in handy," advised Mara though she was beginning to see a possible problem. Maybe the device would only work on the current time's technology, not the homeworld of Thunder. The men they had dealt with brought that product to the book world. Mara hoped that Star's world had not developed technology as yet.

Star had packed lunches for the travelers allowing them to go straight through, except for a stop every two hours to allow everyone to stretch their legs, hit bathrooms, and fuel the vehicles when needed. Having departed home at six AM, they were at their destination by four PM. Pat had no trouble finding the shortest and fastest way to reach where they were going. At the last stop, Pat and Mara traded places for a call had to be made to the specialist to advise where they were.

"Dr. Dan Seismore's Office."

"This is Mara Jacobson, and we are here with my daughter and grandson Joy and Joey. I was to call in as soon as we were in the area. We are now on the outskirts of town."

"I will notify the doctor. What road are you on?"

"We came in on West Hwy Ninety. My family is in two vehicles, a car and a pickup pulling a horse trailer behind. It is necessary to stop at the truck stop here and get fuel before doing whatever is required."

"Please remain on this call, and I will use a different phone to reach the doctor. That way, you will know right away what he wishes," replied the woman.

"Thank you; I will wait," Mara replied, then covered the phone speaker.

"Pat, would you get us fueled up? I must wait for the doctor to speak to me. Granda can go inside and see if they have anything to eat, should we need to meet with him immediately," Mara advised.

"No problem, how do you pay?"

"We will be using a credit card that has Granda's name now. I ordered my credit card and also a debit card. Will get you duplicates if needed later," replied the young woman.

Pat advised Granda that they were going to the station for fuel. The pickup was in one line, and the car just ahead of it. Windows got washed as well as the headlights and taillights. When the fuel tanks were full, the units moved to one side, where the dog and horse could have a little bit of walk around before they departed again.

"Yes, I am here," replied Mara to the new voice on the phone, for she had walked to where Pat parked the car and truck. She liked the fresh air and a chance to stretch her legs as well.

"This is Doctor Seismore; is this Mara Jacobson?" asked a firm male voice.

"Yes. We are fueling up at the Riverside Truck Stop. Need to let a horse out for a little bit then can be wherever you want us," Mara told him.

"Stay where you are. I am sending someone to lead you to my private clinic. That will give my staff time to assemble, for we knew you were on your way. There are several fast food places at that place. Don't feed the baby, other than his normal. Oh, that's right. I'm to look at Joy as well. Ask her not to eat either," he told Mara.

"She has not eaten today as she is rather nervous. She did breastfeed the baby, though. The rest of us will eat here and be ready when your guide gets here," responded Mara. In all honesty, she was thankful that this doctor would check out both. It would mean aid for them both much quicker than to wait until they were again home.

"Good, the person who is coming is my wife, Georgine. She will be driving a blue Lincoln sedan. The license is ICU4MED. It will take her about thirty minutes to get there."

"We will be waiting. Thank you, doctor, for doing this for us; we are on a rather tight schedule. However, these two need to be taken care of as soon as possible."

"I assure you they will be. My first line team had today to rest to be ready for tonight. Everything is in place, and you folks arrive, we can take a look-see."

She could feel the man's good humor and be heartened by it. Hopefully, Joy and Joey would also be relieved.

They met the doctor's wife and found her a very likable person. Soon they were at the clinic. How thankful they were for the guide, for they would not have found the clinic otherwise. The streets seemed to run in, most confusing circles.

The clinic was in a quiet area next to a park. They put the horse trailer in a group of trees that allowed them to have shade while not being seen from the main road. Pi and Shira were allowed out though warned to return to the trailer if it appeared anyone was getting too curious. An unkept piece of ground was off a short distance, and they could use that as a relief stop, Mara advised.

Dr. Seismore was waiting inside for them. Joy took one look at him and fainted. Her face was white as a sheet, and she stopped breathing. Mara was at her side immediately and was thankful that Granda was carrying Joey as Mara grabbed Joy to keep her from slamming her head into something.

"I think we better find out what that was all about," said

Mara to the doc, who was totally in agreement.

Soon Joy lay on a bed in an exam room.

"Doctor, would you allow me a few moments with my daughter while I get some answers?"

"Certainly, I've had a variety of responses to me. However, no one has ever fainted when they saw my face," the man said with a look of concern.

"I will return shortly," Mara told them and walked into the room where Joy was resting.

"Joy, how much do you trust me?" asked Mara.

"You are my mom and said you would teach my son to be a kind person. I would and have trusted you with my son and my lives," replied the girl with no hesitation at all.

"You have my word that you will not be in a room alone with someone who has frightened you, regardless of the reason. Will you please tell me why the doctor scared you so badly?"

"He looks just like my stepdad, the one who beat me again and again. My mind says we did all this moving only to be in his hands once again. I'm not sure I can handle another beating," said Joy in all honesty.

Mara could see she was fighting not to weep, as she concentrated on her son was first in her thoughts.

Joy had shown both strengths and weaknesses in their journey, yet never did she complain.

The young woman's first thought was always for her son. She would do her best to care for his needs in a better way than her former relations had cared for her. Now that she had a mom who cared, the youngster was doing all she could to be the kind of person her new mom would want to call her daughter.

Mara was so proud of Joy and would do all in her power to make a loving home for both Joy and Joey. It was something that brought her a lot of joy to contemplate as she watched them grow even in the short time they had been together. As time went on, Joy's past diminished, and her life with Mara became her only life.

Chapter 10
Looking for help

Granda and Mara were having a chat. Things needed discussing without others hearing what was said.

"The trip could not happen without all of us taking part. We need Gwen and Dan to keep the horses taken care of for a week. Eva is with my mom, and she never takes a day off during the week. Therefore, those two will be busy. Kennet must remain with us, as do Pi and Shira. Pat can take navigation if she is willing. We need her to get us places we need, like the one found for the whole team. She has been up for three days and needed some shutdown time. I did have her sleep some on the trip here, for she knew what was ahead. You have been up too long, and my three days are up at six tonight. I can sleep with Joy and Joey in their room. Won't push the doctor and get Shira to join us," Thunder explained.

"You have been up for three days? Where was I?"

"I was in three days of surgery, though managed to get the location moved to show twelve hours for you while it was three days to get both done," Thunder told her.

"Since I slept in the room with Joy while Joey was in surgery, I got enough sleep. I do not feel at all tired. It sounds like you might need a bit of a nap; however," replied Granda.

"Yes. I know. At the same time, if I ask Joy whether she wants to stay in a new area without us or with us, what her response will be. She knows Star and trusts her to a degree; however, Star did not adopt, which has bothered her. Perhaps a new way of explaining needs tried. Like I adopted her because I can come and go to get her medically repaired and am the only one, other than Kennet, that can. He can't either now that I think about it. He tried to lead the last train out, and they didn't move until I took the lead," Thunder responded.

"Thank goodness. I have enough fun trying to keep track of you without everyone being two people and popping in and out all over the place," Granda chuckled, for she always tried to see the humor so that her new granddaughter would not be overwhelmed.

"You think you have trouble, try being me. Who do I answer as now?" asked Thunder and chuckled too. "How about we put Joey in a car seat in the second seat of the truck, and you can have Pat as co-driver with Joy sleeping on the second seat there. She is not as tall as a full adult, and it will only be for the trip home. We can't put her in with Pi and Shira. Don't want to chance any disease to the new surgeries."

"May I enter this conversation?" asked Pat.

"Didn't know you could. Go ahead," replied Thunder in surprise.

"You told me to guard and take roving duties. That is when I got issued the key. My suggestion is to turn in the car since it was rented and pick up a cargo van. We can put a king-sized mattress in the back for the two patients then move on with the program. I could drive the truck, once awake, while you can still check them at each stop," offered Pat.

"Granda, would you object to driving a van with the two patients?" asked Thunder.

"Not at all; my next question is, are we continuing or going home?" Granda replied.

"If we continue, we will manage to get it all done and meet the deadline. If we go back, we lose at least a day, which might be the one we need the most. I think everyone must get a good night's sleep before we do anything, including make that decision. Some decent food would be a plus as well," Pat told them.

"True. Find us a place to let us sleep close to here. Turn

in the car and have them bring us a van with the required mattress. Suggest that we get ones for the sides and back of the van so that the patients don't hit a wall or door if we must stop suddenly. It is warm enough that the patients can stay in the van with Shira on watch overhead and Pi on the ground, which will give us all time for dinner and nap," directed Thunder.

"I'll call a motel plus take care of the vehicle and get it correctly setup if you want to handle the rest of it. At a guess, you will have to learn how to take care of Joy and Joey along the way," commented Pat.

"Feel free to join us anytime. Don't leave Joy alone, though," replied Granda.

"I'm asleep. However, no one would dare enter this room while I'm on guard," said Pat, who then departed the conversation to make the calls.

The women laughed, for they did not doubt her in the least. Twenty minutes later, a van pulled up outside, and Pat sent for Thunder to relieve her so she could make sure the paperwork was correct and that the vehicle had the mattresses as requested. Instead, Granda took the call to watch Joey and Joy while Thunder moved with Pat.

The doctor's staff knew that the family needed to depart as soon as possible. A few people remained on standby to aid in loading Joy into the van. A copy of the x-rays went to Thunder and her family. All medical information was on its way to the doctor who sent them. They also had a copy in the case of problems with the young woman. They found out later those were the only records in existence.

Pat led in the van, and soon they were at a new location. It was a nice motel, and at the back of the property was a meadow. Thunder took Pi there and told her to run well, for it would be a few long days on the road. When the mare was ready, she returned to the horse trailer though she did not get inside. She and Shira would watch over the van and truck, which were parked side by side.

The family, minus Joy and Joey, ate inside at a restaurant.

Thunder fed Joy food from the restaurant after eating her meal inside. The van was spacious; therefore, Thunder crawled in next to them.

Granda, Kennet, and Pat slept in the motel though Thunder used the shower in the morning after taking care of Joy and Joey. By five AM, all had eaten, and the group departed for the next location.

Pat had the list of places they would need to stop and the towns where they would have to file on the properties. They had the court declarations that allowed them to register the various locations owned by the corporation that Mara led. They stopped at the county court first and recorded the change, then they asked about having a map showing where the properties were in that county. Some of the areas had more than one business that would now be theirs. The nations would have to wait until after getting their pilot licenses or perhaps by fax and mail.

"Pat, do you know any real professionals in this area? We need to find a manager for a ranch, furniture store, and a car dealership," said Mara.

"I'll make some calls," was her standard response.

Granda and Mara laughed as she started making calls. They first wanted to see the properties before leaving any of them in some stranger's control. There were applicants to meet with them as soon as they reached a location. The only candidate missing was the one for a ranch. Meantime they prepared to meet those who would control the other businesses.

When Pat had things organized, Mara asked her if she had received a finder's fees on their captured men.

"Why should I? The bust happened, and you were the informer. You get the finds, not me," she replied in all honesty.

"You identified when you signed the receiver for it. Check your bank account," laughed Thunder.

"Alright, though, I think you are wrong," replied Pat with

a grin.

"Think about it, sister. We got all the property, and you get the finder's fees. When we get home, the corporation has to record a change and put you on the board. That will make you part owner of what I control," said Mara.

"Now just a minute, I didn't do anything except follow your directions," replied Pat in surprised shock.

"Don't argue, Pat; she will win. They don't call her a judge or lawyer for nothing, you know," laughed Granda.

Thus, they passed the time from one location to another.

When the group reached the first ranch, they thought it must be the wrong one. It was a thoroughbred horse farm and covered four thousand acres, per the paperwork. The buildings were in excellent shape, and in the fields were many beautiful animals. There was the main house, bunkhouse, and several stables. The stalls were on both sides of the building and allowed the animals outside when the weather was decent.

When they stopped, a woman came out of the main building to speak with them.

"Hello folks, what can I do for you?"

"We are here to meet the manager at this location," replied Granda, for she felt a tension in the air.

"I'm the owner, don't know of any manager. Do you have the right place?" asked the woman.

"I am a police officer sent to identify these folks and see that they receive the property that the courts awarded them. This property is one of those places," Pat told her.

"There has been no notice of such an action," replied the woman.

"The return signature shows receipt by a Meg Starsa. Is that you?" asked Pat.

"Yes, that is me. I wouldn't sell this ranch for anything.

It has been in my family for four generations. Who said it belonged to them?" asked the woman.

"A man on death row claimed ownership. He tried to kill a family to gain their property. I am the one he fired at, and under questioning, he said this was his ranch. The courts processed it, and the judge gave us what is here," replied Mara.

"Give me a few minutes, and I might have some answers," said Pat, who then walked away.

"Pi, I understand there are three stallions at this location. Would you mind translating?" asked Mara though the family knew it was Thunder asking.

Her horse partner backed out of the trailer and looked around. She nodded her head and followed Thunder to where the first stud was in his stall.

"Mara, would you call for backup, please. Kennet, please stay with your sister and her child," said Thunder to Pat, then Kennet.

"They are on their way," replied the woman.

As they entered the first stud's location, he reached his head over the corral's top pole.

"Hello fellow, we are your new owners, and this woman is trying to keep us from taking possession. What is your opinion?" asked Thunder.

Pi pushed Thunder toward the corral.

She opened the gate and moved inside. There she mounted the stud and called to open the gate. Pat/Mara opened the gate. Thunder rode the stallion out of the corral without saddle or bridle.

The two moved as one, and the two were entirely in motion together. The animal returned to its corral as Thunder told him of the other ranch and the stallion that led there. This new one was called Thunder Road. He bowed to her, thanking her for the ride, and calmly walked into his corral.

They moved to another area, and another stallion trumpeted. That animal heard the same question, and again Thunder moved inside to mount the horse. A short ride without saddle or bridle and another bow from a horse before it returned voluntarily to the corral.

"She does not want me near the third one. I can feel her fear," whispered Thunder to her team, yet they moved to the third location. The lead stallion was loudly vocal. The difference was this one was trying to get out of the corral.

"Pi, tell him what is going on and why we are here. His focus is on the woman behind you. She fears him. Ask the stud to do as the others did and to not go near the woman. I will deal with her," Thunder directed.

The stallion immediately quieted. Thunder entered the corral and mounted again without saddle or bridle. The corral gate opened, and the ride began. The horse did every trick it knew, and Thunder met him on his terms. He entirely ignored the ranch woman coming and going though he too walked into his corral without a hand or rope on him.

"I think they have voted. None of those stallions will ever answer your call again. Nor will those under them. The ranch is now mine, and you are to leave. Since we knew you would be a problem, the local law is here to see that you depart immediately," Thunder advised and turned toward the officers coming up the drive.

There were patrol cars for city, county, and state in the grouping. The vehicles remained in the parking lot, and the officers moved toward where the Thunder group stood to wait, though Pat and Thunder watched the ranch woman closely.

Suddenly the woman moved. She pulled a weapon and grabbed for Thunder.

Pat reached her first and had her down and in cuffs before she could move. Thunder had reached for her sword yet knew she could only remove it from the sheath as a last resort.

"Officers, thank you for coming. Would you, gentlemen, please give me your oaths? It will not jeopardize any of you. It is to protect you and us. Mara, will you ask the questions?" directed Thunder after receiving the oaths.

Thunder ordered a court, and Granda made sure no one could speak that shouldn't and that the area was kept free of others entering.

Mara asked the woman to identify her husband if she had one. She named him. What were their actual names, the name of the ranch, the real owners, and then she asked what the game was that they were running?

The woman answered all questions in truth, and all information was in a written format to give the officers. It seems the pair stole the property from an elderly couple who died soon after. They had been the ones who kept the place up so well.

"Officers would like one of you to research who that couple was and if they had any family? However, we still own the property and want to know if there are any more like this woman in the mix," directed Mara.

"Also, I need to know if this woman owns anything anyplace. She has now forfeited it to The Guardian," ordered the Judge.

"Agreed," said the lead officer.

"This woman is charged with attempted murder and will be given a death sentence. She has set charges throughout the property to blow it up rather than turning it over. Shi, would you lead the officers to those locations, please?" directed Thunder as Judge.

When the law enforcement officers departed, they had everything they needed to see that the woman never saw daylight again in her short life. The officers thought it strange that the woman never spoke after giving her testimony against herself and the man she called her husband.

Mara wasn't sure if the paperwork would catch up with her, so they could get all properties recorded and working, or if it would be at Granda's Ranch when they returned.

When the property was empty of everyone except Thunder's team, they began to go through the place. Dogs came out of hiding; horses returned to the stables. Pi and Shira discussed with those who lived at that location.

Thunder went to the van as soon as the woman prisoner departed the premises. She had asked Kennet to remain with the patient. Joy was crying, and Kennet was trying to help.

"What's wrong, Joy? No one is going to bother you here. Do you want to get out for a while?" asked Thunder.

"Joey needs changing, but I can't do it. I tried and tried. Please, will you help him?" asked Joy.

"Yes, I'll take care of it," Thunder replied with a smile as she tended to the baby.

"Granda, would you please come to get Joey? I'm going to have Pat help me move Joy into the house or onto the porch. She has had enough of the van for a while."

Granda picked up Joey, and Kennet ran into the house to find what place had a lovely room for Joy, for she was miserable being in the van for so long. He found one with a beautiful bedspread, a window that looked out on a pasture full of horses, and some birds in a tree. He knew that Joy could not do much, so he pulled the covers back for her to lie on the bed though he left the spread so she could see it.

"Thank you, Kennet, the right choice. Joy, what can I get you? We will spend the night here at least," advised Thunder.

"I checked the pantry, and it is well filled. We can quickly fix a meal for tonight and tomorrow. The hay and grains bins are full for the upcoming winter. The dogs have a good stock of dog food. It seems like she was planning on a siege, yet somehow she was caught unprepared for us," commented Granda.

"What do you want me to do?" asked Kennet.

"What should we fix? Something that Joy can eat lying down. How about a hamburger for everyone? I noticed that there is a lovely garden growing out there. You can pick what you want on your sandwich," advised Granda.

They had an excellent meal, and Joy even managed to join them for a while.

"I have a suggestion. Since this place has a piano, how would you like some music after our supper settles?" asked Mara.

"Oh, mom, I didn't bring my guitar," said Kennet with a frown.

"Any of you that wish to learn to play will be taught by me if you will promise to do as I tell you and practice. As you improve, we can maybe start a family band if you are interested," said Mara.

"Oh, could we? Once I'm out of this brace, I want to learn, and maybe Joey can as well," said Joy with excitement.

"Each of you will have private lessons, and you pick the instrument you want to play. You cannot change what you play until you have mastered the first one. Now let's clean up the table and sit down to rest a little before the concert," laughed Mara, who loved to play.

"Pat, what do you play?" asked Mara.

"Marbles, pool, poker, let me see..." she replied, for her mind was elsewhere.

"Musical instruments silly," said Mara with a smile.

"Oh, never learned how actually," replied Pat after a bit of thought.

"Pick an instrument when we get home, and lessons are available," replied Mara.

"We shall see. What I'm thinking about now is someone decent to run this ranch. You do not want it to go downhill due to being so far from your home. It would be great if we had all your horse property in one area. However, that isn't too likely," Pat told her.

"This ranch is only about two hours from home. We move farther away as we claim the properties. We need some folks that have a background check on them, are honest, love horses, and will work to keep this one as nice as it is now," responded Thunder.

"I agree," said Granda.

"Guess I'm beginning to see why I have to learn to fly. We have at least four properties that are out of the country. Those might need to be moved closer to home, though," Thunder commented.

"You need to train a team to claim these properties for you. Not to sign for them, to have a group that can take over an enterprise immediately when you sign the papers until you can hire someone you are happy with to run it," Pat suggested.

"Oh, is that how you do it?" asked Mara with laughter. She had never thought about it before.

"Yes, now I begin to see what I am here for," laughed Pat.

"You are needed, told you that," replied Mara.

"I spoke with some of the officers who were here. They mentioned a woman that lost her home a month ago; a heater was at fault. Anyhow she has four kids and no place to live. Understand she has a clean record, kids are in school, and she loves horses. Do you want me to invite her here for a conversation? Don't think we should take Joy and Joey around strangers for a while, though they could remain in the house while you talk with whomever."

"Let me see; it is about two in the afternoon. We can feed the horses and dogs while we wait or have an evening meal, then feed," replied Mara.

"Animals should come first. Have you noticed plenty of lush green grass for them, and none of the grain bins show use? There is a date sticker on each of them as to when purchased and when opened. The open date is blank," replied Pat.

"Are you saying we don't have to feed them?" asked Mara with a frown.

"It is best that you give them a little grain to keep them friendly to you. Hay is usually for winter, and barley, oats, and such are called treats in the summer and feed in the winter," Pat told her.

Pat was getting quite a chuckle out of her new family. She began to see that Mara had learned all her degrees the hard way by living the subject. Pat needed to earn her keep. She made a phone call, set up an appointment, then departed for the stables to start feeding. Thunder had a daughter and grandson to take care of, as well as a son. Granda was doing meals, and Mara entertained, so horses were her duty.

When Pat entered the first stable, she sensed something. Carefully checking each stall led to finding a mare and newborn. That wasn't anything new to her. After taking care of the needs there, the search continued. Pat found three mares with new foals. These would require a bit of checking on them though all seemed healthy. Pat dried off the latest offspring, and she watched as each tried to stand, then succeeded. When each was eating, she circled again to check on the next one. Once they were doing well, she moved to the stallion corrals.

"Would you please call in your group? I will see that they get some feed and check them for any cuts or other injuries," Pat advised.

Horses began to run to the barn. Pat opened all stalls and waited for them to sort themselves out.

Each horse was checked and given a treat of grain. Then Pat moved to the next stable and repeated the process. After the horses were fed and brushed, she called for one of the dogs. Then it was a repeat to check them for any injuries, brush them down, and fed.

She was tired but happy when she returned to the main house. She was also dirty, so a shower came next, recalling it was a good thing she brought clean clothes from the truck.

"Where have you been?" asked Mara in surprise when Pat went looking for everyone.

"I brushed a hundred horses, watched over three new deliveries, fed the groups then called in the dogs, and found we have two batches of new pups, cleaned the adults down, and fed them. Guess that is about it," replied Pat with a smile.

"You need a steak dinner, not a hamburger," said Granda in surprise.

"I won't turn down either one. Did the woman come for her appointment?" replied Pat with a smile.

"No, I have not seen anyone since you disappeared. Could that be the lady?" asked Mara as she observed a vehicle entering the property.

"Probably. I can introduce you. Where do you want me to take her for you to have a chat?" Pat asked.

"Since you have the stable all cleaned up, let's start there," said Thunder, for Mara wanted all senses entirely in place for this one.

The woman got out of the car and shook hands with Pat. She turned to the car and left a reminder.

"If you cannot behave now, you will when we get home," cautioned the woman.

They walked out to the barn and around to where the studs were in corrals. There were strong walls between each of them.

"This is Thunder Road, who oversees the mares in the first stable. There are two other studs on site. Three of the horses delivered young today while we were cleaning the house. Also, have a few new pups as well."

"Oh, I love the young ones. They are so fun to watch as they run and play. The woman who had this ranch used to have a game time with her animals, and what fun it was to watch," responded the woman who said her name was Sally Bestra.

"We inherited this ranch; however, we need a caregiver for now. My daughter and grandson both had surgery a few days ago, so they are traveling with us now. That is why we met you in the barn rather than the house. Joy cannot get around very well, for she is wearing a body brace. It is my understanding that you have a clean background, four kids who are still in school, and are familiar with the requirements of a ranch," Thunder shared once she was sure all was well.

"Would you allow my kids to see the new animal babies? It might give them a reason to want to be here," said the woman with a smile.

Pat departed to get the kids.

"Your mother suggested that you might like to see some new colts and pups. Don't scare them, for they can barely move yet. The puppies' eyes will remain shut for about ten days. We will see how you do with the mothers of the animals," suggested Pat.

The kids were obviously on their best behavior, for they whispered around the new ones.

Chapter 11

Training Continues

"Mom, can I take care of this one?" a twelve-year-old girl said.

"We shall see. Remember, if we agree to this, it must be all of us, and the ranch and animals should come first. That means before fun things. You must keep up your studies and care for the animals. We will do all the chores together, that means everything. There will be days when it snows and is cold. However, the horses still come first. Are you still willing?" asked the woman.

"Jack, I want to do my best. Will you help too?" asked the first girl of a boy who could have been her twin.

"Jill, you knew I would be in when they mentioned horses," laughed the boy.

"Can Jason and I do the dogs?" asked another girl.

"Means you train them, feed them, clean the kennels, and still help out with the other stuff," replied the mother.

"We promise, Mom. You said we could have a dog someday. You didn't say a whole kennel full," laughed the second girl, who proved to be a twin also. They were Fourteen.

"Okay, we will do it. When do you want us to start?" asked Sally Bestra.

"We need to leave early tomorrow. Must be on the road about six, if possible. We have appointments for the next six days," replied Mara for Thunder, who was satisfied and faded away.

"We will drive over a little before six to see if we can help. Then we will move personal items once you are gone," Sally told them.

"The feed is in place for the winter, the pantry is full, and there is a piano if anyone plays. The house comes fully furnished, as you see. I will give you a tour before we leave. Right now, my daughter is resting. A body brace is a problem in cool weather and a beast in summer."

"That works for us. No, you may not take a pup home, this will be home starting tomorrow, and you will be taking care of them right where they are once the mother permits you. Now back to the car with you," Sally directed, and her kids took off on the run.

"They are good kids and love animals. They are very excited about this place for we have been sleeping in the park. We don't have much of anything. The land is still there; however, it would be too expensive to do much, and they would still make us pay for it," Sally said, yet she had a smile and moved on.

Pat was on the phone to the county treasurer to get information on the woman's property to secure it for when her kids were of age to make use of it.

"We need your signature on the manager agreement, and anything else can be taken care of by mail or a quick drive over. We will pay you on the first of every month if you give us your bank number. Every horse has a saddle, and the studs know who I am. They agreed to the transfer to me. Now we need to ask them if they agree to have you working for me," said Mara though she knew that Thunder would have to take over again.

She led the way to the first stallion box.

"Hello Thunder Road, this woman has four children, and they have no place to live. Would you object to them managing things here for me while I catch up on some things between here and there?"

He backed up from the gate which Thunder opened.

"Do not recommend you do this. However, TR will behave for me," warned Thunder.

The horse stood quietly before the new woman.

"Looks like he plans on keeping you," said Thunder.

He turned and reentered his corral.

The next one was the same and answered to Thunder Dream; however, the third one might cause problems, and Thunder wondered if the former manager's mishandling would cause problems.

"Thunder Pride, I know you did not care for the old manager and would prefer not to have that happen again. This woman has four children, and they have no home as theirs burned down. Would you be willing to work with her in keeping things in order here?" asked Thunder.

He tried to open the gate until Thunder realized what he wanted.

She allowed him outside the corral.

"He wants to meet your kids; it seems," Thunder told the woman.

"Please don't be startled, I will call them," Sally whistled a sharp whistle, and the kids came running to stop at the edge of the stable then walk to where the group waited.

Their eyes got very wide when they saw the massive animal.

"This gentleman has asked to meet you. He wants to know what kind of kids you are. Will you be kind, feed them on time, and speak with him when you are in his area," said Sally.

The horse nodded his head.

"We need a place to live, and this lady needs someone to take care of you for her. We all like horses and dogs. We have already agreed to help mom take care of the place and put the dogs and horses first. Have to keep our grades up, or we must move and need to maintain the place looking beautiful," said the fourteen-year-old.

"Our job is the dogs though we will help every place we can," spoke up the twelve-year-old.

Thunder had to chuckle, for it was the girl children who replied.

The stallion moved to Thunder and waited.

She jumped onto his back, and they rode into the field.

"She does know that is a stallion, I hope. She uses no saddle, bridle, or spurs. I hate those sharp pointed things; however, do we have to ride the rest of the horses bareback?" Sally asked Pat.

"You ride how you are comfortable. I do not recommend you try what Mara is doing. Do you see the way he is moving? He is showing her his talents before we leave. No one else is to ride any of the stallions on her order," directed Pat.

"Love to watch them together. We better get out of your way and see you in the morning. Have a good night, and thank you for the job and home. We will do our best for you," said Sally.

The woman and her children departed, and Thunder returned the stud to his corral. A quick shower had her ready for supper.

"Does Joey need a change before we eat?" asked Thunder.

"No, Granda showed me how, and I'm careful," replied Kennet.

Granda immediately began a steak dinner for their newest member.

"Pat, where do you want to be placed in this family?" asked Mara.

"What do you mean?"

"Granda is my grandmother; next comes my mother who had me. I have Kennet, Star, and Joy as my kids. Star has Gwen, Eva, and Dan, while Joy has Joey. If you want to be adopted, tell me where you want to be in the family line," repeated Mara.

"How did you know?" asked Pat with surprise.

"How did I know what?" asked Mara.

"I got into law enforcement due to a kid who killed my family then shot himself. My ranch is taken care of by some friends who needed a home. Mom met dad when they went to college after being raised in an orphanage. Both worked their way through. They bought a piece of property from the government for a dollar. When they reached the property, which they had not seen before, it turned out to be a two-thousand-acre ranch complete with everything. They went to work, and when I came along, I did the riding of the horses, training of the dogs, and I became an extra pair of hands. Something told me I would be leaving, so I started moving everything I wanted to keep to a secret place. One day mom came to me and said she had a secret to share. She took me to an entry that I thought was the pantry. It led to an underground city. Along the way, she introduced me to the AI, which controlled the property. There was even a vault, and it was full of a lot of things. She gave me the combination then took me to the barn where she again showed me the underground entry, only this time, it was for an underground stable that would house a thousand horses. Everything there was automated. If I had to be away for a week, the animals still get care. When we returned to the main house, dad was in the barn, so mom went there. I got my secret stash and moved it to the house underground. Once it was all put away, thought it time to check on what mom wanted for dinner," Pat paused to quit shaking, for she recalled the horror again.

"Take your time. I will not cook your steak until you finish," said Granda with sympathy and understanding.

"Dad was dead, and so was a teenage boy. Mom was still alive, though. She said the ranch was mine and where the deed was. The kid had gone to the wrong place, by his idea of what he wanted to do. Destiny had it set up just the way it was. Mom died before the ambulance could get there. The mortician was with it. Law enforcement came and checked out the whole area, then determined that the boy was the only one involved. The boy lived in another town and thought he was at his stepdad's place. When dad surprised him, he shot before he realized who it was and then felt he had to kill mom too, or she would tell on him. Finally, he realized he was in the wrong place and shot himself. The boy told mom that his step-dad would kill him as the man had already tried a few times. He also apologized for the mistake. She said he was crying when he killed himself. I went to law school and became an officer. The stepdad was put on death row, not for the boy, however, for a few other people. That is when I moved after hiring folks to take care of things for me. I felt lost without a family. I was shocked when you told the officers that we were family. Now you are asking where I want to be in the family structure; I do not care if I'm the washerwoman if Pat can belong again," said the woman with tears in her eyes.

"You are now my twin sister. The reason being you need to be able to go where I go, and that would make us equal. You know all of us, where we are in the family line, and the tasks. Mom accepts us, as you know. She doesn't comprehend who we are, what we do, or how it fits together only that we are related and that she is a part." Mara was surprised that Pat suddenly spoke about so much. She knew there had to be a story. However, none of them would push her, and they would hear it only if Pat chose to tell it.

Pat found herself enveloped in a group hug, then she heard another call and ran to the bedroom of Joy for a hug with her as well, for the girl could not come to her though she listened to what was going on.

Finally, they settled down to listen to some music on the piano. Joy was brought out and placed on the couch with Joey at her side.

Thunder awakened in the night and knew something was amiss. She slipped out of her room and where Joy and Joey were sleeping. A check on Granda found her asleep as well. Kennet was in his bed; the only one missing was Pat.

"All right, sister, tell me where you are and don't hide from me," said Thunder.

"I'm not hiding from you, we have company, and I don't like it," said Pat softly.

Thunder moved to where Pat sat in the darkness, looking out the window. There were people in the yard running around.

"We need two Lightning Swords, one for me as Thunder Press and one for Pat as my twin." Thunder then held up her right hand, for she was right-handed, and Pat did the same with her right hand. A blade landed in the upraised hand of Pat.

"Quick information; do not let a friend get in front of you when the blade is unshielded. If we move in lockstep, it will help. Do not lay the weapon down anyplace. Keep it on your body always or at hand's reach if showering or sleeping. Only you and I will see the sword until released from the leather. Keep it out until all duty for that event is complete, which includes sentencing the felons. For now, I will be the judge, and you will be a lawyer as I have credentials for both."

They opened an outside door and stepped through, being quiet as they moved. Thunder felt something behind her and started to turn, then stopped. It was one of the studs, and Pat had another meeting with her. Mara and Pat mounted then moved in the shadows. The house had every door and window locked by the computer as soon as the women departed.

The stallions seemed to know where they were going, and the riders just rode. They went to one of the stables and could hear the men inside.

"Meg said that it has to be in this stable. She checked all the others. Per her, there should be millions in a vault on-site," said one voice in a whisper.

"Ah, come on, no one would keep that much under a stable," said another.

"If she told me wrong, we pack up and leave. Should she prove to have told the truth, for a change, we will be rich," replied voice one.

Thunder thought a moment then directed "lights" in a

soft voice after warning the horses and Pat. Lights instantly illuminated the whole area. About thirty men were reaching for weapons though blinded by the sudden light.

"You are trespassing," said Thunder.

"And that is not a good idea when you know there is a watch on this place," added Pat.

"It's just two women take them," voice one called.

"That's easy for you to say. Where did the women go?" asked voice two.

One of the women was at one end of the building the group was in, while her twin was at the other end. They were on stallions that could move very quickly if required. The rider nearest the ranch house began walking her ride through the stable, driving the men before her as the second woman sat her stallion by the exit. The women forced the intruders to a corral where the third animal was waiting. The gate was open, and the people walked inside. The women dismounted and moved into the open gate.

"You were told you were trespassing. Not listening can cause some problems for you. Sister prepare," directed Thunder, and they pulled the leather-encased swords from their backs.

"You idiots, that's Thunder, and now there are two, have you no sense at all? Get out of here," shouted one of the men.

"A little late now, wouldn't you say?" asked Thunder Two.

The man who was shouting pulled a weapon and fired. A stallion hit him as he aimed, and the shot went into the ground. However, it was the key to uncovering the swords. The women unsheathed the swords and began meeting the incoming fire.

"Concentrate," Thunder One told Thunder Two.

"I have your back," said another voice.

"Please call the local law," replied T1.

"Done," replied Granda.

Pi must have sent a message for the three studs moved behind the Thunders.

Once again, a court convened, and T1 was the judge though T2 learned how to use her talents.

Pat was concentrating on what was happening and trying to recall the first time she served as a Thunder Court lawyer. She wanted to be sure she had a clear recollection of what to do.

"Who leads?" T1 asked those inside the corral.

The court was a repeat of a lot of others she had held. Once the men had each given their testimony, names, ownership of properties, and dealings they were in, it was in time to see a line of vehicles entering Mara's property.

"Shira, is that the law enforcement or someone else?" asked T1.

The wolf turned and bared her teeth at the prisoners, then turned toward the incoming and flagged her tail.

"Okay, would you lead them here, please?" asked Thunder.

"Hold them in place, Sister. We need to get the studs put away. Thank you, stallions, for your aid. Now we must get you in your corrals before those men see you lose, and we get a fine."

T2 ran toward the corrals, and the stallions each entered their holding pen, which she closed before running to join Thunder. Pat was the second and therefore needed to leave T1 in charge of the prisoners while the horses got put away. In time, she would do it all; now, she was in training.

T1 gave the officers the depositions, confessions, and court judgment. T2 gave them the prisoners. The patrol cars had come silently and left the same way though Pat verified who they were before they got the information.

The two women entered the stable and checked on the new foals. They were sleeping, so the women moved into the tack room and sat down.

"Secure," said T1.

"Confirmed," was heard.

"Any questions, T2?"

"Each time I learn something new. How did I end up with a sword? I knew you had one. However, my having one also was a bit of a shock."

"If you are to be my twin, you need similarly equipped. Now you can be a judge or lawyer. The only time people can tell us apart is if we use Pat and Mara's home features. The rest of the time, all they can do is guess who is who."

"I noticed the stallions followed me, whereas they usually followed you," Pat commented.

"They will even let you ride them now," Mara chuckled.

"Would love to try that out only, not in the middle of the night in the dark," responded Pat.

"The time will come when we must do that; tonight was the training session," Thunder cautioned, for she had quickly learned that whatever she learned was usually used before too long.

When everyone was up the following morning, they were amazed at how rested they felt. The adults packed and loaded the night before, except for what they would need upon rising. Granda had breakfast ready for each one as they appeared from their bedrooms. Beds were stripped and remade with clean linens; the laundry went into the washer and dryer; dishes were done and put away, and the evidence of anyone having been there was gone.

Mara frowned a little, then smiled.

No sooner did they finish feeding the animals than they saw a car coming up the drive. In it were Sally and her four kids.

"Hello, Sally, how are you this fine morning?" asked Mara.

"We are reaping the blessings of the Lord," she replied with a smile.

"As are we, the animals are fed, the house is ready for you, and your paperwork is on the table, as is the contact information for the corporation that now owns this spread. In plain English, that is us," Mara advised.

"I'm glad you are the owners, for you are wonderful. We promise to take good care of this spread you are entrusting to us," responded Sally.

Sally had explained to her kids how they came to have the job. A friend on the police force had recommended them. She was thankful to have a home before winter, for living in the park would not be a viable solution once temperatures dropped.

"We have to get moving. Have a good day. Now my daughter will be brought out to the car, and the trip begins again," said Mara.

"The kids and I said prayers for all of you to have safe traveling mercies. Please come see us again when your daughter is better so she and the kids can get to know one another," Sally said with her eyes sparkling.

"It will be done when time is available. Two of us begin university in a week. Therefore, we will be busy this fall and winter. Don't look for us before spring, at a guess," responded Mara.

Granda came out with the baby, then Pat and Mara went in to aid Joy. She insisted she could walk and did a fair job after having had surgery only two days before. They supported Joy on each side to make sure of her not falling. Once she was comfortable in the van, they put Joey with her, and everyone took their traveling seats. Kennet rode with Granda so he could help with Joey if needed.

The rest of the businesses went by so quickly they couldn't believe it. There weren't any problems, and people were in place with backgrounds completed to do the job required. All of them were folks that the twins readily agreed to.

As they pulled into the road leading from the highway to the house, they had to chuckle at the horses lining the driveway.

"Don't suppose they are glad to see us are they?" said Mara with a laugh.

"Spoiled is what they are," replied Pat, who also smiled.

All but Joy and Joey departed the vehicles.

The horses each came by for a pat before returning to the pastures where they belonged.

Star was standing on the porch, watching it all. When her turn came, she got hugs from everyone.

"Good to be home, daughter mine," said Mara to Star.

"You have no idea how glad I am to see you, even if it has only been two days. Did you run into problems?" Star asked.

"Not really. The doctor there decided to do surgery on both Joey and Joy. She is getting around well in her brace, though she has to be careful not to fall, so one of us moves with her in case. Joey is gurgling up a storm and trying to talk," Mara filled her in.

Pat looked on and kept quiet.

"There will be none of that, Aunt Pat, get over here for your hugs too," said Star, and Pat did as directed.

"Just because you are twins is no reason to think we would ignore you," said Dan in welcome.

When the greetings were over, Pi and Shira unloaded from the truck. They ran around for quite some time enjoying home. The animals then seemed to be updating one another while Joy had help getting inside.

"Where do you want to be? The front room, kitchen, bedroom, porch, or back in the van?" asked Pat.

"Please, not the cargo van; any of the others will be all

right." Joy replied, frowning slightly.

"Just teasing. Where do you want to be?" asked Mara.

"I get so tired of lying down yet know it is necessary to heal. Hope that doctor here finds I am all healed," commented Joy with a chuckle, for she knew it was just a dream, not reality. She recalled that the doctors both said she would be in the body brace for a year.

"One never knows," responded Mara, who had been noticing some things with her daughter. She seemed to have grown in the ten days they had been gone, yet Star said they had only been away two days. Both Joy and Joey seemed healthier than either of them had been in the time Mari knew them.

On Tuesday, by Star's calendar, they returned to the doctor's office for Joy and Joey to be checked out.

Mara said that everyone would be going, and they would eat out just for fun.

The two girls climbed in the back with the boys. The van was loaded so that Joy could lay down for the trip. Star and Joey had the third row of seats.

Mara went inside the clinic while the family remained with Joy.

"Hello, may I help you?" asked a pleasant voice.

"I'm Mara Jacobson, and we were to bring Joy in for a checkup today. She had surgery in the East."

"Yes, we were expecting you. Do you need assistance?" it was evident the woman was speaking by rote, for the eyes kept looking here and there like she was expecting trouble.

"Yes, how about a bed with wheels, so she doesn't have to stand up to wait," suggested Mara.

"No problem, we will put her in a private room immediately. In fact, why not drive around to this door, and she can come in that way. I will get the transfer bed," the woman told Mara.

Pat heard the message and moved the vehicle, where the nurse said.

When they saw all the narrow doorways, stairs, etc., the women elected to do it the way they had been. Pat took Joy's feet, and Mara took her shoulders to get her inside. Granda carried Joey while the rest followed and stayed out of the way.

Joy was laid on an empty bed in the room assigned.

The family each found a place out of the way.

"I'm sorry, I hurried as quickly as I could," said a different nurse.

"We moved Joy for the stairs would have been a problem," replied Mara. If they treated their patients this way, this would probably be the last visit for this family.

"The doctor is very busy," began the nurse.

"We have an appointment, and I called ahead to confirm it before we came. Is there a problem?" asked Mara.

"We don't have any such record," finally the nurse told them.

"In that case, please send an x-ray tech to do pictures of her body, which I will read, so don't bother charging me for a doctor since I am one. We will see how her body looks then, take her home," said Mara, who was getting very irritated.

"But... you can't do that. Joy should be in a hospital, not at home," the nurse replied.

"Watch me! Dr. Sanderson to the front," Mara said, and the speakers in the entire building repeated her request.

The man came a few minutes later.

"Is there a problem?" he asked.

"Yes, we have an appointment for my daughter Joy Jacobson for today. Your nurse doesn't feel we scheduled though you are the one who sent us to Bashire to see a specialist and selected this day as when to have a follow-up. He elected to operate on her there. Now we are bringing her in for a checkup, which he requests you send him a copy of for his records," said Mara politely.

"I recall sending you to the other doctor. However, that was a month ago; why did you wait so long for a checkup?" the doc asked.

"We told you we were going on a trip that we could not avoid, and it came up suddenly. Our return date got moved some, and the return was yesterday. Since you do not have office hours in the evening, we waited until today, which was Joy's actual appointment, to come in. The doctor there asked that you take x-rays and forward a copy of them to him. We will also want a copy of them," Mara repeated yet again.

"Nurse, call in the x-ray tech and get this done, please. We are a bit backed up; however, the x-ray room is open. Tell her we need three copies," he directed.

The nurse went to get the designated person. When she returned, she had an older woman with her.

Chapter 12

How to use new knowledge

"This is Myrta, our tech. She will take the pictures required," said the nurse.

"Are you ready for us?" asked Mara.

"Yes, come this way," said the woman.

Once they were in the room with the door closed, the woman spoke again; only her whole demeanor had changed.

"My name is Myrta, and this has been a crazy day. What do you need?" she wanted to know though she spoke in a whisper.

"My daughter and grandson both had surgery in Bashire where this doctor sent us. We have an appointment to get x-rays taken of Joy's entire body and Joey's head. The Doctor said to get three sets. One stays here, one goes to the doc in Bashire, and we will take the rest with us since I am a doctor as well," said Mara.

When they were in the x-ray room, the woman handed Mara a handwritten note; it read as follows: [Suggest you take all the pictures with you. Strange things are going on here the last week, and if you want those x-rays, take them with you. Otherwise, you might never see them again. As soon as I finish what you requested, I am leaving, suggest you do the same. I tell you honestly; this place is not a healthy one.] Mara read.

"We figured that out when they expected us to use a bed on wheels to get upstairs with Joy on it plus wanted her to remain in the hospital although no one knew if they had taken care of her problems. Please, will you do this for us? I will pay for the x-ray, and that is all."

"Don't even do that; this clinic will be looking for new

owners by tomorrow. Remember me if you get involved in it," said the woman, who then took a full set of x-rays on both patients. She made two sets and gave them to Mara, who handed them to Pat, who laid them on the bed, then departed for the room where the family was, pushing Joy on the wheeled bed while Granda carried the baby. The other kids waited in the place where Joy had been.

"Come on, kids, we are leaving," said Star when she saw Pat and Granda with no Mara.

Pat and Star moved Joy to the van, and Granda took the driver's seat.

"Take them to the restaurant we were at before. Do not wait for us. Pat and I will meet you there. Go now before anyone tries to detain you," Mara said into the microphone she was never without and connected Granda, Mara, and Pat.

Granda did as directed, and soon, the family had a quiet room in the restaurant out of public scrutiny.

Meantime at the Clinic, the twins were trying to get some answers.

"Pat, this place is closing down, and not sure why. I think we better get some answers and soon. If it is going to be for sale, we might want to take a hand. We need a regular doctor to run it as it will be close to home. This one will need to be good at fixing legs or have a partner that is. We have a man who needs that kind of help, which I'll explain more about later. Now we are going to ask some questions. Keep Lightning handy though hidden. I may need my hands. We will meet everyone at the restaurant," said Mara quietly into the collar mike that connected her to her family, unless she desired it to be either broadcast or a one on one call.

They returned to the x-ray and caught the woman just leaving.

"Before you depart, would you please explain what is going on here? No one will hear you except us," directed Thunder after asking oath from the woman.

"Someone finally got tired of being sent all over the country for medical needs when the doctor here should have been able to handle it. Mind you: I said 'should have' been able. I never met a more incompetent pair, and it will be a blessing for the community if someone would buy this place and the hospital—someone who will give good service to this town and the university. We charge people for doctor visits and do nothing for them. The bill they get is many times inflated, and no one gets anything from the group who quote-unquote owns these two places," Myrta explained.

"I want you to do something for me. Find out who will take it over, and when it might happen," asked Mara.

"The county attorney will work with the city one to get it closed. Then the county treasurer will have it put up for auction. My guess is it will be done today and probably about four PM. If you can be there with money in hand, I'm betting you could get it for pennies on the dollar. I know the honest staff if you want them to give me their information for you. We would gladly work for you."

Mara knew who the county treasurer was, for that was the office that handled the transfer of title from Granda to her. The twins went to see that person next though they gave Myrta their contact information.

The twins walked to the Treasure's office was located.

"Hello, may I help you?" asked a voice as they entered the Treasurer's office.

"We are looking for the County Treasurer about a property," said Pat, for Mara was looking at something she had in her hand.

"Just a moment, and I will get her. Did you have an appointment?"

"No, however, it is rather important, and we just found out about the issue," said Pat.

The woman departed to locate the treasurer. When she returned, she had a very professional looking woman with her.

"This is Mrs. Trison, the treasurer."

"Thank you for getting her. May we have a private conversation with you, Ma'am?" asked Pat.

The woman led them to a glass-enclosed room. They went inside and closed the door behind them.

"Hello, Mara, happy to see you again. No one can hear or record in here. Will this do?" asked the woman.

"Yes, thank you. I am Pat. We have been out of town and returned to find the medical clinic and hospital about to be closed. This town has only one of each that will create an undue hardship on this area's residents. If you could quickly claim it as soon as it is closed, we are willing to purchase it and interview for positions within the facilities. We are both doctors. However, other duties keep us busy. At the same time, we can question and be sure that those hired are capable and willing to do the services required," said Pat.

"My goodness, are you ever timely. Sign these papers, both of you. I will send a courier to get them where they need to go. First, I will run you a copy of them. You will own the two places in about two hours. It will take that long for the police to move everyone out," said the Treasurer.

She waited as the twins signed the required documents.

"Would you be willing to take it over as is, where is? We can't help you with startup capital. However, grants are available, I understand. I understand that there should be quite a bit of money in the bank for those places. We froze all funds at six this morning. That is the best we can do," said the woman.

She departed the room, and they saw a young boy run out with the paperwork in his hand. As quickly as the treasurer left, she was back.

"Now, let's get a look at the bank records on those two places and the people who owned them. I thought as much. The head doctor has millions in his account and only a thousand dollars in the clinic account. The other head doctor, his wife, runs the hospital. Same thing there, and it looks like they were getting ready to leave. A lot of money came in from a Swiss bank, which gives us an account number there. She has the money, and the hospital has no money in the account. It's a good thing that we froze their accounts. Give me a place that the funds can go to until things settle," said the woman.

"Send them to this account at this location," said Mara. The money disappeared from the accounts and was in the vault under the stables.

"Do we need to be present at the sale?" asked Pat.

"No, we marked it sold, and it won't go on the block. Thank goodness we don't have to deal with all that would entail. The hospital is full of patients, so a nursing staff will need to cover their care until the transition is complete. The license is current, with taxes paid in full. I will have to change the title to show new ownership. Okay, everything is updated. Here is a bill of sale for $1. Thank you for giving me a solution," said Mrs. Trison.

"Thank you for working with us. All paperwork is complete here to include registration of the two locations, I take it," Pat said, and once confirmed with titles in hand, they left.

"When the runner departed, he was taking the paperwork to registration to be sure your name was on it. I had them register it as M&P Enterprises. You can always change it."

The twins thanked her and departed for the next location.

"One change we will need to make is put it under a corporate umbrella. We don't want anyone looking for us when someone finds out the new owners live here. Want to hire that woman who gave us the information and any she feels are good workers. There is plenty of money there to run the two places while we get staff in place. In case you wondered, the Swiss accounts no longer have funds for at the same time we saw the reports, those numbers released all funds. Every account either has any place now is empty with the funds in our control."

"I will work on getting the word out on the net via information media. Then we need to meet with our family for dinner. When we get home, Granda will set up another corporation for each place. Now we must hire some managers for the new corporations. We won't have time to do it all. Delegate Pat," laughed Mara.

"Remember, you start your testing tomorrow," advised Pat.

"How can I forget? In case you didn't realize it, you have to take the exams too. When that is over, we need to bring a patient to our new clinic for an appointment to get his legs fixed. We will need resumes from all applicants, for they will have a background check by Thunder before we hire anyone," Mara said, for she had directed a silence bubble over them as they moved.

"We also have to check the x-rays on both the kids. I hope Joy can get out of that harness. It must be uncomfortable, yet never hear her complain. She takes care of Joey with Kennet's help and seems content, yet I've seen her crying more than once."

"Wouldn't you in a similar situation? We need to look at those x-rays as soon as possible," Mara replied.

By the time they reached the restaurant, they were tired and hungry. Granda had fed the rest of the brood, although Joy had to have her meal in the van. Star provided her meal since the other two were gone.

"Sorry, folks, we hit a snag; I will explain at home. What are they having that is good?"

"They have a great cherry pie or a strawberry/rhubarb that was excellent!" said Kennet.

"I think you would eat nothing except pie if I let you," said Mara with a smile.

"You need to learn how to make them," said Kennet.

"I know how my son; it is a case of having the time. Did you have anything besides pie?"

"Yes, I had a pot roast and all the trimmings. I couldn't decide which kind of pie to have because I have never had either, so the waitress said she would get me half of a slice of each," replied Kennet with a smile.

"Okay, if you ate a full meal. Thank you, son, for all you do to help us. Today has been a bit stressful. However, tomorrow will be better. Let us eat; then we will head home and have a meeting," Mara advised.

They ordered their food and relaxed though the Twin Thunders were very aware of all around them.

"What are you expecting," Granda asked.

"That's what it is. I'm waiting for someone, wonder who? We need a hospital and clinic administrator. Need them immediately because I won't be available tomorrow, nor will Pat," said Mara.

"Ah, so that is what it is," replied Pat.

"Which pie did you like best, Kennet?"

"I liked the strawberry/rhubarb one. It was scrumptious."

"Then, on your recommendation, I will have the same."

The waitress took the order, and as they were finishing it, two women stopped at their table.

"Excuse us for interrupting. Did we hear you say you are looking for a hospital administrator and a clinic one as well?" asked a woman in her late twenties.

"You heard correctly. Why, are you interested?"

"We have both graduated from college, and those are the positions we both have been learning. Everyone says we must have the experience, as in having held the jobs. Both of us went to OJT or on-the-job training; however, no one wants to accept that as training. I spent my high school years working with the hospital admin, and my friend spent hers with the medical clinic one. We went to school during the day then worked another shift with them. I have a resume with me and four letters of recommendation.

Neither of us has had any trouble with the law. You can still check, though."

"And who might you be?" asked Pat with a smile.

"Oh, sorry, I'm Pennelope Price, and this is Adriana Shore; we are called Penn and Addy. We studied together because we both needed the same subjects and had little time. Then became friends and now hope to work in this town and not have to move," said the first girl.

"We need some oaths, folks," said Mara.

They gave them readily and passed her their resumes. Each girl also had a police report showing they had no wants or warrants.

"My sister and I are both doctors. We can double-check you in the beginning. However, our time is limited. We have business at the university; then we have classes to teach before getting back to you. Can you locate some doctors looking for jobs?"

"Those selected must know their professions and put the patients first. We can check their work. We are not going to pay them a fortune. However, they will receive a regular doctor's salary. By that, I mean the highest hourly wage in the state for a starting position with raises offered if earned. They will be required to work semi-regular hours."

"The reason I say that is if there is an epidemic, a flood, fire, or an earthquake, they might have to work some extra time. Otherwise, it will be up to you two to see that they do not overwork the rest of the staff and that people are where and when they need to be. No one will work twenty-four-hour shifts. There will be no bullying."

"Individuals not present for a duty shift three times in a month without calling in will be released. Those with a doctor's certificate of reason will report to you ladies if a valid reason is proven."

The twins noted that the women they were speaking with recorded any information about their new duties.

"They will work no more than twelve hours out of twenty-four with overtime paid for anything over ten. At shift change, people will be in place to take over from those who have already completed their duties. Are we in agreement?" Mara asked.

"Yes, we are. I know the good medical staff who quit due to lack of time with families and worked to death while getting less pay and benefits. Would you allow us to start with three shifts? That way, we can have a backup for the other two to have a break. Another concern is the benefits. The employees need good medical coverage and sick leave. If they are sick three days, they have to furnish a Doctor's written determination."

"Set it up the way you feel it should be, and we will back you. If it doesn't work, we will do a review in a month and can make any changes we feel are needed. That will require your input," responded Mara.

"We will do our best for you," replied one of the girls, and the second woman nodded.

They were given a contact number for the twins, and the pair shared their contact info.

"Let's allow things to settle at the hospital while we get our first appointment met. Then we can get with these two and do some housecleaning," said Mara.

Pat chuckled at all that was happening and then realized what Mara had said. Would they both be doing testing? How and why was she going to be doing that?

The following morning found the twins up and dressed by six, for they had to be at the university by six-thirty. Pat drove her car, and they were on their way. When they reached the university's main building, they saw a sign saying new students and moved to that door.

"May I help you?" asked a passing student.

"We have to take some exams today for entrance into classes," said Mara.

"No problem, come with me. The miser is usually in by now. However, his real name is Masherra since few passes his tests, we call him miser," said the cheerful young man.

"Thank you for the escort and information," said Mara with a smile.

They entered a large classroom where one person was already in place. They looked around and saw stacks of tests on tables with a sign that said DO NOT TOUCH.

"Mr. Masherra, you have some takers for your tests. Good luck, ladies," their escort told them and departed.

"And who might you two be?" asked the man.

"I am Mara, and this is Patricia Jacobson. We are here to take pretests for master's degrees in a few areas."

"A few, my goodness, you are expecting a lot, aren't you?" he replied with skeptical surprise.

"We shall see," replied Mara.

"Indeed, we shall. Give me a list of those exams you wish to take, and we will get you started." Mr. Masherra told them though the instructor was going to watch these two close. He was intrigued that they felt that knowledgeable. Most of his pre-test applicants were dreamers who didn't even have a basic knowledge.

"We would like to test as medical doctors, surgeons, nurses, hospitalists, medical and clinic administrators. Then we will do Legal as in Law enforcement officers, lawyers, and judges. Next will be equestrian, veterinarian, and ranch operations. We need business degrees, bookkeeping, accounting, CPA, and marketing degrees. Writer, lapidary, leather master, musicians, marksmanship, weapons, and arms plus black belts in at least four disciplines. Real estate buying and selling, architectural drafting and design for homes, businesses, and airplanes. Also, both of us need testing for pilot's licenses. Would it be okay to start now?" Mara asked with a smile at Pat, who was in shock.

"Trust," was all that Mara said, and they sat down to the

first exam.

The girls were placed on opposite sides of the room and given different tests though they would take the full list.

Mr. Masherra called the Bandmaster into the classroom and asked her to test them on every musical instrument on the site.

Mara began on the piano while Pat started with a fiddle.

The examiner offered them lunch, so they ate before returning to complete what they started.

"I know you listed equestrian. However, we don't have any horses at the moment," the man apologized.

"Granda, would you send Pi and the stud to me?" asked Mara.

"They will be there in about thirty minutes," replied Granda.

Mara advised the exam director, and they took the next exam. They had finished all areas by the time the horses arrived with Shira escorting. Both wore saddles, and Mara knew their reins were in the saddlebags behind the saddle seat.

"Will you show us where you wish us to ride please," Pat asked, for suddenly, the day was not as daunting as it had been. She had managed to answer every question.

He took them to an open field and told them to ride. The twins rode side by side and put on quite a show. The horses changed steps, walked sideways, backed up, raced, and went through every pace they knew. The girls never seemed to move and rode like they were part of the horses. When done, they returned to their starting place. They had taken the written portion of the exams while they waited for the horses.

"That was quite a show with both the animals and the instruments. You ladies were serious, without a doubt. I graded your test papers as you went and, for the first time in my life, I have seen real masters at work. We will grant Master Degrees to each of you for all areas you tested. No doubt, you will return as you learn. It will be my pleasure to test your knowledge as you grow. The Dean and I will discuss when and how to get the degrees administered for both of you. We will be in touch," he told them.

"We have one request; please, we prefer no notoriety. We do not want our pictures in the news or any of that. We are busy with some new businesses we recently received. Therefore, we do not have the time to deal with the media. The degrees are to prove our talents as we do what is required of us daily. Thank you for your time," Mara told the man.

"But this would be such good publicity for the university," he began.

"We did not learn here, only tested. Why would the school claim any part of our education? Please issue the certifications under the university letterhead. I understand that there is a list by number and kind of different Master's Degrees qualified for within the academic year. You are not to use our names or faces in any way," Pat said.

The man continued to try to persuade until Pat reached up for her sword. She did not draw it, just laid her hand on the pommel. He didn't seem to notice. However, he no longer tried to persuade them. The letters, certificates, scores, and membership to the university arrived by mail the following day.

"Well, Sis, how does it feel to be well educated?" asked Mara when they reached Pat's car for the trip home.

"Fantastic, though not something I ever expected to be," replied Pat with a smile. She said she had never smiled so much as she had since joining Mara.

"Pi and the stallion have departed for home. We need to look at those x-rays on Joy. On a rather well-educated guess, I would say that we need to remove her brace," said Mara.

"I agree. I think the year was up the day we left the second doctor's location. It seemed like no one even knew we were gone. No bills, no nothing," replied Pat.

They noticed that the stud and Pi got to the stable at the same time they did. Both animals were put in their stalls by Mara while Pat put her car away.

"What time do you have to go in tomorrow?" Granda asked.

"That depends on us," said Mara though Pat smiled.

"You didn't... you maxed them all?" asked Granda in a stunned yet enthusiastic manner.

"Yes, we did. We now have a few Master's Degrees. Now we have a daughter to get fixed up," replied Mara.

"I will get a light," said Pat after asking Granda where to find some foggy glass.

"Most anything you want or need would be in the workroom in the basement behind where the vehicles are parked."

Pat took off running. She soon returned with an old window frame that still had the glass in it. A can of paint for bathroom windows so folks couldn't see in had been sprayed on the glass. She sat it on the counter, leaned it against a cupboard, turned on a light behind it, and they were ready to look at the x-rays.

Everyone went to Joy's room.

"How did you two do?" asked the girl.

"We passed all tests," replied Thunder.

"Wow, that is quite a feat," said Joy though she didn't quite understand what that meant.

"Now we have one more course to accomplish. Will you help us with it?" asked Mara.

"Sure, mom, what do you want me to do?" asked Joy.

"I want you to lie perfectly still while we remove your

braces," Mara advised.

Joy's eyes began to sparkle with tears, yet she said not a word.

The neck brace came off first. No problems that they could find. The neck moved freely, and Joy didn't have a headache. Next were the arm splints, and after removing them, Joy was to move her arms and check her mobility while they placed their hands on her wrist, then elbow, and shoulder. No grating, no pain, and all seemed fine. By the time they had removed everything, they had asked her to stand and found she had grown a few inches. She was now sixteen and nearly as tall as her mom. They looked a lot alike, which pleased them both, and even Pat commented on it.

"How do you feel?" asked Mara.

"I don't ever remember feeling so good. You are both excellent doctors. Now you need to purchase medical bags so that you can look professional," replied the girl with a grin.

"We just received our degrees today. Now we must go before a medical board before we are licensed to practice," replied Pat.

"Better hurry if you are going to be running a hospital starting today," replied Joy with laughter.

"There is some truth to that. Okay, we are on our way. See you all later. Pat, you need to use your car again if you will," Mara told her twin.

They left for Prescot, laughing at how well Joy was doing despite the doctor that refused to even look at her x-rays. They couldn't find the pins or screws that Mara saw installed.

"Pat, I'm not finding fault; I would not do that; however, you and I both need vehicles. Would you have a problem with turning in this one and getting a new one?" asked Mara.

"Thought about getting a new one. However, it wouldn't fit the UC role I had to play. Why have something you can't use?" Pat replied.

"Then let's both get new vehicles. That way, we don't have to worry about breakdowns or to get a mechanics degree anytime soon," Mara laughed.

"I draw the line at that. I'm not a mechanic. Well, maybe," said Pat with a smile, for she had often helped her dad repair things around the farm/ranch.

"I thought so. Now we must take another test," Mara laughed again and again. They turned in Pat's car and purchased two new ones. Pat's was blue, and Mara's was red though they were the same make and model. The choice was minivans since they never knew when they might have to take a family member someplace.

Since both had name changes, it was time to get their vehicle driving licenses updated. They got their pictures taken as Thunders then as Mara and Pat. Those at the testing station did not even seem to notice the request for double licenses.

Chapter 13

Watch what you wish for

The medical board had called and said an emergency meeting was due to doctors requirement at the new hospital, so they took the exam. Once their certification was in place, they went to the hospital to see how things were going. Penn saw them enter the area and ran down the stairs to meet them at the door.

"Hello, folks, happy to see you. Would you come this way, please?" she said with a welcoming smile.

They moved to a conference room nearby.

"No recording devices in here, though some rooms do still have them for security. Thank you so much for giving me the job. I love it. The hospital is full of patients that the clinic sent to us. Would you be willing to do a walkthrough?" asked Penn.

"Certainly," replied Mara, and they followed their Administrator through the hospital.

Everyone seemed cheerful and busy. No employees are sitting about or lounging in the break room. When the tour was over, they drove to the Clinic and repeated their visit there. They spotted Myrta when they got to the lab.

"How do you like your job?" asked Pat without making it apparent that they knew the woman.

"I love it, and the information you asked for when you were last here is in that box over there," said Myrta pointing at the designated container.

"We will use it, I assure you," said Mara.

Those who passed the Thunder test continued in positions they had filled before as if they remained at the changeover.

They applied for licenses in all professions that needed them and took the exams. The one they were wondering about was the pilot's exam. That was done by each taking a turn at flying with an instructor.

The next stop was an office supply store. There each picked up folders for a hundred professions. Inside were placed their Master's Degrees, letters of congratulations, followed by permit and license for each one. Each had two sets of records for Thunder was one and their home name as the other.

They stopped at a small café and found an out of the way location where they could sit and visit. Mara called for no recordings, whether voice or photo.

"Sis, we are now caught up again though we still have to do the overseas places. Have you any questions thus far?" asked Mara.

"I'm so amazed at all you do, and to think I have the same requirements boggles my mind. Thank you so much for allowing me to join as your twin. What a blessing. Did you notice that some of our new professions require special clothing too? We must get headgear, surgical gowns, suits, western gear, and the list goes on. We will need an entire house to keep track of that stuff, and how do we do that?" Pat wanted to know.

"Keep them at the locations where they are needed, could have a real runaway here; however, let's only acknowledge them as the need comes up. I don't want to be so in demand that the family gets lost, or we don't cover the bases that started all this," Mara replied.

"I agree. Yes, I do have some questions. You said we depart on Monday; which direction will we be going? How will we be traveling?" Pat wanted to know.

"I don't know, although I know we depart on that day," Mara smiled.

"How about picking up some business suits and flying gear? Anything else can wait," Pat commented, for she had looked over the paperwork showing what degrees she now had.

They did just that. The pilot's helmet was made specially and sent via special delivery to their home. In another box was the pilot's jacket and cap. They were there before the twins got home.

"That means another course, another license, and all that stuff costs," said Pat, who was thinking about the little plane they tested in and the big one that would be necessary for the family.

"Didn't you notice the subjects in which you now have degrees? The thing is, I'm not sure what kind of plane to get."

"You need one for a hundred people, and it must be a jet. That way, you can take the family plus anyone else that needs to go. How are you going to take horses?" Pat wanted to know.

"Guess I thought they would swim home," said Mara with laughter.

"In answer to your question about what we took the test in: I was scared and knew I didn't have that kind of knowledge, yet you said trust, and so that is what I did. I didn't look at the subject, just answered the questions as they came up," replied Pat in all honesty.

"Me too," replied Mara with a smile.

"You mean you learned that way too?" asked Pat.

"Yes, in fact, all my training has been placed in my head until needed, it seems."

"What do you have on the schedule next?"

"We took care of exams, Joy, permits, licenses, special gear, and all that. Even did the hospital and clinic tours plus hired a full staff there. We have reliable new vehicles. The more we can get done, the sooner we can leave. Granda would like to go with us to find Grace, a new home, and a shop. Everyone else, except Kennet, can stay at the house while we get it done," Mara told her.

"Okay, mom is next, then we need to look at the help for Granda if we are elsewhere. She used to live alone and now has a housekeeper, stablehands, and cook. Guards are around when we are gone. She seems to like being the monarch of the group. She doesn't want your job; she wants a place of her own where she could participate. I think that position is the right one for her. I'm so thankful that we can do a month's worth of work in one day to get things covered before we are again on the move," said Pat, who was enjoying her new position and life.

"That reminds me," said Mara as she turned on her headphone.

"Granda, we need some grants to cover the hospital and clinic opening. The doctor and his wife took all the funds. They no longer have them, however. At the same time, the more we can keep in our hands by getting grants and the like, the more we will have to work with if this continues to happen," Mara commented.

"It is done. Sent out the request the day you purchased those two places," Granda laughed. She was so enjoying the challenges the family was giving her; it made her feel young again.

An activated sensor activated the garage door, and they drove inside.

"Hurry, hurry, we want to see what you accomplished this time," said Joy with a big grin.

They ran into the house and saw the pile of folders on the table.

"Granda, we each have folders for all our Master's Degrees. We need to put any licenses with the folder to which it pertains. We will do the same with permits, plus a list of phone numbers for each business and who is in charge. My thought is to leave the original folders on file here. I also ordered briefcases for us. That way, we can put the information in one before meeting with someone who needs confirmation of what we know. Or we can tell them to contact the university and ask if we have a given talent.

"I think we will need everything when we fly out. However, I prefer that we never take the originals along, just copies. Wonder if our plane will have a vault onboard? We leave on Monday, therefore, have only a few days to get things done," warned Mara.

"Kennet, have you been working on your riding and exercises to include knives?" asked Mara.

"Yes, can I take my horse and guitar this time?" he asked.

"No, the guitar is still at the inn, as is mine, and we need to pick up one for Pat. However, you can take your horse. I want to purchase two of those twelve-string guitars that Mr. Spritzer makes. Tonight, we will leave Star in charge while we take care of business for my mom. When we return, what would you all like to do that is fun?" asked Mara.

"Could we have a concert?" asked Joy with a smile.

"Can you play?" asked Mara with a smile, for she had a hunch if she and Pat played, they probably all did.

"Don't have instruments," replied Joy in sadness.

"Then let us take care of this trip first. Tomorrow morning, as soon as the stores open, we will take everyone shopping for your instrument or instruments of choice," said Mara with a broad smile.

"Do you mean it? Really, oh what fun," said Joy, for she wanted so much to be like her much-loved mom. To her mind, T1 was the surgeon for her and Joey.

"Granda, grab your keys and let's go. We will take a vehicle that will hold five people, three of us, and the two we will pick up at mom's."

They were immediately out the door and on their way.

"We made it; I thought they would all want to go," said Mara.

"They did, however, the promise of a trip tomorrow to get instruments had them pleased, and they will behave," Granda commented.

"I've been trying to think of places that are in the neighborhood where mom lives that would work for a house and store. It seems that the coding makes that impossible unless she lives in the country, then no one will want to go out of their way to find her. Have you any suggestions?" asked Mara.

"Yes, I do. That is why I took the driver. Look at this and see what you think," said Granda.

They drove toward the center of town and property that Granda had seen advertised. It had been a home and store plus was on a twenty-acre lot. The house had an apartment, and the store was spacious with easy delivery access and parking for patrons. The drive-by had them excited, and they went to get Grace and Eve.

Grace was called and told that Mara had a surprise, and they were on their way. As soon as the passengers climbed inside, they drove to the location they had passed before.

"A realtor is to meet us there. That is probably her in that car waiting," said Granda.

Everyone got out of the van and walked to meet the woman who also got out.

"Hello, are you the folks who want to look at this property?"

"Yes, we are looking now," said Grace, though she wondered why.

"If I had the funds, I would buy it myself, for it is a sound investment. At the same time, realtors are exempt from this purchase. It has new everything. All appliances are new, plumbing, sewer, electric, heating, and cooling. All buildings have new roofing, blown-in insulation, and the house even has sheets, towels, blankets, and all that. Zoning allows a business that does not require a lot of long-term parking needs. There is a six-car garage by the house. There is an additional incentive; however, let me show you the store first," the realtor said as she opened the door to that building.

Grace stood in shocked amazement, for she had seen this store in her dreams, and it had everything she wanted or needed. It was a three-story with an elevator. There was off-street parking, a large storeroom for fabric, cutting tables, good lighting, windows to display garments, and an attendant area.

The place was spotless. None of them said anything; as they looked at what the realtor was showing them. She had given them each a printout of the property. They then moved to the home. It was also spacious and clean. Everything looked as if newly built, new cupboards, counters, carpets, but the most amazing was it came fully furnished, and that too was new. Both buildings had heat and cooling with solar as the source.

"Why are they selling such a beautiful place?" asked Grace.

"The woman found out her husband was unfaithful. She is suing for divorce, and the judge says they must sell one of the houses. She agreed to sell it and would do it herself. The kicker is it will cost you one dollar as the first person to show interest. That is all she is going to give her husband," said the realtor.

"Can she do that?" asked Mara in shock.

"Yes, she can. You see, she holds the title, and the Judge said the x-husband could have the property's value. That is the price she wants. He paid for the overhaul of the real estate top to bottom, intending to move his girlfriend in as soon as the contractors finished, for that person wants it. You are here before he even knows it is on the market, and the wife says the first person to offer gets it."

"We take it," said Mara.

"Oh darn, and I was hoping to get it," said Grace with sadness.

"Not so Mother, dear, I am buying it for you," responded

Mara.

"What? You can't do that. You still have your college education to pay," replied her mother, who was sure the price was a lot higher than one dollar.

"Maybe and maybe not, Granda, will you calm her down? Ma'am, when and how soon can we close? Also, what form of payment do you require?"

"She wants cash of two fifty-cent pieces, to pay him off immediately. He can keep one and give the other to his mistress. I have the paperwork here, and if you will sign it now, it is yours. There are even orders to pay all closing costs to ensure the paperwork gets done properly, the plat is available, and a record of all work done is in the package. There is a five-year warranty on everything already paid, and you can continue to pay the monthly amount when it runs out if you wish to continue with it. Don't worry, she wants it this way and says to tell you, if you are not the girlfriend, that she has plenty of money and he will see none of it," the realtor told them.

"Thank you for your time and the opportunity. My mother has long wanted a place like this as she is a clothes designer and seamstress. With her is her apprentice. They will be moving in as soon as we can line up the movers," said Mara.

The home had four bedrooms, each with a bath. There was also a large master suite plus an apartment.

"Grace, she can do this, and it has long been her desire to do it for you. Your twins are giving it to you, and I would have helped pay for it if needed. Now start thinking about who will pack and move you. Also, make a list of what you want to take with you and what you want to leave behind. Understand your current property is debt-free, so maybe you could sell it for one dollar and pass on the blessing for you will keep the value in this place," responded Granda.

"How can they sell it for so little?" asked Grace again.

"Does it matter? The woman who owned it said she was not short of funds, which is how she wants it done. Your daughters have passed all their Master's exams. Shhh, we will discuss it when we are out of here as I don't want to say too much. They want to tell you," said Granda, though the girls could hear her.

No one mentioned the other properties. Granda knew what the mother's focus would be, her daughters, and their education. Focus her on that, and it would take the pressure off the girls.

Grace was so excited about the new living and working area that she wanted to move that night, so they hurried home where they pulled the seats out of the van, took the pickup and horse trailer plus Granda's car, and then picked up everyone before going again to Grace's old one. With guards on duty, the property had protection.

Eva, Gwen, Kennet, and Joy put things in boxes while Star and Dan moved them out to the vehicles. The intent was to take just what was needed to live until movers were available. Grace pointed out what to pack at the house. It had to be personal and not business-related, for big movers would move that and be tax-deductible as it was a business expense. Her equipment and large fabric rolls would require healthy people to move.

Before they thought it possible, everything was at the new home Grace wanted to keep. She called to see if a moving company was available late at night and was surprised when a crew and large trucks appeared in thirty minutes. Anything left after the commercial movers finished could remain with the house.

Pat and Mara chuckled when they looked at the clock at home. It said the whole thing took two hours. They knew better than that yet thanked the powers and told everyone to take a shower before bed. Joey had been with his mom and was sound asleep through it all.

Mara told her family that all chores had to be taken care of before they left the following morning. The trip to the music store had the result that Mara thought it might. It required that a delivery truck take their purchases home for each person was allowed two instruments, except the twins who had a copy of everything the rest did to teach them how to play. Mara, Granda, and Pat decided that two pianos were enough. One to practice and one to train on, or for the twins to both play simultaneously. Like Mara told her family, once each of the kids showed proficiency, they would be allowed to add another instrument to their collection.

Grace took her piano to her new home, although the only one who played it was Mara, as far as Grace knew.

Mara spoke with the people at the music store, and they agreed, for a fee, to move her piano from her mom's old home to the new one. Since the music store delivery would not be there before one, they went out to eat early to allow plenty of time to get home to transfer instruments.

Upon entering the restaurant, they met a woman none of them recognized, and she approached the group.

"May I speak with you?" she asked.

"Certainly, you may. Would you care to join us?"

"I won't take much of your time, I promise."

"What would you like to speak about?" Pat replied for Mara was checking out the area, and the waitress was setting them in a quiet corner.

"I am from this area and need to return due to family issues. I need a job to remain. I had a dream that you would be here and that I should ask if you had an opening. It seems strange, I know, but, before the woman could continue, Pat took over."

"Not in our world. What kind of work do you do?" Pat asked, then nodded at Mara to take the interview.

"I've done many things. Worked as a waitress, cook, dishwasher, was a wrangler on a few ranches, a couple of which were beginner variety. I was once a dance instructor, was in the military, have a background in law enforcement, owned a business or a dozen, did medical record translation, cleaned houses, rode horses, ran a pet store, worked for one state Bureau of Investigation. I worked on radar, teletype, recruiting, helicopter mechanics, unit administrator, and logistics. I spent some time as a volunteer in a terminal cancer hospital. I was a chauffeur, have ridden horses, elephant, camel, a miniature horse, Shetland pony, a buffalo, and operated a kennel where I trained dogs. Checked new homes for anything missed before the owners took over; repaired rental units for the owners. Traveled by car, truck, bus, train, boat, tour ship, and military ship; plane, helicopter, twin-engine, superjet, transcontinental flights; motorcycle, snowmobile, bobsled, regular sled. Over time have been in a few countries, almost all states, and have a current passport. I have a Jetplane although I may have to sell it," said the woman.

"We need your name and an oath," Mara replied with a smile.

Pat led, and the woman who repeated it.

"Would you be willing to sell us your airplane on paper? How large is it?" began Mara.

"At one time, it was part of a corporation, and when it went bankrupt, I bought the plane cheaply as I had been the pilot. We just received notification that the manufacturer has a recall of that make and model. They are replacing them with a newer version. The manufacturer wants to find out how well it held up. A friend of mine was my copilot. However, we both lost our jobs at that time. She came with me and is also looking for work. A hundred could ride comfortably in it. My name is Shandra Tridine. My pilot's license is current if you also need a pilot," she explained.

"Okay, sign over the plane, if you will. We will need to put it in a corporation to cover it with insurance, maintenance, etc. Call your co-pilot and tell that person they, too, are hired. We need your services and will pay you both a regular salary. There is a requirement to fly to a few different nations on business. Our entire family will probably go if they are free at the time. We travel with a wolf, and if we can figure out how, a horse or three," responded Mara.

"You are kidding, aren't you?" asked the woman with a smile and a laugh.

"Afraid not, my friend," Pat told her.

"Okay, if that is what you need, I will see what we can do," replied Shandra.

"Call your partner and go to this address. The sign says N-Sign Ranch. It is about forty miles west on the highway. We have an appointment there at one. Bring a picture of the plane, your partner, resumes, and if you happen to know another set of pilots, bring them along if you will. Now that is not to say we won't put you to work in other ways as well," laughed Pat, and Granda nodded.

The woman immediately departed, and they could see her on the phone in her car. After completing the call, she left though they saw her fist shoot into the air and a shout of "Yes," as she backed out of the parking place.

It was a rental vehicle, and since they flew in, that was most likely how they were getting around.

Granda had always wanted a piano in her home, even though she did not play. Now she would get to hear one or two as her family played them. Granda was so looking forward to it. Might even learn to play a little herself, she thought.

They put the vehicles away to empty the driveway for the delivery truck. It was right behind them. Then they saw another car approaching as well.

"I'll handle the movers; you two meet your guests," directed Granda.

The rest of the family moved inside and out of the way. Mara wanted them out of the way, for they couldn't do anything to help and could be injured. They assembled in Joy's room until the movers left.

"Hello, Shandra, who is your friend?" asked Pat, for Mara had to go in and decide where the more prominent instruments, like floor harp and pianos, were to go.

"This is Cherry Nightwind, my copilot. The other pair hanging back is another pair of pilot and copilot. We have worked with them before, and they too lost their jobs due to downsizing. Somehow, they managed also to gain a plane. Think before we go any further you need to get some oaths, however," replied Shandra.

When done, Pat learned the second string was Gretchen, called Gretch, Passuer, and Michelle, called Mike, Grinson.

"Did you bring pictures and resumes?" Pat asked for she already liked the four.

"Yes, do you want them now or when we get inside so that the wind does not help you sort us out," asked Mike with a laugh.

"Inside is fine. Say, do any of you play musical instruments?" Pat wanted to know.

"That is how we first met. We all play something or other, in fact, maybe a few something or others," responded Gretch as she looked at her friends for confirmation, and they nodded.

"In that case, let's go inside. Once the movers leave, we are going to have a jam session. My twin is the leader of the band," laughed Pat.

They ran up the stairs and met the movers running down. Everyone waved and kept going.

"Pat, would you help get the instruments tuned? The pianos sound okay now need to work on the rest," directed Mara.

"We have four new participants if you want to add them in," said Pat.

"If you gals have a seat for a moment, we will see what my family can come up with first," laughed Mara.

"This is all family?" asked Shandra with wide eyes.

"We will introduce ourselves as we go," replied Mara.

"Granda, what makes you think you can sit there doing nothing? Have a seat at the piano, and you can move on from there," Pat directed.

Granda did as her granddaughter told her, though with a frown. She played a few keys, then brightened and added a few more. Mara picked up her sax, and they played together. Soon everyone was playing. As each did a solo on one of the instruments, they introduced themselves and their relationship to the bandleader.

"Now, it is your turn. We have a few other musical instruments," Mara offered.

The guests got up, selected some horns and strings, and then began to play their music style.

"Okay, everyone gets an instrument, or if we run out, you can trade-off," said Mara as she sat at the piano and watched Granda pick up a trumpet and frown at it.

"Trust," she whispered to her benefactor.

Granda looked at her in surprise; then, a wide grin filled her face. She picked up the horn and played taps. The twins were elated at the surprised look on her face.

"By next time, you need to have your instruments with you. We may need to present a concert to find who and what we seek," Mara told the new ones and advised the family at the same time.

"Has anyone asked them where they are staying, how much time they need to cover whatever brought them back here, and what their long-term plans are?" asked Granda in a whisper.

"They just flew in this morning. The instruments are on their planes. It seems that the reason they ended up in Preston was a message came that their family needed them. When they arrived, they found that no one in town knew them, which was not a surprise to the foursome, for none of them have a family to their knowledge. Shandra said she would follow up on a lead she had, which resulted in her finding us. On a guess, might we be the family they need to find? In that case, they need to stay in a suite here," responded Mara.

"Suite?" asked Granda in shock.

"Didn't you notice? All the bedrooms are now suites. Even yours was made larger. We can now house about a hundred, I understand, for that is the number of suites we have though there can be more in each suite. Everyone will maintain their suite, while general use areas will share maintenance with everyone doing a part. I was going to request a building that is heated and used just for concerts. However, we don't want to let folks know where and how we live," Mara advised.

Chapter 14

Pat breaks them in her way

Granda departed immediately to see her new enlarged area. She was thrilled and had tears in her eyes as she turned and found that Mara was right behind her.

"Dear one, we would never exclude you. If we get an upgrade, so do you," said Mara.

Granda stood in one place, not knowing what to do.

Mara hugged Granda, then realized her calm grandmother was crying due to Mara, including her in all that was happening.

"I can never thank you enough for the opportunities you have given all of us. If you had not opened your book to me, your home to my family, and your heart to all of us, we would not be who we are. The impossible happened, and we are the only ones who know it. We now need living quarters because most of us are women, and in time some will marry. Each suite has three bedrooms, which can be for kids, guests, or whatever. The AI says he likes the new form. The garage now will house twice as many vehicles as there are rooms."

"How do you like being a musician? Also, those degrees that Pat and I have? You have them as well. We will need them; I understand we now know several foreign languages."

"However, we must deal with those different properties first. The Twin Thunders must return with Kennet and our guards to your book. We must finish what we started there. Give the new women suites and duties. The airplanes are now part of my corporation, and therefore the corp for the planes owns a hangar at the airport to keep our air units out of the weather. Once the new women choose quarters, their belongings will join them," Mara explained.

"Dear child, how are you getting this all done?"

"Have you looked at what has happened in the last week?" asked Mara.

"As I recall, we met on Sunday, and you came home with me."

"True, and I moved on Monday night, I believe. The trip to the first doc was Tuesday. You said we were two weeks on the road. The med clinic said we were gone a month, while Star said it was two days. We drove nearly a full day to get to the second doctor. The surgery took three days for the two children. Those who worked on the kids forgot we were even there."

"After we spent a day driving and two days at the first ranch, we caught up the area. Then we did all the rest of the stops and came home. That was when Star said we were gone for two days. That would have made it Thursday."

"Pat and I took all the exams on our first day back after getting the x-rays on Joy and Joey. Next, we got mom squared away. Now it is again coming on Sunday and in one week look what has happened. I guess that we are preparing for some major duties once we depart. Presently don't know if it will be a book or overseas. However, we will be going to work on Monday," Mara advised.

"At least you can go to church with your whole family," said Granda with a chuckle as she regained her balance.

"Let me see, that means thirteen in a sixteen passenger van, that is unless we use the vans that Pat and I have," laughed Mara.

"Where will the new four fit?" asked Granda.

"That is up to you. Do you want more children, or would you prefer that they fall under me?"

I've raised my brood. Now it is your turn. Put the four new ones under you, if you have no objections," Granda suggested, for she was in her fifties.

"Granda, they are mine," said Pat with a chuckle, for she felt that she needed to do her part as well in this fantastic family.

"Only have about two to go, and you catch up with me," replied Mara with a laugh. She didn't care who went with who as long as everyone felt included in some way.

Mara and Granda returned to the group and met Joy, returning after feeding Joey and changing him.

"Okay, let's take a break. You four can pick out living spaces. No, you do not have to share. Each is authorized a suite in case you later marry. For now, don't care where you sleep; only claim a suite for your own. Since I am now your mother, you can expect visits from me while learning more about you. Meantime you will be learning as well. If you ride, we have racers in the stables. Gwen is the one who rules in that area. If you do not, I would suggest that you give it a try. we have the time, we, the Twins, will join you. Granda rides as well. As far as I know, the only non-rider is Grace, my mother, unless you count in Joey, who is a bit young though he likes riding with his mom," explained Pat.

"Would you like to go to the airport with us and see the planes while we pick up our belongings?" asked Shandra.

"Granda, think you need to go along, Kennet, you know you go. Joy, what is your status? I rephrase that: who is not going?" Pat asked.

"Can we stay and play the instruments?" Dan wanted to know.

Mara knew that was also Joy's wish.

"Not more than one more hour, then you need to do something else for a while. You will have time set aside daily for practice like you have with the horses. I will devise a schedule for all of us. As soon as the tutors arrive, you will begin to learn. The Twin Thunders are going to take our new members out to meet the horses before we depart. If the stallion doesn't know who they are, they might not get back in," laughed Pat, who was enjoying her new role.

"Come on, ladies, we have some horses to visit," said Mara, and the twins led their new members to the stables.

"This is the way the twins ride," said Pat, and she called for a racer while Mara asked for the stallion. Instead of the racehorse, Pi came, and the ride was on. They put on quite a show for the new members, with Pat riding the male horse.

"You are kidding. You expect us to ride like that?" asked one of the new women.

"Certainly, as we own a few ranches, and you might have to deal with stock to show you have that kind of knowledge. You may select mounts when we come back. Gwen, my granddaughter, will help you, for she knows the horses well. Also, my son Kennet may make suggestions. Everyone practices before breakfast, on horses. After we clean up and eat, we have classes of various kinds," explained Mara.

"I'll call Kennet and tell Star we are leaving," offered Pat.

"Thanks, Sis, I'll get the van out. Never know when we might need more room," laughed Mara.

Soon the eight were on their way to the airport. They entered the lobby of the private plane side of the airport.

"Hello, I am Shandra. My airplane remained here while I contacted my family."

"Ah, yes, the one with the shadow, what can I do for you?" asked the man at the counter.

"We need to have access to the planes. Do we need a key, combination, or handprint?" asked Shandra.

"You sent the people to put the hangar in place. They are getting ready to leave; why not ask them?" he replied.

"Thank you," said Shandra as they departed for the hangar. It seemed quite large to accommodate two passenger planes though it looked large enough for four such units.

"Hello Brison, thank you for getting it done so quickly. We need access to the hangar. Did you put in the palm print pad as I asked?" Pat said though she knew any name would work.

"Here you go, the pad for the side door is here, and the one for the main door is here. Push this button, then put your palm on the pad. Now lift your palm when the light comes on. Okay, press the button twice, next. Now you need to lock the pad for those who just signed in while giving one-person override authority," he led them each through the process.

When all had tried it and had quick access, he left.

"Before you get concerned, he will not recall having been here. Nor can he tell you who owns this hangar only that it has full security, and no one is allowed inside without permission from the corporation that owns the planes inside. Go ahead," directed Mara.

They entered the hangar and waited while the pilot of each plane unlocked it, then lowered the stairs to get inside.

"Hangar two-twelve, please respond," said a female voice.

"Go ahead, this is hangar two-twelve," replied Mara.

"We have two planes landing that request to meet with you on private business."

"Tell them the message received, and we shall wait. Opening the hangar doors," Mara told them.

"What is going on?" asked Pat.

"At a guess, I would say the new planes are here, and I assure you these are not one hundred passenger airplanes. They are private ones, jets by the looks of them," Mara replied.

The women watched as the planes landed then taxied to the open hangar. The only one that was open as it happened. Two people departed each plane and moved toward the women.

"Are you the owners of the eight-ninety-fours?" asked the person in the lead.

"Yes," replied Mara, for she realized that it was best to have her handle it. After all, she was head of the corporation.

"They told us that you would accept two planes to replace what you have. We will fly the older ones to the factory. If you wish to remove anything from the inside, please do so, and we will wait. If you don't object, we will use the tug to move the older planes outside and put the new ones inside. Tomorrow, we will fly out the older ones," directed one of the pilots.

"Kids, please get your gear and put it in the van," Pat suggested.

"May we enter the new ships?" asked Mara.

"Of course," replied one of the incoming pilots with a smile as they knew how much of a shock this would be for the new owners.

"Pat, we need to check them out together and allow the girls time to get all they need to," suggested Mara.

They entered the nearest craft, for both had been left open.

"Would you look at this!"

"This is not a commercial craft."

"No, thankfully, now let's see what we have."

It had two levels, three with cargo. There were four bedrooms on the top level, assumedly for the pilots as there were only four, which would be necessary for transcontinental flights. There was a private stairway leading to the rest area for pilots from the cab of the craft. The seats were well-spaced on the main floor and could be reclined almost flat; they even had privacy panels if desired. The lowest level was cargo, and there were stalls in a small part of it centered on the aircraft for balancing the load. The horses could even lay down during flight. Accommodations for about ten, it looked like with air pumped in. Everything was new and shiny. Mara had the paperwork in her hand and found out that the planes were fresh off the assembly line. The titles were there, and all they had to do was register them.

It wasn't long before Pat's girls joined them to check out the new airplanes. They were shocked at the upgrade. When they had completed their inspection, they departed the planes. There was a moving tug waiting to change out the aircraft. One van had a full load then moved outside the hangar to allow the new planes; however, there was still room for more. Once the aircraft garage was secure, they departed.

The first stop was registering the aircraft in their corporate name and showing certification to fly the new planes. Granda and Kennet had remained with them. They filed their information and departed.

Shira had remained on the van to be sure no sensing devices were on the unit. Pat checked with her electronics to be sure. Once satisfied, they loaded up and departed the government building's parking lot, where they got things updated.

Grand was driving, and they headed toward home, for it would soon be supper time. Each time they entered the property Granda recalled her promise to herself to get the drive resurfaced. She would get that call made today.

"What do you think of the new planes?" asked Mara.

"Only one problem, we don't know how to fly these," said Shandra in sadness, for she loved to pilot.

"Oh, I doubt it will be a problem. It is the school you went to after all," said Pat with a chuckle.

Her daughters looked at one another in total astonishment.

"Your mother will never lie to you," said Mara.

"Okay…," replied Shandra with a smile, for she was relieved that they would not have to take another six-month-long training course.

"Mom, we are being followed. They picked us up at the place you got your license," Kennet told Mara.

"Then we shall see how good of drivers they are," said Pat.

The van stopped, and they changed drivers without either woman leaving the vehicle. Pat was now driving.

"Keep Lightning handy," was all she said before departing the parking spot. Pat maintained at the speed limit until near the highway, where she quickly entered it and pushed the speed some.

"Still coming," said Kennet.

"Okay, guys, and gals hang on to your hats," said Pat.

Everyone checked the fastening of their seatbelt.

As she hit the accelerator, the following vehicle did the same; she switched lanes, so did they. Suddenly she was facing them, and as the van stopped, Mara and Pat departed with hands on their swords.

The oncoming vehicle stopped where it was and would not run.

"Granda, freeze," said Mara.

"Ladies, watch and learn," said Granda to those in the van. Kennet moved out the side door and stood to the side and behind his mom.

The family van was directly behind the two women and the safest place they could be. Those in the other vehicle also got out.

"May we ask why you are following us?" Mara asked. She would not become Thunder until she saw a reason that would hold up in court.

"Seemed as good a pastime as any," replied the first man out.

"Doesn't make sense to me," replied Pat.

"Pretty girls, beautiful day, nice ride, what more does one need?" he told her with a grin.

"Maybe something like a valid reason?" Mara offered.

Pat and Mara turned to reenter the van. However, Kennet was watching.

"Twins down!" he shouted.

The men froze, and the bullet-headed toward each of them froze as well. The Lightning Swords came out, and the battle was happening. The swords returned the shells to those who sent them, including those firing from inside their vehicle, although those took the most direct route knocking out the front window of the adversaries' unit.

The eight men hit the ground, and the court began.

"S, give testimony of what you saw," directed the judge.

Shandra moved to where Kennet was and gave the required information.

When all testimony was on the permanent recording and confessions heard, the local law received a call. Pat met them and explained the situation. The prisoners had orders to walk back to town, and the squad was right behind them. Pat drove their car though it was not in decent shape, it was still drivable. The men and a vehicle were dropped off at the police station since the event began in town.

"Now you have an idea of what your family does and especially the Twins," said Pat.

"Granda, would you be open to a stop for a treat?" Mara asked for she requested Granda to remain with them in the case of a call. That way, the vehicle would return home.

"You know I never turn down a treat," replied the woman with a smile.

They were near where the Pie'd Piper Restaurant was, which made Mara think of it. Kennet so loved the ones they made there.

The group went inside and sat where they could watch their vehicle so that no one put any more electronic bugs in or on it.

"Would you mind explaining?" asked Shandra.

"Only when at home," replied Pat, for training needed to begin immediately.

When the pie came, they noted that the waitress brought Kennet two pieces once Mara gave the okay. He was of slight build and had never had sweets until going home with his new mom. He was going on eleven and was always on the run.

General questions about the area, climate, and amenities of the city were safe areas of discussion as that was public knowledge of all-around their table. The new four learned a great deal that didn't relate to their new family.

At home, they explained why to use an initial instead of using a name. The information about Thunder's family was to remain private.

They learned what the walking felons were involved in and why the family was the court's target. For some reason, there were a lot of folks on the loose who wanted what the N-Sign Clan owned.

"Will we all be given swords?" Cherry wanted to know.

"I don't think so. Mara and I both carry them because we are twins and share the leadership role. None of the others have them," explained Pat.

"Thank goodness!" responded Cherry.

"Why do you feel that way?" asked Mara in surprise.

"I never was good at dancing," replied the young woman with a smile though it was because she had never learned.

Mara laughed a lot over that one. The girl was a musician yet couldn't dance? That didn't make any sense.

"She will learn," replied Pat, who knew what her twin was thinking as well as what her daughter was thinking. Another lesson to teach and this was one that Pat indeed knew. Not only had she learned to dance as the various fads came up, but she also took ballroom dancing. Thus, they each learned to use a sword and dance.

On Sunday, the entire family went to church in two vans. The weather had turned so hot that they needed breathing room. Pat took her four in her new car, and Mara took the rest in hers. Just in case, a second sixteen passenger van was also in the garage.

When they unloaded, the first person they saw was Grace, followed by Eva. Eva ran to give everyone in Mara's van a hug, starting with Mara. The others followed suit. The family moved inside and took up two rows. Mara took one with her brood and Pat the other with hers. The congregation saw it as the way it had always been. They claimed their seats then milled around visiting with those in attendance.

"Hello, Mara, we missed you last week," said the pastor.

"We had to take my daughter and grandson to a doctor out of state. They had surgery and are now both doing fine," she replied.

"Your family has grown," he commented.

"Come and meet the clan," she told him.

He moved to where Pat and the group sat.

"This is my twin Pat and her daughters Shandra, Cherry, Gretch, and Michelle. You already know Shelly and Grace, my Mom and grandmother. Meet Joy and Joey, my daughter and her son, my daughter Star and her kids Dan, Eva, and Gwen."

"You have a beautiful family. It is nice to meet you. You are very welcome," the pastor told them.

He moved on to greet others that were coming in. His wife joined him, and they continued to welcome their parishioners.

"Wonder how he will keep us all figured out?" asked Cherry.

"That isn't a requirement. The first Sunday of the month, name tags are worn," laughed Mara.

When they departed after the service, Pat and Mara were

suddenly in Thunder mode. Their family remained behind them as they moved. Mara stood guard while Pat walked around, checking each vehicle. As they already knew, the units carried electronic devices. Pat signed for silence, and all entered the cars. They drove out of the parking lot and to the highway headed North. They saw the following car immediately.

"How about dinner out?" commented Mara.

"Have you someplace particular in mind?" asked Pat.

"I thought maybe we could have an excellent buffet in Crator a few miles down the road," replied Mara with a smile.

"Ah, yes, I know of that one. Let's do it if Granda has no objections," responded Pat.

"You two know I never turn down food," laughed Granda, though she never gained a pound for her, and Kennet had similar metabolisms.

They used a back road to reach the restaurant holding the Sunday buffet. Pat was leading; however, Mara could now drive as well as her twin did. For the pair to know how to do something, it only took the one with the knowledge to use it.

When they reached the location, they found the parking lot was full.

They parked around back, and there was the outdoor BBQ for any who didn't find room inside. Near the setup was a large corral with the gate open. Again, Mara smiled, and Pat knew what she had in mind.

Mara spoke with the owner as she passed.

"Would you object if you had a bit of a show added to your meal?" asked Mara.

"Not at all if it does no damage," the woman replied with a smile.

"Just tell your patrons to remain seated for the show and under no circumstance to participate," Mara advised.

Pat and Mara moved to the restroom, where they changed into their western gear. Jeans, shirt, boots, and hat was more in keeping with the decor of the place. Pat moved to the corral and picked up a rope she saw. Soon she was doing rope tricks with it. Shira moved to where she was and began jumping through the line as it spun. Thunder One and Thunder Two were soon in operation as they kept alert for the following group. They had to find a way to get that bunch to challenge the Thunders.

"Hey, where did you find my dog?" yelled one of the men belligerently.

T1 kept doing what she was doing. T2 followed her lead.

Kennet moved to the Corral with the two women, for he too now wore jeans and boots. Soon he was jumping through the ropes with Shira. He tumbled and lay down to let Shira jump over him, or he did the same to her. He was watching those outside the corral.

Star decided it was time for her to take part.

"We don't have your dog and never have had. Come on, and I will prove it to you," directed Star as she pushed two of the men into the corral.

Two more came to object and were also escorted inside, only by two of T2's kids.

Once the Thunder group was inside the corral, the gate closed, and the family climbed the corral fencing to watch what was going on. They were careful to remain behind the Thunder Twins facing the restaurant so that nothing would hit the customers when the firing started. The return of the shell always hit the sender.

"If you didn't find my dog, then you stole her," said the man.

"Shy, how many years have we been together?" asked T1.

The dog barked up to ten.

"That's right, about ten years. Thank you," T1 told her

guard.

He kept harassing and interfering, yet the women kept doing what they were doing, and the man was getting angrier. He finally reached for T1 to spin her around. She laid him out on the ground.

"Now, what is this all about?" T1 asked the group that now had no leader.

"We are to mess up whatever you have going on," said one of the men though he tried to hide before speaking.

"Speaker to the front," directed Pat, for she knew that her sister was making sure everyone was out of the line of fire. There were open fields on three sides; however, using two sides would keep all bullets away from the restaurant's patrons. The front of the corral, nearest the restaurant, had become transparent to those eating while fon inside the fence was solid.

The man moved forward, for he could not refuse a Thunder order.

"Tell me, what brings you here? Who are you, and why are we your targets?" asked T1.

He gave the required answers, even providing everyone's name and the name of the person who sent them. This individual became part of the group they were meeting.

"Return to your friends!" she directed the man.

Thunder turned her back on the group and appeared to depart.

"Twins, down!" shouted Kennet.

They dropped immediately to their heels to move fast if needed. Then they turned to face the armed men who were frozen until they were ready to return fire. The bullets shot at the two women were transferred so fast that people could not even see them. Once all were down, it was time for another court.

T2 became the judge while T1 asked the questions, and

Kennet kept watching with Shira.

As at all their court sessions, the proceedings would be in a recording, and the confessions signed before T2 made a phone call. Soon authorities came and removed those detained.

"That was quite the program. Come anytime. Now may we give you a free meal?" asked the owner.

"Thank you for the offer; however, we pay our way. My family is rather large, and it is best we pay as we go. We appreciated the use of your corral," Mara responded, for as a law enforcement officer, it would be considered a bribe.

"It looked almost like Thunder was here," said the owner.

"They were," replied Mara as they moved in the door to find places where they could sit together.

"May our guard come with us? She will remain under my sister's chair unless more are foolhardy enough to challenge us," asked Pat as she passed the owner.

"Yes, she may. I can see she is well behaved and will not bother the other customers without reason. You and your family are welcome anytime."

Chapter 15

Keeping the Balance

Once they finished their meal, they prepared to depart, and the owner stopped them.

"Look, I told everyone that you would not accept payment, but they insisted. Our patrons took up a collection and want you to know how much everyone appreciated the entertainment. Many have been wishing to see Thunder in action," the woman told them.

They took the money not to create a scene. However, Mara gave it to a local food bank. The family was shocked when they saw how much the locals had paid for the entertainment. The restaurant was a popular place to eat. However, it only held about a hundred people. The amount collected was in the thousands, which significantly aided the food bank.

The trip home was a silent one, for the family knew the vans had electronics aboard. Pat had her kit out and was deactivating all of them as soon as the two vans stopped.

It was a good thing that Mara kept shot records, copies of x-rays, and medical info on her entire family. Even if the former owners of the two medical establishments were inept, the new ones were not, and the information could be necessary for various reasons. Some examples would be blood work if anyone were to get married, so close relationships they didn't know about didn't create any problems. The medical record of each person was kept up to date and included a full blood report. She realized that the short physical given was not what she wanted. They still needed x-rays of all of them.

"Granda," alerted Mara.

Those in the van didn't hear the conversation.

"Go ahead."

"I just realized that we still need x-rays of all of us, and I need them as both Mara and as Thunder. We still don't know if we are leading people to us," replied Mara.

"Why not look at who we have, and who would still need them? You know Joy and Joey already have theirs on file. Kennet and Star's group got theirs when you had the first doc look them over. The x-ray tech took films of everyone; I made sure. The Pat branch won't need the inspection, for they have not been there yet," responded Granda.

"Thank you for keeping me focused. You are correct. Pat and I need to take the new four to get familiar with the town. That way, they can aid you while we are gone, wherever we are going. If by air, then we all go. If by land, then only Kennet, Pat, and I will go plus the guards, as far as I know now. I'll run to the hospital and get mine done early tomorrow or late tonight as it shouldn't be as busy then."

"Not doable that I can see. You said the mission begins tomorrow yet didn't give us time information. We have no idea if the planes are involved or the usual transport. Have you received further information? All passports are in to include Pat's bunch. Shots were updated when you took everyone in for the physical. I made sure of that. Also, show that we have x-rays of everyone, including you," commented Granda, for she had everyone's put together and had personally requested that they all have x-rays by the tech they met.

They had located a room in the mansion to use as the record room, and it was where they kept all medical and legal documents. The AI hid the location from anyone that shouldn't have access. It would be a lot easier to locate if needed, and the room locked with AI control.

Mara departed the house and walked to the stable. She met Shira partway, and Pi soon followed. They walked with her to the pasture, where the Twins had dealt with many of the felons. She knelt in the grass and bowed her head. When she rose an hour later, she found that the stud and her twin was there, as was Kennet.

"Book is first," she told them and shared the timetable.

Everyone went to their assigned quarters for a night of rest.

"Thank you, Granda, for keeping my back covered. We do not have time for x-rays, for we leave at four, and I am the cook for those going. Talk to you on the road," advised Mara.

Pat notified her kids of the schedule, and all would be ready.

Early the following morning saw the seven riders mounted for departure. Mara was in the lead. Granda stood with the book in hand until all were lined up and ready to follow. Mara rode Pi, Pat rode the stud, Kennet rode on his favorite, and the four new women had selected sturdy mounts.

"Are you ready? Remember to trust," directed Thunder, then suddenly she turned, and Granda set the book down.

Thunder was on her way, and the rest followed. The horses knew the route and quickly followed. Shira had moved with Thunder and Pi.

They landed in the underground stable in Thunder's part of the UC.

"Okay, as of this moment, you are deputized by me. Give out no information and stick together. The gangs here will soon be making targets of you if you are not careful. I must see a man in an underground city store for he might have some information for me. The reason for bringing so many animals is we might need them. Kennet, I need to know what is going on. See what you can find out without leaving the UC. By now, they know you work for me, and that could be asking for trouble. First, see how stable the UC itself is, then we will go from there. I am going to the music man if you need to find me," Thunder told him.

She put the horses in their stalls, removed their gear, brushed them down, and gave them grain before departing for the upper city. The animals were in open stalls so that they could go to her if the need came up.

"You five need to move nearby me until they realize you are part of the UC. Then you can move around and see what you learn. There is a group of businesses that are around the city. That is where I am going. If anyone asks who you are, tell them a friend of Kennet and nothing else. By the time I get there, word will have passed, and you can move on your own. Do not call me by any known name in this location. The only one who knew any was Star. The only way anyone else knows who I am is if they see me in action, and then their memories are lost to them. I must remind you this is not a safe place, so please use caution. Are you armed, as I suggested?" Thunder asked.

"Yes, all have been tested and are ready to go to work," replied Thunder Two.

T1 showed them the secret way to her private ranch to return if trouble came their way though she told them always to make sure no one followed them and that there wasn't any watching when they left.

Mara moved around the outer circle of the UC until she located the music man. Entering his store, she received a welcoming smile.

"Hello, Mr. Spritzer. How are you doing?" she asked with a smile of her own.

"Not a lot of business today; however, we are safe and secure, which is wonderful. What can I do for you, Kennet's friend?" he asked.

"How many twelve-string guitars do you have available for sale?"

"Not much demand for them, I'm afraid. How many do you want?"

"At least a dozen though twenty-four might work better," she replied.

"A dozen?" he stammered.

"I know it is probably beyond reason. However, I do have the need," Mara replied with a smile.

"There are two finished though it will take a while to get the rest done. I will gladly take the order, however. Is there anything else?"

Yes, I also need that many traditional guitars as well.

You make gorgeous instruments, and I prefer to get them from someone who I know to be a talented artisan," Thunder commented.

"I probably have two dozen of those on hand. It takes a very talented person to use a twelve-string, which you certainly are," he responded.

"Figure out what it will cost and time frame. How much do you need upfront to get the materials you will require?"

He was quickly writing on a piece of paper to keep track of what they agreed to. He gave a price, a time frame suggested, and she told him there was a business to take care of; therefore, she could probably pick them up before leaving again.

He was the one who made saddles and had crippled legs.

She again was met with a welcoming smile.

"Hello, Kennet's friend; I have not seen you since I moved in. What can I do for you?" he inquired.

"Could we have a private conversation?" she asked.

He nodded and told her to lock the door, then moved to his workroom in the back.

"I have a proposition for you; however, before we can discuss, I must require your oath. It is to protect both of us if you please."

"You are a friend of Kennet, no need even to ask. Certainly, I will do so. What is the oath?"

She led him in the oath then sat down to visit.

"My names are many and my occupations as well. What I would like to offer you is a trip someplace you have never seen where your legs can be checked out and maybe repaired. If you want to move there and take your tools and materials with you, you can do that. I have not asked anyone else, so; please do not share anything you know about me or those who work with me," Mara cautioned.

"For the chance to get my legs back, yes, I would like to go," he replied with his eyes wide.

"If it is as successful as we think it will be, you might not want to return. The only hitch there is you could end up putting up with my team for the rest of your life," she explained.

"You honor me. When do we leave?" Myster asked.

"Has there been more trouble here?" Thunder questioned. She had sent Kennet to check things out also; therefore , only she and the man would know of her offer, plus her family.

"My full name is Gary Myster. I'm a master leather craftsman. If someone wants something made from leather, I'm the guy for it. I am thirty years of age though very beat up now. Yes, to moving regardless. When do I pack?"

"First, we need to find a way to move you comfortably. We travel by horse to the new destination. If you need additional pack animals, let me know. Your leather products must go on pack horses for the trip. For now, keep it business as usual. I will get back to you when there is more information to share. Right now, it is necessary to check out the status of the town. Do you know what is going on out there?"

"Oh, yes. An unknown removed the guys trying to take over. They had been gone about two weeks when another group tried to move in. We weren't letting them get even a toe-hold this time. The people who live up top built a strong gate across the entry to the town, and there is a watch on it day and night. No one enters without proper identification. A couple of the more persistent ones tried to force their way in, and the guards killed them. Things have been quiet since. Though, wonder how those in the outlying areas are doing. I think especially of the woman who is running a ranch with small children and no man to help out."

"Thank you for the information; now I know what to check on. I will be in touch to let you know the timetable once the situation here is taken care of," Thunder said and departed.

She went to the room she rented on her first trip, for it was time for a conversation.

"Are you there?" she asked the air.

"Yes."

"We need the farm, where Jennie Parsons is the owner, secured in some manner. Gary Myster is coming back with us to have a doctor look at his legs. His wish is to remain. Is there another shop in Prescot where he could have his business? He makes beautiful leatherwork. He crafted the saddle that Kennet uses. We might want to purchase some property near home for his shop, which needs to have living quarters in it someplace. We need a home where those we must bring back can have their homes and maybe a tourist attraction to sell what they make. I want to bring the music man back as well. However, another would need to take his place to keep a balance here. He will need the wood for making guitars for sure. He has an order for two dozen regular guitars and another two dozen twelve-string ones. I wasn't happy with those I saw at the music store."

"There is a need for a farm here as well. With as many horses as you have, it would help keep down costs. I will see what I can find. It seems to me I recall a ghost town about ten miles from here that is due to be sold. That might work out well. Set it up like an old west town with modern living for the residents. Their shops can be old style with homes under them or in a separate area."

"It seems like those called Kennet's friends might need to return with me. To do that, you would need to replace their characters there. Some, like the woman blacksmith, would not fit. However, most would do well there, and they make excellent products," Mara responded.

"Are you sure that is what you want to do? Why not leave them where they are and purchase their products from them at that location so they are in a place familiar to them, and you don't have even more to oversee, plus the prices would be more reasonable?"

"Which puts us back to where we see how the surgery goes for Gary Myster, then have a meeting with you and Pat," replied Mara with a smile.

"Sounds like the best idea to me," laughed Granda though the smile was evident in her speaking voice.

Mara heard a knock at the door, and she rose to answer it. The one there was Kennet.

"There is trouble above. Can we go?" the youngster asked.

"Pat trouble, watch for us and move when and where we do," sent Mara, who then moved through the UC on her way to the outer gate exit.

"Kennet, what did you find out?" asked Mara.

"Someone attacked the mines and the farm where Star bought her feeds," he replied.

"Granda."

"Yes."

"Jennie Parsins Farm and the mines have been hit. We are leaving for there to check on the situation."

Pi and Shira were waiting, with the rest of their mounts. They led them out through the stable and mounted once outside the town. The group was soon at a gallop, for the ranch was about ten miles out. They asked Pi to pace the horses as they moved. When they were a mile from the destination, they looked for a high place where they could see what was going on. There didn't seem to be any activity at the location, which there should have been.

"Sis, we can't afford to all be captured. I am the best qualified now, so Shira and Pi are going with me. Stay within shouting distance; however, let me lead the way. As soon as I have some answers, will send them to you," Mara then dismounted when at the line of shade trees in front of the farmhouse.

"I am going to have you watch my back while I try to find out what is going on," she told her guards. Pi's bridle remained in the saddlebag where she placed it before leaving the stable. Therefore they were ready.

Thunder crept up to the house and listened to the windows. Hearing no sounds, she continued to move around each side, checking.

"T2, check out the barn and see if there are prisoners there," directed T1.

"None," was the reply.

"Okay, I am going to try something. Let me check upstairs first, then will create a bit of a commotion," T1 warned.

She called for Pi and mounted, then she stood on the saddle seat to reach the porch roof, and from there, she could check out the second floor. Again, she listened though there wasn't any noise. There were no unlocked windows. Moving to the edge of the roof, she spotted Pi waiting and transferred to the saddle once again. She rode the horse quietly to the farm entry. Then she turned and began her plan.

"Hello, the place. Hey Jennie, I have an order for you from town. Where are you?" she shouted.

She felt rather than saw someone move. Pi moved immediately, and when she stopped, Mara dismounted. Standing in the doorway of the barn was a disheveled woman and three kids.

"Who are you?" asked the woman, for she had to protect her kids.

"A friend. Do you know, Kennet?" asked Mara with a smile.

"Oh yes, any friend of his is a friend of mine. How did you know to come?"

"A friend told us. Where is a safe place to talk?" asked Mara.

"Are you alone?" asked the woman.

"No, there are seven of us with our horses, and one of the riders is Kennet."

"They will try to steal your horses. Everything of value is below in the lower chambers. That is where we were when you came," she whispered.

"In that case, may I call in the rest of my group and go under with you? We need to ask some questions and see what we can do to aid you if that is alright," said Mara in the same soft tone.

"Yes, please, come and do that."

Mara sent Shira to get the rest of the group. Soon all were in the barn. They then were shown the passageway for the horses, and all of them departed to the lower ground.

"Come with me. We have a place that no sound can leave. Even if they set fire to things, they will not find us," the woman informed them.

"G?" said Mara.

"Here," came the response though only Mara and Pat heard her.

"The farm woman has an underground, thank you for that. She sure needed it. Now must figure out how to salvage her crops, the house, and the other outbuildings. We are going to a meeting and need you to listen in. That way, you will know her suggestions as soon as she gives them," Mara advised Granda.

"Now, would you please give us an idea of what happened?"

"The kids and I were cleaning the house below. When we leave the upper house, we lock up and secure all stock. Once we were below, the kids went to their room, and I moved to a pipe that gives me an easily identified sound. They were talking about needing to take over the farm as a source of income. When they found no one home, they departed. One was for burning the place down. However, the leader said no, they would have to come up with the money to rebuild if anyone did that. They would return at another time. Then they left. We have been down here ever since," said the woman.

"Did you know any of the people, were they all men or some women too? Did anyone call another by a name that you recall?"

"The leader has been here before. Said he wanted to purchase some of the crops. I didn't like the feel of him and didn't want him near my kids. I told him that I have a waiting list from town. At that time, he said his name was Manor Parsons with an o. A strange spelling seemed to me. The horse he rode was jet black and afraid of the man. He double tied it with a halter and a rope around its neck. I do not like to see folks mistreat horses. They are necessary to our lives, yet he would abuse one?"

"Can you give us a description of the man who called himself Parsons?"

"First, his name is spelled with an O while mine is with an I, and he seemed to think he could waltz in here and claim to be my husband or something. He stood about five-ten maybe weighed one-fifty. Broad in the arms and chest, although he had a slight limp; Dark hair, beard, glassy looking eyes; wore jeans and a lumberjack shirt; was carrying for I saw the handle of two pistols and boot knives when he moved wrong."

"He will be back if he has already been here twice. What would you suggest to capture him when he returns?" asked Thunder. She saw T2 raise an eyebrow in question.

"We need ideas," she told her sister in a whisper.

"First off, I would remove his horse. He can't go far without one. Then take his weapons. Then, let's send for Thunder and see if he has any luck with her," said the woman.

"And how do you propose to do that?" asked Thunder in

surprise.

"I never met her; however, I hear a lot about her, and she is the kind of person I would like to call a friend. She gets called, takes care of the problem, then moves on, my style of a woman indeed. It would be nice if she stuck around a bit more. However, all I hear about her says she is good folk," the woman said as she stared at a wall in the room.

"Afraid we are on our own this time. Last I heard, Thunder was taking care of a town where she acquired some property," replied T1.

"She earned it, I'm sure. I had a friend in Morrison who met her once, said she was very nice, not pushy, and was an excellent shot. That was all she would say as she was oathsworn. Guess that means she can't talk to us about Thunder. Only the songs tell us what she is up to," said Jennie.

"Why do you wish to meet Thunder?" asked T2.

"I would like to train under her and be the guardian of this area. My kids would also like to learn from her to take over when I can no longer do the duty. If I had the skills, I wouldn't be so afraid all the time and would try to be the kind of person that Meisha says Thunder is."

"Hold. Does it sound like you want to put a new Thunder at this location? It seems reasonable to me now that we have so much to oversee. Give her the memories she will need and a special sword. I am going to keep my sword, as is Pat and her daughters. No doubt, we will need them no matter where we are. The ranch here remains mine, for it has the gold mine."

"You will need her oath as well as that of the children."

"Agreed."

"Resume."

"Jennie, how well do you follow orders?" T2 asked for she could feel her twin's concern.

"Depends on who is giving them," the woman replied.

"You have some training to attend, and your children must remain here. We will be nearby though not in the underground," T1 advised.

"What kind of training?" asked Jennie.

"Thunder," responded T1.

"Yes, any directions from her I will take. May I have the oath first?" asked Jennie, who smiled once then concentrated on what she needed to learn.

T2 gave the oath to her and her kids then they got busy.

"You are now fully armed and need to know how to use what you carry," advised Thunder.

"I felt them come. The kids will not leave their rooms unless I tell them it is okay to do so. They have everything they need in that one room. The herd dogs will keep them company and warn of problems," explained Jennie.

"I think we better start with hand to hand here, don't you?" T2 asked her twin.

"No, she has that knowledge. We have only as much time as we need to get her using the sword," replied T1.

They moved above ground then noticed that Pi, Shira, and Kennet moved with them. Mara never looked for them; she just knew if she moved, so did they. She was glad to know they were with her.

Mara noted that the farm woman was muscular and wiry. Moving all those stacks of hay must have done it. They heard only silence and a view bubble. Then the drill began.

"Never turn your back on an adversary. That could be the bullet that kills you. Always face them. Try to keep any observers and your team behind your working hand. You could shoot a friend otherwise. You may have to do that soon, so check your memories and remember you are qualified to do what you have asked to do. Another request you made was to be trained by Thunder. Since we are Twins, you are being trained by both of us. You will need a fast horse and a wolf partner if one is willing. Here they come now," said Mara with a smile.

Shira moved to the wolf, and they had a conversation. The two additions walked to where Jennie waited.

"You need to be made known to the wolf. Sit here on the porch step. Relax and open your mouth. The wolf will get your scent so that she can find you anyplace. Give her a name you find easy to remember," directed Pat, for Mara was checking with Granda on another issue.

"I will call her Shadow, for she will be close to me always," replied Jennie.

"The horse is of racing blood. The animal can outrun any horses except ours. Both animals understand human speech. Tell them what is going on. Ask their aid, do not order them. They will do all you ask if you treat them well. The one thing we cannot train you to do is to use the sword. That is done by instinct though we will be here to make sure you can handle it. Relax and concentrate. Listen to the voice in your mind. It will sound like it is speaking outright to you, although no one else will hear it." Mara told their new pupil.

"Watch us, and you will see what I mean. We will use short swords to give you an idea. When you pull Lightning, it is real, and it is like having a loaded gun in your hand. Your sword will ride on your back with the handle in easy reach of your dominant hand. You will discover that in time, you will be able to use the sword in either hand. Like this," said Pat as she called forward one of her daughters and had them do the drill.

Shandra moved from side to side, and as she steadily moved, she switched hands on the weapon's pommel. Then she began guarding to left and right, each time changing hands though there was always one hand on the sword. The guard moved up, down, left, right, overhead, and was a constant movement. Mara could well see what Cherry meant by not knowing the dance.

While Shandra was still doing the drill, Jennie stepped up

near yet slightly behind the woman doing the maneuvers and began to do the same. She had confidence in the exercise flow as she only stopped a couple of times when she couldn't get a shift. Then one of the Thunder twins stepped up and aided her in the transition. One of the daughters replaced the one in place by picking up the drill. Cherry did the exercise flawlessly, then Mike followed by Gretch. They kept the training going until Jennie said she had it.

Chapter 16

Why so many

They heard the silence bubble when it disappeared. Coming up the walkway to the house was a group of men. In the lead was the man on a black horse. The women spread out to allow them room for fighting. Jennie stood in the center with a Thunder on each side and two of Pat's daughters on each end of the group while Kennet stood behind them.

"What may we do for you, gents?" asked Jennie.

"Came to purchase your farm since you won't let me buy your crops," Manor Parsons.

"Seems to me I heard someone tell you the harvest wasn't for sale," commented Jennie.

"That is why we are here to see her. I'm sure she would be willing to listen to our offer," Manor replied.

"I doubt it, as she isn't available now, however," T3 told him.

"We shall see," he said as he dismounted.

Pi sent a message, and all horses dumped their riders then departed behind the barn. None of the passengers saw them during the men's visit.

"Now, why did you go and do that? You owe me a horse and preferably the one you just spooked," Manor demanded.

"Don't think so besides which not one of us moved, so how do you figure we are the ones that took your horses?" T3 answered.

"Because we are the only ones here," he replied.

"Are you sure?" she asked.

"I see seven of you that look alike and a kid. None of you moved, yet my horse knows better than to depart without me. I'll deal with that one when they return," he said.

"Doubt it will return," replied T3.

"What makes you say that?" he asked.

"You are an unkind master who abuses those under you," T3 told him.

"That horse is the one that threw me and busted my hip."

"And I suppose you didn't do a thing to make it happen. After all, the horse only wanted to get you out of the path of that rattler," T3 advised.

"What rattler?" the man asked with a frown.

"The one you put there to get even with a man who took a woman you wanted," T3 told him.

"No one takes from me that which is mine!" Manor roared.

"The woman was not yours, the man is dead by your hand, the horse is gone, and you are afoot. My bet is this is not the only instance of your trying to control life in your favor," T3 replied.

"A guy does what he has to do," the man told her without apology.

"No, a man should do as the Lord directs and take care of those he is over. A man should treat them fairly and be kind. A man should aid, not demand, love not to control, share not keep, and be a man of his word, not a manipulator. You are in the wrong on all counts. Look it up if you don't believe me."

Suddenly one of the women returned a shot fired at them. Then the battle was on. Everyone had an injury on the male side by the time it was over. A court setting opened, and the group tried. T3 was the judge, T2, the prosecutor, T1 the guard, and four daughters serving as witnesses. The men gave their names, the reason for being where they were, any other illegal actions, and where they lived. They mainly targeted women that didn't have a husband on site. The lead man confessed to putting a rattler on the man who died and other such events. The individuals within the group admitted to causing the deaths of many folks. When the court was over, T1 opened the way to the prison that already had a few people in it. The new group joined them, bringing the total incarcerated up.

"Now you have an idea of what Thunder's duties require. If it is truly your desire to take on the role, have you any questions of us?" asked T1.

"My goodness! Yes, this is what I have wanted since I first heard the name. Questions? How do you know who to ask to aid you? Do you have some backup of your authority? Can I continue to live on the farm? If things begin to get out of hand, may I call on you? Guess that will do for a start," Jennie replied. T3.

"The voice that trained you will also aid you, and we will know if there is a need for us to return. You have an undercover license that allows you to call for assistance when it is needed. At the same time, I suggest you build a reliable team of your own. An example would be to find someone knowledgeable to run the farm, in case you must cover duties elsewhere. Be sure they are oath-bound to you. The farm is yours and will remain yours if you filed with the legal authorities to own property here, I would imagine. You must have a legal title for it to be yours. Since you are now a lawyer and judge, the way to do that is in your memory."

"Another question: what do I do with those horses?"

"You now own them, for you were working as Thunder when acquired. Unless, of course, you want to say that since Pi directed them to leave and is owned by me, that I do. That is your decision," said Mara with a smile.

"We have horses to ride, to pull the hay wagon, to go hunting, and for just general use. We do not have time for much more. When the girls are a bit older and can care for their own, I would like to get them each a horse; however, now have all I can handle," said the woman.

"Then they will leave with us. We will check in on you from time to time and wish you well. Start training your kids as soon as they can hold any weapon. The more they understand the cautions and uses for those items they require to fulfill these duties, the better they will be able to use them. Now it is time for us to take care of a few other things that got out of hand while we were gone. That way, you will be left with a clean slate and can start from there," Mara advised.

"I accept and thank you. You have made my dreams come true. Thank you is all I have, although it is heartfelt. Consider yourselves welcome any place I am. Thank you for making me part of the Thunder team," she said.

Shira and Pi came when T1 called, and the horses of the men were with them. Thunder removed each headpiece from the new animals and asked Pi to speak with the man's black to let him know what was going on and the requirements.

Pi nodded her head and stood to wait for Mara to mount. The other mounts of the ladies were doing the same. Kennet was on his horse as soon as it came in sight.

The next stop would be the mines. As they departed the area, they saw another group headed toward the farm. Mara chuckled, for Jennie could more than hold her own. No one was going to walk over her.

When they reached the first mine, they met outriders. Kennet spoke with them, and they moved on.

"Those are the ones who should be there. The rider says they had some trouble. However, the riders repelled them. He says he isn't sure how the other mines made out, for they had their hands full here. He also advised that the guy in charge rode a black stud. It sounds like that problem is solved," smiled Kennet.

"It would appear so. It looks like we may see some more property changing hands, though think it will go to Jennie, not us," commented Mara into her communicator for T3 would need the financial support that would give her. The N-Sign family had enough now to live on plus pay quite a few salaries of folks who needed the money to live on as well.

They found all mines secure; then, Mara had a sudden bad feeling.

"Granda, which way do we go, town or the ranch? We have been challenged in two areas and not sure which group is particular to us," sent Mara.

"The ranch is excellent in Jennie's hands. You must take care of the town, however, as she is busy. She is learning to use her newly acquired skills."

At a signal from T1, the group departed to town at a gallop. Shira ran ahead to check out the location, and the stud passed them going the same direction.

When they reached the town, they found the gate closed. However, the stallion was no place to be seen.

"Pi, where is the stud? We need to join him," said Mara.

Pi took off running, and the rest were riding behind her, including the riderless mounts. She raced to a back wall, and there she slowed to duck inside a gate with the others doing the same. Then she was running again. They heard the animal before they saw him. He was screaming in rage. The group slowed, for they knew they were near and didn't want to run into any trouble until they knew what was going on.

They found the stud in the center of a street with ropes on him from all sides. When he saw the team, he whirled and pulled all lines from the hands of those who had thought him captured. He shook the ropes off, and he then turned on the men who had tried to catch him. In terror, they began to run, right into the Thunder Clan and their arrest.

"Nice job, stud. Have you a suggestion about what to do with this bunch?" Mara asked as she walked over to the black horse.

He stood before her, ready for her orders. She thanked him and patted his neck, then went back to work, for she had things to do.

The number of animals they controlled swelled as those owned by the men captured were joining the group. All carried saddles though no headgear for Granda wrote in that bridles were removed though no one had time. Those animals became the guard for the men captured while Mara and the team continued cleanup.

The stud pushed her with his head toward a building nearby. She was puzzled at the request yet did as directed. Thunder reached up to knock; however, he shook his head.

Feeling his cautious warning, Mara opened the unlocked door and stepped inside with her family right behind her.

"You fire in this building, and you won't live to leave it," said a voice.

"Then come on out and discuss what is going on," responded Thunder.

"Who are you? Not that Mason! Come in here and let me see you," said the voice.

Shira moved by Mara, and bared her teeth at her partner, then walked into the room where she heard the male voice.

Sitting at a table was a man in his late twenties. Before him on the table was a row of loaded weapons.

"And who might you be?" he asked the wolf politely.

She moved to his location and sat up to shake his hand.

"Are you on my side?" the man inquired.

The wolf cocked her head to one side and waited.

"Ah, you want to know what side I am on?" he replied.

A nod was his response.

"I'm on the side of the law. I won't say I have always been, though since that Thunder woman was here, you couldn't pay me enough to go against her. Does that answer your question?"

She nodded and turned to depart the area. When she returned, the team was with her. While she was gathering them up, the man unloaded the weapons and put the shells in containers by each device for next time, for no doubt there would be one.

"Hello, my guard says you wish to speak with me and are ready to take the oath. May I have your name first off?" asked Thunder.

"Name is Jeffers; folks call me Jerry though my legal name is Jerome. What may I do for you, folks? Your partner says you are to be trusted," he told her.

"We are, and this woman will give you the oath required to work with us," responded Mara, for she was going to do some checking around the location.

"Shira, this place is dangerous for us. We need to get him out and try to take care of what is wrong. Will you warn him since he trusts you?" asked Pat as she watched Mara move around the room they were all in.

"Please explain to me the structure we are in," said Mara into her speaker though it was at a whisper.

When she had the information, she went through a door located behind the man. Shira moved inside that room immediately, and Mara was running at the next step for Shira was there to guard not to lead, so something was very wrong. Shandra and Cherry remained with the man and Kennet while Pat's other two daughters moved to the room they had entered by, and Pat departed behind Mara.

"Mister, reload your weapons. We may need them, though, don't use them from your location behind us unless we tell you. We must stay faced away from you. Do not try to pass us, for it could mean your death. Trust us as you trusted our messenger," said Shandra quietly.

He nodded and did as directed.

They heard footsteps on the stairs from above. Gretch and Mike each took a side of the stairwell then waited. Coming down the stairs was a woman with a weapon in hand. It was an enclosed stairway, so she did not see those waiting for her. When she departed the last step, Gretch removed the gun from her hand and, with a nod of her head, directed the woman to the room where the man waited.

She did as Gretch told her.

"Ma'am, have a seat. We may be here a while yet," directed Shandra in a soft voice.

At a nod of the man's head, the woman did as directed.

Meantime Mara and Shira were moving quickly, with Pat right behind. They ran through a hallway, then up a flight of stairs, though they were careful to stay to the side of the stairs. They were in what looked like a boarding house, for there were doors all along the hall. At the top Shira stopped a moment and moved her head from side to side to make sure the area was safe for those following, then she moved again, only this time it was with her nose to the floor and at a slower pace. Pat moved backward behind Mara to be sure no one came on them, unaware.

Shira moved to one door and stopped. She lowered her head and shoulders as if asking to come in. A Thunder Twin stood at each side of the door, and Shira scratched at the door. When it opened inward, there was some space; Mara quickly was inside with Shira. Pat followed.

Inside was a room with a bed, a dresser, and a chair. That was all the furniture. On the mattress were four children, and sitting in the chair was a man with a gun he was cocking with it aimed at the children. Shira had his hand in her teeth immediately. He screamed, and T1 laid him out while Pat dealt with the one behind the door.

They checked out the room for any hidden problems then took the children and prisoners to where Jerry Jeffers was.

"We need you all in one place until we can sort this out," directed Mara as she saw the woman added to the collection.

The man, who threatened the children with a gun, was tied to a chair though he no longer had that weapon or others he carried. Shandra guarded one door, and her sister the other while the other pair controlled the front room.

"Is this all of them?" asked Mara of her wolf guard.

The wolf sniffed the floor, then a nod of the head was the response.

"It appears that you feel we have captured those who entered this way. There are other entries as well, are there not? Open the door to the front room so that everyone is involved," directed T1.

The four sisters were standing by that door with two on each side.

When Thunder understood who the people were, why they were there, and how much blast powder was in the building, they had a little better picture of the problem. After removing all weapons, the people from inside moved outside to join those watched by the horses. The four children learned that the horses were on duty; however, if they wanted to sit on the saddle while the animals moved around, it would be okay.

Mara wanted the kids off the ground. Due to their size, it would make them easier to see, plus the horses would watch over them if mounted.

"Do we have any others we need to round up?" asked T1 of Jerry once one of the horses went forward to serve as his mount. Thunder told him to climb from the porch to make it a bit easier for him.

"Ask your partner; I didn't know about the ones you have captured. We knew that trouble was here, yet I cannot move fast enough to take care of it. Know the two folks, yet didn't know they were here to create problems," the man replied, for his clubbed feet made walking a chore, and running was beyond his capability.

"Okay, we are now going to check out the entire building. I recommend that everyone remain where you are. Two of us are staying with you," warned Mara before moving into the boarding house via the front entrance and up the stairs that the woman prisoner had come down. Shandra and Cherry took the guard post of those the horses were watching over while Mike and Gretch covered the leader's backs.

Again, Shira led. She ran up the stairs, then stopped and checked the area before moving on. She used the same procedure to get each door opened. There was gunpowder in four of the rooms. Had anyone fired at the activator, the place would have gone up in smoke, taking most of the town with it.

After securing the building and all powder removed, they could have a trial for those they were holding. The group returned to the holding space, and when Mara mounted, the horses formed a half-moon behind the prisoners and pushed them to the main gate, which opened for them. They moved to the open field beyond the gate though Mara asked if the gate guard would be responsible for the four children. A woman stepped up and said yes, she would stand bond.

Jerry Jeffers gave the oath, and the children dismounted, with help.

Jerry was to remain mounted, however, to stay behind the women. He did as told. However, his mount would make sure he stayed safe until the trial was over.

"I call this court to order under the control of the Thunder Clan," directed T1.

"I represent prosecutor for the Clan," directed T2.

"We four stand as guards and have other guards with us," Shandra advised.

"Who stands accused in this case?" asked T1.

"That is yet to be determined, your honor. Someone is said to have placed gunpowder throughout the building, intending to set fire to the whole town. Two men were threatening four children. A woman with a weapon came from one of the rooms where the powder was," replied her twin.

The people Thunder had tied up were allowed to tell their stories, one at a time.

By the time the court was over, they had one hundred prisoners. Each admitted to their part in the problem and signed confessions. They also gave lists of all property of value that they owned. Each included the address where to find it and the market price if known.

"G?"

"I am here."

"This is more of the same bunch that started this mess. Somehow, these men found a way to get in, and they were taking over. We must locate the source. I know you did not write this part of the story," T1 told her mentor.

"Will consider it."

"The Thunder court sentences all standing here, that is not part of my team. Any others need to give a reason they wish to remain here," she said.

"May I speak with you?" asked Jerry.

Mara moved to where he was though she made sure that he remained in the safe area until the court was over.

"You said something about maybe getting my feet fixed. Does that offer remain open, or am I now being sent to prison?" Jerry asked in a whisper.

"The offer is open, and you have been found innocent of any wrongdoing. Are you related to any of those we have before us?" Thunder questioned.

"No, though would hate to see those four children without a mom," Jerry replied.

"I assure you they won't be," responded T2.

"Might have to share," commented T1 with a chuckle though only her team heard her.

Then they returned to business and put those who had been found guilty in prison.

Upon their return, Mara spoke with the guard, who was

watching over the children.

"Do you know who claims these children?"

"No, I have seen them around. However, no one seems to claim then. I understand that each is eight years old and share the same birthdate," the woman replied.

"In that case, they are headed to a new home. Thank you for watching over them during the trial. You won't be able to tell anyone you took part in it, for that would put you in danger. However, there is another one of us who will be patrolling this area. Offer her your services when she comes through. She is setting up a team to keep the area secure," Thunder advised.

"Thank you; you honor me," the woman replied. She then put each of the children on a horse that stood to wait. The adults walked by their horses. However, the children and Jerry could ride.

When they were in the stable at Wren's Nest Inn, Jerry's mount took him to a stall at the back where he remained on the horse he rode until Granda wrote in bed for him. It could be a bit of a wait.

"Jerry, we are leaving tonight, if we can get everyone together. Do you have anything you need to take with you?"

"No, you have my weapons, which I handed to that gal who was in charge of the guards so that I could keep them if not found to be part of the problem. She still has them — anything else I can replace when I get where I'm going. What are you going to do with the boarding house?" he asked. He worked at the boarding house to log in patrons. His income was hidden on his person, for he wanted to buy a piece of property of his own.

"Why would we do anything with it?" Mara asked with a smile.

"Since you got rid of those who owned it, it seems to me you now own it," he replied.

"G." Mara wanted to see if Granda heard the need.

"On the way."

Mara told everyone except Kennet to remain in place. He was to meet someone at the gate. He took off at a run. Duster, his mount, would stay with his mom at his order, for one could not run a horse in town.

The children had help dismounting from their mounts though Jerry was found asleep on the bed Granda furnished.

The female guards went to get Gary Myster.

Mara suggested that they take the black stud that they had inherited. He seemed to be a stable mount and had a secure gate that Gary would need to get home. She was still thinking about the horse that had volunteered to take Jerry with them. Now to get mounts ready to take the children on the return home. There was also a load to pick up at her mine.

"Kids, come with me. I am going to put you in a room that belongs to me. If you stay there until my return, you will be placed on the horses again, and we will leave. A lot of folks are going with us, so please be patient."

"Thunder, Ma'am, are we going to have a real home? No more having to run all the time or beg for food?" asked one of the braver ones.

"That is the truth. What are your names, by the way?"

"I'm Preter, called Pete, as no one understands why there is an r in my name. That is Jaimes; his name got mixed up too with an I in it. The girls are Nan Cee and Trace Cee. They are twins, as are my brother and me. The only one we will miss is our dog though you probably have ones where we are going, and maybe if all of us behave, we can have another one someday," the eight-year-old boy told her.

"Shira, would you be willing to try to locate the dog these kids had? I need to see it, then will decide whether they remain here or go with us. It might be best to get them some when we get home," said Mara.

The wolf departed, and Mara knew that the dogs would

get some good homes. However, they weren't going with the children.

As soon as the kids were on the bed, Mara and Pat left at a run. Kennet was in the stable with some folks.

"Hello, Son, what do we have?" asked Mara.

"These folks said they are here to run a boarding house for some women who can't stay to take care of it. They need a job, and they have everything they own on the wagon parked on the street. Do you want me to take them over while you get things done here?"

"Appreciate the offer. However, you need to remain here. I will take care of it. You need to help get things lined up here. We must go to our ranch and pick up the bags, then line everyone up on mounts. We have four kids and two adult men returning to base with us. We have about a hundred horses, I would guess. My sister's girls are taking care of Gary Myster getting here."

She had to be the one to interview the new people, get their oaths, and make sure they had what they needed to do the duty asked of them. Mara chuckled to herself when she saw a stray dog going by with the female guard who took care of her kids.

It took about an hour to load the pack horses with ore. The men were mounted and tied onto the saddle due to the racers' speed. Mara directed the four new women to do the same with the kids, though someone explained the need. Some of the riding animals agreed to carry leather tools and equipment for Gary.

Pi was to take the kids and men's horses to the main house where the riders went inside. A storage room in the basement would store Gary's gear until he decided where he wanted to live.

Chapter 17

A hospital wing

As soon as the group landed, Gwen was ready with grain in every stall. The AI filled the stalls as a horse went inside, not to waste the food. She never knew for sure how many were coming. Therefore, she ordered one entire stable to prepare for incoming. The pack animals walked to where the bags were the last time. The saddlebags dropped to the floor, and the packboards removed, then the horses were free to enter their stalls.

"Stud, we have another of your species joining us. Please share the area. Not sure yet what the solution is; however, I inherited this one as I did you. We will work it out, I assure you. We need to take some people to the hospital to get the repair done to their legs.

They are the ones waiting at the main house. We will get them inside and cleaned up to take them to the hospital to see a doctor. Guard the place and train the new horses in what is required, please. Pi will have control. I must move the bags we brought back, and Pat will help me. We will see you as soon as the men get a new living space."

Pat passed the bags to Mara. Then what they brought back was checked for electronics before being put in the vault for later transfer to the Gold man.

Once inside home, Mara explained to Star about the kids and the two men. She said she would give the kids beds in Joy's room if she didn't object and went to ask.

"I don't object to sharing. However, don't you think these should learn as I did about having a suite to claim? At least put each pair of twins in a room of their own. Will do all we can to make them comfortable and welcome," said Joy with a smile.

She was faithful to her word and got them up each morning, took them to the ongoing training, made sure they cleaned up for breakfast, and that their rooms were clean after breakfast. Joy did not want to see Granda cleaning when the occupant of that room didn't do what they must. It happened once, and it would not happen again if Joy could do anything about it.

"Okay, sis, we must get these men inside and cleaned up, then we will take them to the doctor and see what can medically correct their problems. We might end up bringing them back with us until the doctor works out a schedule. Make sure we get x-rays of everyone that returned with us. That means the kids go as well. Alright, let's be about it," advised Mara with a smile.

Granda walked in about then and had some questions of her own.

"I have the names and ordered passports. There are clothes here to fit everyone for now. Now that we have the elevator, they won't have any problem getting to the suite floors. It's my understanding that the new twins will share a suite as twins. Who is going to claim them? That way, you will have time to do the kids before making the trip to town," Granda suggested.

"Good idea. I'm not sure how we should do this. Do we go to the clinic, and they set up the necessary treatment of surgery or whatever?" Mara wondered.

"Yes, the clinic comes first unless a life-threatening event sends one tagged as an emergency, which gets them sent to the hospital direct. Your N-sign doc should have an appointment available since she knew you would need one for each of the groups you gained. I set it up, and she will see them today at one," Granda advised.

The team departed the book home in the evening yet arrived at Prescot's beginning. The men were to rest in their suites until one of the women came to get them for the trip to town. The AI secured the suites, and the rest of the family went to their riding lessons, followed by music ones.

Kennet got his wish and brought back his guitar on this trip. Mara also had two six-string guitars, the one used to train Kennett, and two violins, as she wasn't too happy with the ones she bought at the local music store. She had a goal in mind, and the trip to town would get something else done.

Star stayed home with her three, Joy and Joey also remained due to the new group needing more space in the heat. Pat took her van, and Mara took hers. Being in two vehicles was not a problem due to being connected electronically. Granda was also with them to be sure all areas had someone taking charge.

Rather than have the ones go who had taken care of their medical issues, Mara told them that they would take the men and new kids. Once the doctor gave them physicals, they would return and get everyone else for a meal at a restaurant though it might be on a different day.

The noon meal was ready early to allow them time to reach the clinic for their appointments. Pat's daughters would be the drivers so that Mara could answer questions for the twin kids and the men.

Granda said she would be riding with the two new men. Mara laughed and left her to them while she toured with the four kids and Pat. Two of Pat's girls were in each of the vans. Kennet was with Granda in the case of problems.

They were a bit early at the clinic. The doctor knew of Mara and Granda's pension to being first, so she was ready and at the door.

"Hello, Doctor Meranda. Have some business for you if you don't mind? Your nurse can get the full x-rays for everyone. Since it will take longer for the men, why don't you start with them, and I will have one of my nieces remain with the kids?" Mara suggested.

"We will put each in a patient room separately. There are enough of you to cover. I want to start with the man who can't walk well. It seems to me Mrs. N-Sign said some horses trampled one man. The tech is waiting."

"We all carry the same last names. Gary is the one you are referencing. Jerry is the one with club feet, and I imagine you will want x-rays of him next. I require full body x-rays for our records. The kids are Nan Cee, Trac Cee, Preter, and Jaimes, estimated ages about eight."

None of them were surprised to find the kids were now Nancy, Tracy, Peter, and James per the medical records. Grand looked at the files and shook her head, which got them changed to actual names.

When the kids finished their x-rays, shots, and general health questions, they went to a room to wait. Granda joined them for control.

"I am Granda, do not monitor this room," directed Granda.

"Accepted," responded the room.

The kids looked startled when Granda still sat calm, and seeing a smile on her face; they settled down.

A call came for Granda, and she stepped into the hall to talk with Mara.

"Gary is being referred to the Ortho docs who say they have an opening for both men to be done at the same time, by different doctors, to help us keep track of everyone and combine vehicles. The doctors are scrubbing and will be in surgery with the men in half an hour. Both will have their legs in removable casts, which means they remain here for a couple of days to be sure all went well. Pat and I will scrub. The quad is returning to you. I am betting this will be a late night. Therefore, I suggest that you feed the Quad and take them home. A couple of Pat's girls can drive you then return here to wait on us. It is now about four. Let the new kids eat out once and feel more at home in the area. Allow ice cream for dessert. We will be awhile. Tomorrow, the men will move in the Joy van or an ambulance," reported Mara.

"Be sure to borrow a couple of wheelchairs for the men to get around. You must become the doctor of record once they get home. Gary will be remaining; however, what are you going to do with Jerry?" asked Granda.

"They will both be staying," replied Mara with a smile.

Granda received a call at the restaurant from their private communicators. Shandra was asking for a ride back with them. That way, the current ones could go home and relax while the adult quad would return for Pat and Mara. Kennet always remained where his mom was unless at home.

Star explained to those at home about what might happen and what might not. Dinner was in the might not column. They would eat out another time. For now, the men were in surgery, and it would take a while. Those at home agreed to the change, for the guys needed time to walk better.

Shandra had the keys to Pat's van and moved from one vehicle to the other for the return trip after hugging Granda.

The adult Quad sat in the waiting room for surgery to wait for the Thunder Twins. They read, napped, watched some TV, and visited with others who were also waiting.

When Pat and Mara returned, it was near midnight.

"Hello, darlings, the men are in hospital beds with a private nurse watching over them. Put them both in the same room, so they have someone to talk to when they wake up. I made sure there wasn't any monitoring there. Let's go get something to eat and head home," directed Pat, who was a little weary. It had been a long day.

"Are one of you awake enough to drive?" asked Pat.

"We have been napping, so any of us is up to it," smiled Shandra, who was voted the lead guard by the other guards.

"Pat, what is open at this hour that has decent food?" asked Mara.

"The truck stop on the highway would be the best bet. It is twenty-four-seven and always has good homemade food," Pat replied.

"Then tell them how to get there," responded Mara with a smile, for she knew what was making everyone so tired, the trip into the book.

The following day found everyone getting a late start. Star didn't even start breakfast until she saw some folks were up and moving.

Joy agreed to wait, for she knew the twins had gotten in very late. The new boy and girl twins would need some time to adapt. She took care of Joey and let him play after being fed. She and Star had breakfast with Star's kids, who then quietly left the house to take care of horses and training. Since the four new ones were up, Joy made sure they ate as well.

When Mara finally entered the kitchen, she saw that Joy was there, and that was all.

"Good morning, Joy. What have we missed?" asked Mara.

"Only half the day," replied her daughter with a smile.

"You are kidding; we are that late?"

"It is now a quarter after twelve. That makes it an afternoon. Why was everyone so tired? Kennet went with the rest to training classes. However, he wasn't moving very fast, either. He ate with the kids. The new kids were fine. Haven't seen Granda since she got home last night," Joy told her.

Mara was immediately on the run for Granda's suite. She palmed open the door and moved inside cautiously to not trip over anything. There, in the middle of the front room floor, was Granda. She was sprawled on a rug and not moving.

"Pat, Granda's suite immediately," sent Mara, who had blocked the door open once she was inside in case she needed help.

"Granda, it is Mara. Speak to me, please." said Mara tearfully though she remained in control.

"What's wrong?" asked Pat as she ran in the door.

"Not sure yet; help me get her off the floor," said Mara.

"No, leave her where she is. Call for an ambulance, and

we are going with her. Hurry, we don't know how long she has been down," said Pat, who had dealt with such events before.

Mara directed the AI to connect her to the hospital emergency number.

"This is the N-Sign ranch, Mara N-Sign here. We need medical assistance. Mrs. N-Sign, my grandmother, is down and needs to be taken to the emergency room immediately. Yes, I am checking her vitals. My sister is covering her. We have no idea how long she was down as we were away at the hospital doing surgery. Didn't realize until just now that she had not seen in about twelve hours," Mara advised.

She disconnected the communicator and noted that Pat was out of the room. Mara knelt by her grandmother and spoke to her.

"Granda, this is Mara. How can we help?" asked the girl.

"Not worry," whispered the woman.

"Hang in for an ambulance is on the way. We will have you out of here as soon as we can. You will be out riding horses in no time," said Mara though the tears continued to flow.

"Sorry, had to let Star know what is going on and where to send the ambulance crew, also had to alert the horses that it was alright and to let the vehicle and people come to the main house. How is she doing?"

"She spoke once, said 'not worry,' and that was all. Not sure what she is telling us," Mara explained.

"Star has breakfast ready. Why don't you get some, and I will stand watch? You know we need to eat, for this means we have three in the hospital and are in charge here. Shandra says she will drive the family in once we are on the way. There is enough stress on both of us, and she will be our driver. We will need transportation to move to and from," Pat advised. She knew how shook her twin was and was doing all in her power to help.

The sirens were a notification that the ambulance was

entering the drive, and Pat was at the door to lead them. They put Shelly on a backboard and moved her to the ambulance. Pat and Mara stepped inside the ambulance also, and it took off to the hospital, where an entire crew was waiting to check her out.

The twins put on their Thunder persona and went with the medical teams to look after Granda. They had to scrub, for neither woman would leave Granda alone, even in surgery. There were other doctors with expertise; however, the twins would be present.

Shandra told her twin to get another van, for the keys were in them, and follow the ambulance in. She would be there later with the rest of the family. Cherry immediately took off after the ambulance.

"Star, I'm the one in charge for now. Let's get everyone loaded up and bring them to the hospital if you all want to go. If not, then I will go in to serve as coordinator until mom and Mara can replace me," said Shandra.

"I don't like that place. Could the kids and I stay here and watch over the ranch?" asked Star.

"Certainly, you may. I will see what Joy wants to do then will go to town. Mike and Gretch will remain here for now," the Guard leader told them.

She knocked on the suite door for Joy. It opened immediately. Joy stood there with Joey and dressed to leave. A nod of Shandra's head and they departed for the vehicle in the basement. Joey would have whatever he needed from the looks of the bag that Joy was trying to carry.

"Why don't I take either the young man or the bag?" Shandra offered.

"Yes, please, would you. I'm so concerned about Granda. I should have checked sooner. Hope she will be okay," replied Mara's daughter.

Granda had taken Joy shopping for the items that Joey would need. Today was the first time to use any of it. They saw the stroller waiting by the vehicles, and Shandra put it in the van. The car seat was in place for the growing boy.

"Joy, we are all family here. Please, can you give me an idea of why Star won't leave the house?"

"Gwen wanted to go with us, and so did the new kids, but Star shushed them. I think they have a right to know how Granda is too. She is important to all of us. Can we go back and get them?" asked Joy.

Shandra had not departed the garage, so they called for Gwen and the four new kids. They ran to the van and departed. Kennet had left with Cherry. Dan said he would take care of the horses and for Gwen to go.

It was a very long day and night. None of them would leave for long. Therefore, Pat's kids kept them fed and took care of any maintenance needed. The hospital set aside a room with enough beds for everyone when the administrator learned how many family members were on site.

The following morning Pat and Mara met with the doctors.

"Hello, Ladies. It was not as severe as we thought. Your grandmother has a broken hip that we repaired. She will be able to walk after the bone settles. We had to use a couple of screws to make it stay in place. She says to tell you she is sorry she frightened you. Still a bit tired from the surgery, however you can see her as soon as we catch you up." Doctor Meranda told them.

"The hospital administrator said that she would like to meet with you when you have a minute," added the male doctor.

"Thank you, both, for your care of our family. We now have three in your fine facility," said Pat to lighten the mood. The doctors were tired, Mara was worried, and the whole family wanted to know what was wrong with Granda.

"Will Granda be able to ride horseback again? She so loves riding," said Pat to keep the conversation up.

"Oh yes, though suggest you wait until her hip has a chance to heal," smiled the doc in charge. The twins were true professionals, as far as she was concerned. They scrubbed yet did not interfere, and if someone needed extra hands, one of them immediately stepped up.

"Do we need to know about any particular care she needs? At the same time, we need to know the same about Gary and Jerry," said Mara as she seemed to awaken.

"Just the usual which as doctors yourselves you no doubt know, make them exercise within their various capabilities. Keep any wound sites clean; bathing often is not a good idea with a cast, only bed baths. Bring them in for a checkup in six weeks. We will aid any way we can, even to making house calls due to the number you now have as walking wounded," chuckled their female doc who had been part of the surgical team.

Dr. Meranda was so impressed with the family with whom she was speaking. At first, she was concerned that she would be on call for their needs twenty-four-seven. However, the new hospital admin said that would not be the case, and those women worked under different rules. She had worked at the hospital for a month, which was the first time there had been a need. With three patients from the family, she was kept very busy yet didn't object. None of them were demanding, and if any of the family was with the one healing, they took care of the needs of their family members.

"Meranda, we may yet need you, so don't jump ship just yet," said Mara with a laugh. She was quite serious that the woman would be welcomed and needed.

"You can't get rid of me. I doubt you could get rid of either my husband or me," replied the woman as she nodded at the other doc as he walked out the door.

"Are you telling me you two are married?" asked Mara in surprise. She had missed something along the way.

"Yes, we are both Ortho qualified. However, the hospital needed a GP, so I took that job and helped in Ortho when Jack can't get it all done as fast as necessary," replied Meranda.

"What position are you paid for?" asked Mara, now alert to what was going on.

"I get GP pay," she replied yet continued to speak with a small smile and a chuckle here and there. She was a good-natured woman gifted in what she did.

"That has now been changed and backdated. Since docs have a networking system, will you find me a decent GP and need you to remain as our doc though you will receive the higher pay now. If Jack needs help, find him a partner, preferably male, work with him for you may be on the road, or maybe skies if we can work it out. My Clan is large, and we need to have a doctor that can work with and for us in an emergency, as you have just seen. Our various duties keep us very busy, and there are times when we even need a doctor to travel with us. Would you be willing to do that?" Mara asked for she began to feel that would be necessary for the not too distant future.

"Where do you travel to?"

"When our walking wounded are back on their feet, we are all going out of the country to take care of business and need to have you along to handle whatever comes up medically. Not comfortable with the medical support in those areas. Would you have a current passport by any chance?" asked Mara.

"Yes, actually, it was a requirement of employment here. Now I see why. I would love to go along; when do I need to pack?" asked Meranda.

"How about we give you a week off to join us at home, with pay, of course? That way, you can get an idea of what will be required. Which reminds me, do you play any musical instruments?"

"Always wanted to. However, I was so involved in getting my medical license that the desire did not become a reality," Meranda replied.

"It will now. We will discuss it when at home. Now before we have a revolt, best we go see the invalids, then let you get back to work," laughed Mara while Pat chuckled along.

They moved to the room where Granda was first.

"Hello love, how are you doing?" asked Mara, who immediately moved to the bed.

"Sorry, I upset everyone. Certainly, get wonderful care at this place," said Granda, and they all saw the tears in her eyes.

"Trust," whispered Mara.

"Thank you, dear one, for had you not found me when you did, I might have departed. I didn't want to go. So much yet to do," said Granda on the private connection, for even during surgery, she refused to allow them to remove it. She also knew that Mara had remained in the operation room during the whole procedure.

"Hello Granda, we couldn't let you depart. We need you much too badly. So much yet to do, and we wouldn't be complete without you," said Pat with tears in her own eyes now that the emergency was over.

"Know I will hang on as long as needed now that I see your love for me. You have no idea how much this whole family is loved," responded Granda.

"We will return later with the rest of your family. Most have stayed at the hospital since this began. They all want to see you; however, for now, you have had enough. Rest well, and we will return later. We are going to see Gary and Jerry, let you get a nap, then will bring the rest to see you," Mara told Granda. Mara could see that Granda was in some pain. Therefore, she nodded at Meranda to take over.

They moved to the next location. Mara found the two men sitting in wheelchairs as they visited. Both stopped when the women entered the door.

"How is she?" was the first question from Gary.

"She gave us a scare. However, she will recover, and we hope to take you all home in the next week. Know we have not forgotten you just knew you were in good hands. She broke her hip and needed surgery to repair it. Therefore, the three of you can start a parade in your chairs; however, don't scare the other patients here," laughed Mara.

"When can we go home?" asked Jerry with longing. He didn't like hospitals, he decided. However, if this fixed his walking issues, he would willingly remain.

"Dr. Meranda will give us a couple of days to prepare home for you, and then you will come home. Meantime relax and know we are working as quickly as we can to get you all to the ranch," Pat told them.

When the invalids did make it home, it was to a beautiful welcome by the family. There was a large sunroom where they could sit and visit while recovering, and any of the kids were on hand to run errands for anything they wanted or needed.

Mara and Pat asked to speak with Meranda before they departed for home.

She was there as soon as she finished with a patient.

"Here is the map on how to find us. Once used, please destroy it for too many can find us without a map. Hopefully, you will have a replacement by Friday. Come out after shift that day and plan on spending some time with us as we prepare for the trip out of the country. Our schedule says that the invalids come home in two days. A few things have to be put in place before they come," explained Mara.

"How do you plan on getting them home?" asked the doctor.

"In vans, but don't tell them that. On Friday, we need you to have the x-ray tech take full x-rays of each of them and send them home with us. We will pick them up at four, and if your replacement is here, you can follow us back. That gives you time to pack and change your office location."

"The replacement is on-site and was here about two hours after I contacted her. My husband can fill her in on what is required if you need me sooner. He says I need a vacation.

Will see what he thinks after I am gone a few days," laughed Meranda.

"In truth, we could be away for a few months. We must travel to seven different countries. Have some folks to hire to take with us, then a bit of business in each nation before we can see the sights, then on to the next one. It could take a while, and we do need your expertise," explained Mara.

"Don't tell him that, or he will want to go too. I said there weren't any seats for him," laughed Meranda.

"Well, I suppose we could make an exception..." Pat began with a grin.

"No, you don't; this is my vacation!" laughed the doc.

"One suggestion, don't take a lot with you, except for empty luggage. You may need it to get everything home from where we will be. We are flying in a private jet; therefore, we can bypass the commercial hassle; I will explain more as we prepare. In two days, we will return and pick up the group. Let us know then when you will be free to join us," said Mara.

"In truth, I found a replacement immediately. It is a woman that I have known, and we went to school together. She never wanted to do private practice and should fit in here well. Her knowledge is the same as mine though she prefers only to be backup for Ortho. She likes working with people, having set hours, and good bosses. She stressed the good bosses. I told her she would like the new ones, yet didn't fill her in any more than that. My oath says I don't share such information. We found her an apartment near the clinic. She is a health nut and will be taking hikes, riding horses, swimming, and racing. The offer came as she was packing up to move, though she had no idea where. Now she is settled in and can take over whenever you want her to. Somehow it seems to me that I won't be returning to the clinic. I'm curious yet not anxious, so we march on," replied Meranda.

"In that case, tell her she starts after we kidnap you tomorrow about one. That will give us a chance to meet her and lead you to the ranch," advised Pat.

"I just received word that we have a mission, and for some reason, you are to go along. Can you be at the ranch at six AM, and do you ride horses?" asked Mara.

"Yes, I can ride, though; it has been a long time since I did."

"Wear jeans, a western shirt, boots, and a hat. Gloves are needed as well as a jacket that can handle whatever weather we encounter. Try not to get entirely new. Pick them up at a second-hand store, so it appears you are familiar with the clothing."

"Don't foreign countries have weather reports?" asked the woman in surprise. Then she thought about how many different languages that might require and chuckled.

"Not all," replied Mara though she said nothing more.

"Okay, I can take a hint. Will be there tomorrow morning at six," replied Meranda as she wondered what she was in for, yet she thought whatever happened would be fun.

After work, she ran to the store and purchased the clothing that she had seen the women wear. While out, she ordered a full medkit for ten and asked that the company deliver it to the ranch. No matter where they went, that was an item they would need, and this way, she had a say as to what it contained.

Mara and Pat had some errands to run and departed after Doc Meranda knew what was required. They asked for a silence bubble in the van they were using though Shandra was driving with Cherry in the second seat. Mike and her sister were staying at home to be sure things were covered there.

"We are going to the book, aren't we?" asked Pat.

"After some lunch, we need to hire some folks. I think it is time to take Star home. Her kids are not going, though. She has something there that is unfinished for her, I think. None of the kids want to return. Joy says she will watch over everyone while we are gone, and she will even have the exit ready when we return. That young woman has blossomed since her surgery. What a blessing she has been. Then there are your four, now called quad one. Please, think of the problems we would have been in without them this last week. The new ones we brought back will remain with me for reasons I'm not sure of, yet know it must happen," advised T1.

Pat never said a word, for she knew if Mara said it, then it was so, and she was the one in charge.

www.ingramcontent.com/pod-product-compliance
Lightning Source LLC
Chambersburg PA
CBHW070922190726
48292CB00004B/1063